TWICE THE FILLIES!
TWICE THE FIGHTIN'!
TWO ACTION-PACKED *BUCKSKIN* WESTERNS FOR ONE LOW PRICE!

LARAMIE SHOWDOWN

"Thought you could run over anybody you wanted to, did you?" Morgan asked. "Take what you wanted. Steal and kill and make your own laws. Life don't work out that way. Now you're gonna die, you murdering fool. Think about that."

Morgan stood and swung the Meteor so the twin muzzles aimed at the man's face. His eyes widened in terror. Morgan lowered the muzzles to the killer's chest and fired one round from four feet away.

Fifteen balls the size of a .32 pistol round blasted through the man's shirt and chopped his heart and lungs into a bloody pulp....

DOUBLE ACTION

Morgan tried to roll away. A dozen boots thudded into him. One glanced off his face down across his eye. He could feel a flap of skin hanging down. Twenty, thirty times they kicked him.

"Enough," the first voice he had heard called softly and the punishment stopped.

"Bastard, you come to the wrong town. You picked the wrong boss. Tough luck. That's the way we work up here in the high country. This is your official welcome to hell, 'cause that's sure as hell where you're going to be in about ten seconds!"

LARAMIE SHOWDOWN
DOUBLE ACTION

BUCKSKIN

KIT DALTON

LEISURE BOOKS　　NEW YORK CITY

A LEISURE BOOK®

September 1993

Published by

Dorchester Publishing Co., Inc.
276 Fifth Avenue
New York, NY 10001

LARAMIE SHOWDOWN

Chapter One

The cowboy looked out the window to the west where the afternoon sun drew black shadow daggers across the high valley that stretched two days' ride to the far snow peaks of the Medicine Bow Mountains. A hawk circled, swept lower, then slashed across the high prairie to snatch an unsuspecting mouse from the grass.

The man had enjoyed the past six months here, working the horses, patching up the run-down little spread, and tending to the needs of Virginia and her son Lewis. A convenience.

He had arrived almost broke, heading for an outfit over near Laramie. Virginia fed him that first day, asked him to stay the afternoon to fix up the porch steps and the screen door. Then the barn needed some work on it, and the six head of stock had run off somewhere, and she would appreciate. . . .

Six months now and not a complaint.

Virginia was at the well. It was near the small ravine at the side of the house, thirty yards away from the barn. She primed the pump, then worked the handle until water gushed out. Clean, pure, cold water.

The first shot blasted into the peaceful afternoon when the bucket was full. Virginia looked up to the east, behind the log house. Four of them came storming past the cabin, riding hard. Shotguns spoke their booming, bass voices and Virginia threw up one arm to protect herself, then a full load of double-ought buck hit her in the chest. She slammed backwards beyond the pump and lay still.

Two of the gunners turned their shotguns on the cabin, blasting windows on both sides.

The man inside near the front window had dropped to the floor when he heard the first shotgun blast. He dove toward the back door when he heard the booming sound of the big scatterguns. His Spencer repeater rifle hung near the back entrance.

The double-ought buck riddled the cabin through both windows but he had crawled beyond that line of fire. He grabbed his Spencer seven shot from the hooks and slowly crawled to the shot out window from where he could see the barn.

He put just the tip of the rifle out the window and tracked a rider heading for the barn. The Spencer fired and the man tumbled from his horse.

One rider pulled up, spun his horse around, and headed back toward the cabin.

"Mama!" Little Lewis called. The four year old ran with choppy steps toward where his mother lay.

The man at the window fired at the second horseman. A sudden movement by the rider spoiled his aim and the .52 caliber slug pounded into his shoulder and he slammed backwards, but kept his seat and rode behind the barn.

A third rider raced toward the small boy, lowered his breach-loading shotgun and fired. He came from the left out of the rifleman's sight until it was too late. The shotgun blast tore the head off the small boy and blew his body toward his mother.

Fire, lever in another round. Fire, lever in another round. After the first eight rounds were gone, the man quickly removed the tube and pushed another loaded one into the Spencer. Two shotgun blasts tore through the window, but he was below it, out of the line of fire.

Not even the double-ought buck could penetrate the six to eight inch logs that formed the walls of the cabin. He lifted up and fired again but missed a horseman near the barn.

He smelled the smoke before he saw it. Smoke slithered across the floor of the main room. Then he saw the barn burst into flames as the straw and hay went up from a torch.

He raced to the back door, kicked it open and fired seven shots as fast as he could at the three riders remaining. Two raced behind the barn. The third tried to return fire with his own rifle, but instead took a creasing rifle slug across his arm and rode away into the smoke concealing himself.

The man caught another tube from the Blakeslee Quickloader and pushed it into the stock of the Spencer. Then he fired three more times into the smoke, stopped and listened. He could hear the crackling of the fire, but beyond that there was a drumming of hooves on packed ground.

Leaving.

He raced outside, caught sight of them, and blasted the last five rounds in the Spencer at them to rush the killers on their way.

At the downed raider, the cowboy kicked the killer in the side. There was no reaction. He rolled the man over, his close up weapon, a cut down Meteor Belgium 10 gauge double barreled shotgun, was aimed at the man's head as the body rolled over.

Dead.

He went to check on Virginia, but he knew there was no hope. He knelt beside her. At least she hadn't suffered. He screamed a long wailing protest at the thought. She didn't suffer but she also wouldn't know the joys and happiness of another 40 years of life and loving.

Lewis.

The boy's head had rolled a dozen feet from his body. The man brought it back, laid it beside the rest of him and blinked. Tears welled in his eyes. Not even a chance for life. Not a goddamn chance to know, to grow, to live!

They would pay! One had made a down payment, now the other three would settle up the debt. One way or another, they would pay with their terror, their anguish, their blood and finally with their very lives. They would pay!

Screams of the horses in the corral came through to him now. They had been there in the background, held down, while he checked the humans.

Now he ran to the burning barn. It created a small fire storm of its own, lifting burning clots of hay high into the air.

The horses! He had thirty head, most of them gentled and broken to ride. Now they were locked in near the burning barn.

When he got there he stopped. His anger was so numbing that he fell to his knees. There was no need to worry about the horses being close to the fire. Most of them lay in pools of blood where they had been shotgunned by the retreating raiders.

The blasts had weakened some of the boards of the corral and a dozen of the animals, crazed by the fire, had broken through and now stood fifty yards away uncertain of what to do. He walked toward them. Three panicked and raced away. His best riding horse came to him when he called. He patted the mare and caught a handful of mane and led her back toward the well.

The log cabin burned brightly. It was filled with greedy flames that raced from wall to wall. It would burn long into the night. Most of what he owned lay in a dresser inside. All gone now.

He saw the washing that Virginia had just put out on the thin rope line. Some of the clothes were his. He cut down an unused clothes line and made a lead rope for his horse, tying her to the well. Then he found a shovel in the small garden Virginia had planted and began digging.

No man should have to bury a woman and her child. No man.

Before it was full dark he had finished the burial, erected a crude cross and taken stock. He had two pairs of pants, three shirts, one blanket, no saddle or bridle and a horse. For protection he had the Spencer and two more tubes filled with bullets in the Blakeslee. There were no more rounds for the ten inch barreled shotgun, and he had twenty rounds in loops for his Colt .45.

That was everything in the world that he owned.

Lee Morgan watched the cabin burn a moment more, then took the lead line, grabbed a fist full of mane and jumped on board. The mare skittered a little, unused to such a mounting. He patted her neck.

"Lots of things gonna be different, girl," he said soothingly. "We're going to have to get used to lots of new things again." Then he struck out west, across the valley toward Laramie, 30, 35 miles away.

He saw what was left of his herd of horses. They had stayed together, and had wandered down by the creek where there was fresh spring grass. They had been his stake, his one last try to start a real horse ranch. He had worked for a month rounding up and roping the 30 head of wild horses that roamed the foothills. He brought them back to the place two and three at a time on a short lead line.

Virginia said there were more than 100 that she had seen. He had roped only the best of them. Mounts that would bring $30 to $50 at the ranches around Laramie.

He spent another two months breaking and gentling the horses. Some were ex-cavalry mounts, some wild stallions he could never catch. Many were Indian ponies and all had cross bred for years here in the open range.

He worked hard with them. He wouldn't pass one to the barn corral until Virginia could walk up to it and put on a halter.

Virginia! Oh, damn! Dead before her time. Snuffed out by a bandit with no morals. Goddamn rawhiders without a wagon. They had made their last raid, he vowed that to Virginia.

He and Virginia had started out as a convenience. He had slept in the haymow and been glad for the work and the food. She had no money to pay him. He worked around the place for two weeks, ate at the house, felt secure for the first time in months.

Then one night when Lewis was sleeping, Virginia had come to the barn with a lantern. She talked long and hard and he realized she was trying to convince herself as much as him.

"Lee, I'm not sure that I know why I'm out here. Rudy has been dead and gone for most a year now. I'm a lonely woman. I—I got used to being a wife. Some women don't like it, but I did, the—the touching, the loving. I liked it. I needed it. Then he was gone. My Rudy got gored by that damned range bull and he—he never—he died the next day."

Lee had come out of the shadows and sat in the glow of the lantern.

"Lee, I want you to stay. The place is home-steaded. Free and clear. Proved up, deed registered in the county house. You can have—I mean, you stay and we'll be partners. I'd want you to come to the house to sleep."

She stood and began to open her dress. "Course I guess nobody buys a pig in a poke. I'm no young girl, not what you'd call a beauty. You look at me and if you want me, then we can just live here and run our little ranch, raise some beef and a milk cow and you can breed up those horses you talk about. Must be a couple hundred wild horses around in the valley and the foothills."

She kept talking until she had taken off all her clothes and neatly folded each piece. When she was naked, she turned around slowly in the lamp light, then sat down beside Morgan.

Virginia kissed his lips gently. She made a sound and put her hand to her mouth.

"Oh, nearly forgot. Little Lewis is part of me, so where I go, he goes. He has to be part of the arrangement."

Morgan sighed and kissed her back. "Been thinking about staying. Nice spread. Good water. High country pasture. Some timber and fire-wood. Been thinking."

She kissed Morgan again, then lay down in the hay and held out her arms.

"Enough talking, Mr. Morgan. Come down here. I always heard a body should never buy a horse you ain't ridden yet."

He had stayed.

Now he left.

Morgan watched the darkness come as he rode west. The moon came out and he and his mare kept moving. She turned and looked at him a time or two as if to ask if this wasn't far enough. It was too dark to track the killers. Three of them.

He had no matches to light a torch and check for tracks. They would beeline it for the nearest town, Laramie, the way a honey bee heads for the hive. They would be there.

He would find them.

He would kill all three.

When the big dipper in its trip around the north star told him it was midnight, he found a small stream and let the mare drink. Then he drank, tied the mare to a willow, took his blanket roll and lay down against a young cottonwood.

Strange what life does to a man. He had come as close as he ever had to settling down. Then one blast of a 12 gauge shotgun had tipped his world upside down again.

After Laramie he might have to hit the owl-hoot trail again. If it happened, it happened. He'd ridden that high country, back woods route before. Maybe Laramie would be different. Cow town, some mining out aways. Mostly ranches. The cattle men would understand his vendetta. A lot depended on the sheriff. He drifted off to sleep and to dream. But when he woke he could never remember the dreams. That was good.

A small, brown, inquisitive butterfly lit on his nose and stared at him.

Lee Morgan opened one eye and the small creature no bigger than his thumbnail lifted up and fluttered away a few feet, then came back and lit on his nose again.

Lee lay flat on his back and he realized that his nose was the highest point around for several feet. He coughed softly and the small creature flew off, then returned. He couldn't even feel where its delicate feet touched his nose.

"You better fly away," he said. It took off at his first words, and circled him as he sat up. A moment later the small creature saw another of its kind and flew away on some important butter-fly mission.

The mare made soft noises in her throat as she saw him rise. He took her at once to the stream for another drink. He was always amazed how much water a horse needed a day to survive: twenty to thirty gallons.

As the bay satisfied herself, he moved up-stream, bent low and drank directly from the clear running little stream. He'd never caught a bug yet from fresh running water.

Morgan figured he was halfway there. Three hours later he came in sight of the town. It lay near the Laramie River, and was a division point for the young, strapping Union Pacific railroad. A well traveled stage road led to the south and toward the Territory of Colorado.

He stopped on a small rise and studied the little town. It was larger than he figured. The railroad had a way of doing that, dumping more and more people from the East as well as from Europe in clumps and globs along the right of way. From the looks of things, Laramie had received its fair share of fresh blood.

Lee Morgan kicked the mare in the flanks and rode down toward the town. On this end he saw a livery. That would be his first stop. If he couldn't afford to feed his mare, he'd have to sell her to the livery operator. For the first time he thought to look in the snap top purse he carried. It held one folded paper dollar bill and forty-three cents. A night in a hotel and breakfast. Then he'd have to find a job. He had a feeling this was going to take more than one morning to find the three killers. He'd worry about a job later.

Right now he was interested in only one thing, finding the three killers and speeding their way straight to hell.

Chapter Two

Lee Morgan had left the reddish brown mare at the livery, paid for two days stall and water at twenty cents a day, and said take good care of her. Then he walked two blocks and pushed into the first saloon he found open. Most drinking establishments were not open yet.

The Emporium was better than the average Western bar. It had a long stand up along one side, gaming tables down the other side and a curving staircase that went to the second floor where he was sure there were plenty of small rooms for intimate female companionship.

Only three men were in the saloon. Morgan saw them, evaluated them and classified them in an instant. Then he went to the near end of the bar, dropped a nickel on the polished surface and asked for a draft beer.

It came and he tasted it, wiped foam off his lips and wished to hell he knew where to hunt for the three killers. In the mirror behind the bar he saw the big man moving toward him. He had pegged him as a bruiser and a bully, but not one to pick a fight unless he knew he could win.

Now the six-four hulk stood beside Morgan, not quite touching him, and turned his back to him as he called to the barkeep. "Lewey, when the hell you gonna bring me that damned fresh beer?"

"Soon the hell you ask for one and pay me," the apron said. He drew a beer and held it until the man slid a nickel toward him. The barman slid the heavy mug down the bar. The big man backed up a step, slammed into Morgan and the beer tipped over on the bartop and splashed both of them.

The big man turned, his eyes bulging, his face red. His mouth opened and his jaw jutted out in confrontation. "What the hell, you made me miss my beer!"

Morgan hadn't moved more than half a step where the man had pushed him. He still stood shoulders square to the bar staring at his beer. He ignored the outburst, lifted his beer and sipped it.

"Hey, hardcase, I'm talking to you!" the man thundered.

He rammed Morgan's near shoulder away from the bar, then grabbed at his shirt front.

Morgan's right fist came up and he took half a step forward, putting his 185 pounds behind the punch. It traveled only a foot, but jolted into the big man's jaw like a mule kick. He staggered back a step. By then Morgan's left pounded into the bully's unprotected gut.

He bent over with a grunt and Morgan's right hand powered upward in an uppercut that lifted the taller man off the floor, glazed his eyes and sent him sprawling backwards onto a poker table. The small table tipped and the man tumbled to the floor on his stomach scattering four chairs.

Morgan didn't waste a second glance at the body. He turned back to the bar and tipped his beer again.

The apron turned to the only other man at the bar, a skinny kid with pimples on his face and wearing eyeglasses.

"Gawd, Dave, you see what he did to Brock?"

"Seen, don't rightly believe," Dave said, pushing back his glasses on his nose. "Lucky punch?"

"Lucky like snow in July," the barkeep said. He drew another beer and carried it down to Morgan.

"Compliments of the house," he said. He motioned to the man on the floor. "That's Brock Jansen. Never saw him beat before in a fight. Course you did take him by surprise."

Morgan finished his first beer and reached for the new one.

"Thanks," he said and sipped at the suds.

"You new in town?" the barkeep asked. "You always talk so much?"

"Depends." Morgan said.

From the far end of the bar he heard someone clapping, slow measured strokes. He looked up to see a woman walking toward him, clapping once for each step. She wore a tight blue dress that showed deep cleavage of big breasts. A woman of about 40 who had tried to keep from getting heavy, but lost the battle.

One of her small high heeled shoes prodded the body on the floor. There was no reaction. She frowned and kicked him sharply in the side.

"Brock, wake up and get out."

Brock didn't move.

She looked over at Morgan. "I saw that little exchange. Brock is known in Laramie as a mean sonofabitch who does what he pleases." She looked over at Morgan. "Up to now."

She stood beside Morgan at the bar. The woman was three inches shorter than his own six feet, but still tall for a woman at five-nine. She looked at him. "No lucky punch? You could take him out again?"

Morgan sipped his beer, then glanced at her. He looked down at her cleavage. "Ma'am that sure is a pretty dress, for what it covers up and what it don't." He paused and watched her soft blue eyes. "No lucky punch. I can take Brock anytime, with fists or weapons. Why?"

"He used to be my bouncer and security man here."

"A security man who picks fights with customers?"

"Like I said, he was Brock. He usually kept it quiet in here and no trouble. Sometimes he got a little drunk and said he needed a fight, like now."

"Just a minute," Morgan said. He took his half full mug of beer, rolled Brock over and threw the beer in his face. Brock sputtered but didn't come to. Morgan shrugged, picked up his feet and dragged him outside. He rolled him off the boardwalk into the four inches of dust that made up the Laramie street.

Two cowhands and three miners watched the little drama with wide eyes.

Morgan went back into the bar. He signalled the apron who drew a fresh beer and slid it down the bar to him. Morgan caught it and took a drink.

He looked at the woman who hadn't moved. He held out his hand. "Some people call me Buckskin," he said. "You run this place?"

"Yep, and own it. Me and my partners." She held up two fingers and the bar man brought her a splash of whiskey in a shot glass. She threw it down and slid the empty glass back down the bar where the apron caught it.

"Actually, me and my six girls own the place. I

won it in a poker game five years ago, been fixing it up ever since." She smiled. "Yeah, you're right. I used to work the cribs. Ain't ashamed of it. Worked my way up and out of the tough life into management."

"You need a new bouncer? I'm looking for work."

She pointed at his tied down gun. "I'm not hiring you for gun work. Looks like that's the kind you usually look for."

"Right now I have about a dollar to my name. I just got burned out and shot at, and I need a place to put myself back together."

She stared at him. "Okay. I like your brown eyes, the quick way you handled Brock. Most of the work here will be gentle persuasion, maybe strippng some guns out of holsters, tossing out a few drunks. Nothing complicated. Almost never anything dangerous."

She thought a moment.

"Oh, and if one of the girls gets a real bastard upstairs who tries to hurt her, you'll handle him too. We don't get much of that, mostly locals."

"I could handle them."

"Come with me."

They went behind the bar, through a door into a supply room and back to her office. "I work out of here. The girls manage themselves and Jody is their bookkeeper. Here we all work together and we all get a percentage of the profits. Unusual, but I wanted to try it. It's worked out just fine."

"Gambling?"

"We sell the chips and take 10% off the top. No house players, no stiffing drunks, no wandering professional gamblers or card sharks allowed. Anybody cheating gets thrown out into the alley. We run a respectable gambling, drinking and clean whorehouse here.

"Want the job?"

"Pay?"

"Two dollars a day, pay weekly, and a room in back if you want it. Upstairs we have a free lunch table for the paying customers. Gwen stocks it, she's our cook. You can eat two meals a day with me and the girls, or nibble upstairs, or eat out. I'll show you the room."

It was eight by eight, with a bed and a small heating stove, a wood box and a dresser. A stack of magazines and dime novels lay on a small table.

"You've got a new ramrod," Morgan said.

"You have a name? Or do I go with Buckskin?"

"Buckskin for now. I got some other business in town I'm working on. Might take a little bit of my time."

"So, get it done," She watched him a moment. "This business, will the law be after you when it's all settled?"

"Might."

"Hope not. I could use you around here for a year or so."

"Depends."

"Yeah, a good man is hard to keep in a job like this. My name is Lily. This is the Emporium. Best girls, best gambling and coldest drinks in town. Welcome to our team." She hesitated. "Don't figure you're a man that needs them, but you wanta use one of the girls, you pay like everybody else. Drinks for you are on the house."

Morgan nodded. "One thing. I been ranching. I'll need some better clothes."

"And you need an advance on your wages. Hey, I know how it is to be down and out." She reached in her bosom and brought out a twenty dollar bill. "This goes on your account. You be back for the late afternoon and night. Work from four to one A.M. when we close."

Morgan nodded. "Sounds fair. What store should I go to for some better clothes?"

"Laramie Dry Goods."

Morgan set his hat in place, touched the brim in salute and walked out of the room and the Emporium Saloon.

He was back an hour later with two new shirts, two pair of Sunday Meeting pants and a fancy buckskin fringed vest. He walked back and knocked on Lily's door. He heard a voice and opened the door.

Lily looked up from her books and her frown turned into a smile.

"Wondering if you have a bathtub around here. I'd guess you do."

"Can't have a whorehouse without a bathroom. Up the back stairs and second door on the right. Girls should be out of it by now. A stove in the room if you want hot water. Should be towels, too, Glory, the way those girls go through clean towels."

"Thanks," he started out the door.

"Buckskin—Buck. Glad to have you working here. Never did like that bastard Brock. Oh, be careful of him. He was mad as a whole nest of hornets when he came to." She grinned. "See, Brock has a rep here in town and you dirtied it up. He'll be watching for you."

"Good, I could use the exercise."

Morgan found the bathroom, built a fire and heated up some water, then filled a genuine six foot bathtub set up on claw feet and stepped in. He was halfway through soaping himself when the door opened and five women whooped into the room.

"You're our new boarder, I hear," one of the women said. She had red hair, wore a robe and nothing else, and didn't mind when the top flapped open.

"Just dropped by to *see* you," another said and giggled.

Morgan threw handsful of water at them. They squealed and stepped back. At last he jumped out of the tub and ran toward them all soapy and wet and naked.

They all backed out of the room laughing.

"Hey, you can stop in and see me anytime," a dark eyed brunette shrilled.

"He's built big all over!" another girl said.

"Glad you're hanging out with us," a little blonde said. "My goodness you are hung, aren't you?"

He reached for a bucket of water and they all squealed and hurried through the door.

Morgan grinned at them, closed the door and pushed a chair under the door handle to take the place of a lock so that he could finish his bath. He had just dried off and put on a set of new clothes when someone knocked on the door. He moved the chair and opened it.

Lily grinned at him.

"Hear the girls dropped by to say hello. Forgot to tell you they might do that. It's a little game they play. If you're all done, I have something to show you."

She motioned for him to follow her and walked down the hallway to the door at the end. She opened the door and waved him inside.

"My room," she said. It was her bedroom and done in remarkably soft colors, tasteful, with a touch of class and elegance. Not at all like a whore's room. There was a bedspread with fluffy pillows on the bed, lace curtains at the one window, and lamps with cut glass spangles on the shades sending glinting flashes of light around the room.

She sat on the bed and watched them. "Morgan, I've been over the mountain and back again. I quit working the business because I could afford to. But now and then I get an itch. You know? I see a man who I want, and I just go up to him and ask him if he's got an hour or so for me."

She grinned. "Hell, I know I'm not as pretty as the girls, and I'm carrying more fat than I should, but I'm not eighteen years old any more either. I admit it. But I'm still as damn sexy as I was at twenty. You're way ahead of me Morgan. You got any objections, I'll understand. If not, and you have the time, I'd appreciate it if you could help me scratch this damn itch I'm feeling strong right now."

Morgan laughed softly and sat beside her. Seeing those half dressed women had got him in a mood. He reached over and petted her breasts and smiled.

"Lily, my pleasure." He popped one breast out of the tight dress and fondled it. She sighed and pulled open the buttons on the bodice and pushed out her other breast.

"The girls do like to get chewed on once in a while. Jeez, but it's been a time for me. God, nearly a year. I get thinking about other things and the business and worry. Last year one of my girls got pregnant, and I got her married off to a rancher about fifty miles away.

"She writes. Says it's a hard life, but honest and clean, and she has learned to love the man. She's had the first kid and has a second one in the oven."

Morgan kissed her breasts and she grinned.

"Don't expect me to pretend you're seducing me. The foreplay is fine but I'd rather get right to the banging."

She undressed him gently. When he was naked sitting on the bed, she did a strip tease that excited him more than he wanted to admit. When she was naked and beside him he put his hand down to her crotch, found the node and twanged it about twenty times before she climaxed.

"Oh, god, nobody's done that in a hell of a long time." She panted and rode with the wild humping and pounding, rolled over on her stomach and humped and squealed and panted. Lily looked at him over her shoulder, tears brimmed her eyes as she ground through another wild series of climaxes and fell on the bed gasping for breath.

"Jeez, it's been five years!" She looked at him in wonder, then her hand caught his erection and she gently pumped it back and forth. "Five damn long years since I cum that good. I don't believe it."

"Stand up," Morgan said.

"What? Can't be done that way."

"Stand up."

She got off the bed and moved her feet apart. "Not a chance with me, anyway."

Morgan moved her against the wall and brought her feet back together a little, then came up between her legs.

"Just won't work, darling Buck. Lord knows I tried enough times."

Morgan probed a moment. His knees were bent as he worked into position, then he jammed upward suddenly, lifting her off the floor a moment. As she eased back to the floor she felt his shaft lancing deeper and deeper into her.

"Glory! I don't believe it." Her eyes went wide and she laughed softly. "Jeez, you're in. I'm getting a stand up after all these years."

"Never been your fault, Lily. You just had the wrong partner." He drove hard now with his knees still partly bent, lifting her on her toes each time his thrust reached the top of his stroke.

"My god, I've never been touched in there that way before! Me, finding out something new about the business! Damn near amazing." She grinned and held on to his shoulders.

"Oh, damn, but that feels good. You don't mind me talking while fucking, do you? I always used to. Drove some men crazy. Some couldn't even get it hard when I talked. But I love to talk when we're fucking away. And since it's my party, I get to talk all I want to.

"Damn, you getting ready? You're panting like an old stallion in heat. Glory! You shot that load halfway through me. I'll be tasting that one. Damn! You were not a virgin when we began this little dance, Buck, I know that for damned sure."

Buck finished the racing climax, then felt her taking off again and he tried to keep up with her but there was no second spilling of juices for him. When she at last tapered off her roaring climaxes, she sighed.

They moved back to the bed, still together, and eased down on the mussed up bedspread.

"Damn, now that's a miracle," Lily said softly. "Buck, I owe you. Owe you a damn lot. Nobody ever did me so good, not ever. I've known me some men. None as good as you."

She closed her eyes. "Nap time. Stay right there on top of me. I love to be crushed down into the mattress that way by a strong naked male body."

Twenty minutes later they came apart and Morgan sat on the bed. She watched him a minute.

"Now, Buck. I want you to tell me why you're

in town. I'd guess you're looking for somebody. If you'll tell me who he is and why you want him, I'll be able to help."

Morgan told her briefly about the raid, the burial.

"Three of them left. I figure I owe it to Virginia to set the score even. Wiping out those three bastards won't make things the same again, but it'll set me at peace and let me get on with my life. I should have been protecting those two. Part of my job out there, and I let them get murdered."

"Not your fault, Buck. They probably watched the place and hit when they knew they had an advantage. I seen too many of that kind. But as far as new people in town, that's tough. We get a couple of dozen every day when the train comes through. I never even see most of them.

"Drifters, bums, settlers, cowboys, miners, even foreigners, a little of everything comes on the train these days. But I'll watch for them, anybody who looks like these guys. You do what you have to and I'll understand. Anytime you can be here in the evening, I'll appreciate. Remember, Buck, I still owe you."

Morgan brushed the back of his neck. "Where in town can I get a good haircut?"

Ten minutes later he walked into the Starwell Barbershop next to the Laramie General Store. There was one chair and it was filled.

"Time for a cut today?" Morgan asked.

The barber turned. He wore a white shirt and tie and a white apron such as many bartenders wear. A comb was perched behind his right ear and he held another comb and snapped a pair of razor sharp scissors.

"Yes indeed, kind sir! Always time for one more. The good Lord is sending me lots of good customers today. I thank you for your bounty, Lord."

Morgan sat down in a chair next to the window and watched the town. He could remember only one of the three killers clearly. The man's hat had fallen off and he had an inch wide streak of white hair right down the middle of his head. It stood out like a beacon in the man's head of black hair.

That one should be easy to spot, if he was still in town. Morgan stared into the street, searching.

"You're next, sir," the barber said touching Morgan on the shoulder with his comb.

The man put a cloth over Morgan with a flourish.

"Best haircut in town," the barber said. He held out his hand. "Oh, I'm Paul Starwell. Barber. I also preach at the local interdenominational church on Sundays and hold the Wednesday prayer meeting. You're more than welcome to come and worship with us, anytime."

"Buckskin is the name," Morgan said shaking the soft and clean hand.

"Strange name. Christian name or family name?"

"Only one I go by. Generally not a good thing to inquire too hard into a man's name, Parson. That could lead to his background and more than one man in this part of the country doesn't want to bring up his background."

"Oh, sorry. I'm here only a year or so, and I don't know all of these Western ways yet. I'll learn. The Lord will help me. You see, I figure that the good Lord put me here in Laramie for some good reason. I don't question my Savior. He commands my life. I'm his willing vessel."

"That must be quite a burden to bear," Morgan said. He looked in the mirror. In spite of the sermon, it still was a good haircut.

He paid the fifteen cents and watched the preacher/barber put the cash in his drawer. Might be a good thing to remember the preacher. Sometimes men like him could be a help, sometimes they really became a problem. He'd seen too many soft, gentle men like the preacher just eaten up and spit out in the West. Yes, he would do well to pay attention to the preacher.

Chapter Three

Morgan, who was becoming more accustomed to being called Buck now, went straight to the livery stables from the barbershop.

The owner scratched a two-day growth of beard and closed one eye as he tried to think back.

"Early this morning or last night? Nope, don't remember three riders coming in together. There was two and then one come in. Horses looked little used up, but not ruined. Put all three in adjacent stalls.

"One of them a pinto, brown and white?"

"Yeah, damned if it warn't. These men bank robbers or something?"

"Nope. Just curious. Show me the horses."

The Pinto was gone.

"My boy was here this morning. Pinto must have gone out then."

The other two horses had some old brands, nothing new, a Running M on one and a Bar B on the other. One was a roan, the other a dun. Morgan took out two one dollar bills.

"Give you two dollars if you find out who owns them nags. It's important to me. I want their names and where they're staying. Don't let them know you're curious. Be a big help to me." He gave the man the two dollars. "Hell, you get names and where they stay, I'll give you five dollars more."

The livery man said he'd damn well find out.

Lee walked out of the livery. He'd remember the two horses if he saw them again. He went back toward the Emporium Saloon.

Outside the Emporium, tied to the rail, he saw the same pinto he remembered from the raid out at the ranch. He wanted to storm inside and question every man there until he found the killer. But it was easy for any man to deny owning a horse.

Morgan leaned against the hardware and watched and waited. An hour later a man came out, drew the pinto's tie reins off the hitching rack and was about to step on board.

Morgan touched his shoulder and he turned.

"This your horse?" Morgan asked.

The man frowned, he looked like a towner, or maybe a new man on the range. He nodded.

"Sure as hell is. I just bought her this morning. Paid twenty dollars for her which is damn near a steal. Afraid I don't want to sell her."

Lee scowled. "Who sold her to you?"

"Just some hardcase. Looked mean as grass, but he needed the money and I needed a horse. Can't be a ranch hand without riding in on your own mount. Don't look right."

"What did the guy look like who sold her?"

"Just a man. About my height, weathered some. Oh, took his hat off and he had a white blaze right down his hair. Black hair and that white stripe. That's why he left his hat on most of the time."

Morgan thanked the man and walked away. No damn help there. If one of them sold his horse, the other two would as well. Which meant they would stay in town for a while. Maybe they were short of cash.

Thinking about short, he went to the Laramie General Store and found the counter where they stocked guns and shells. A pretty blonde woman about 30 came over. She was a solid looking, no nonsense woman who smiled at him.

"May I help you, sir?" she asked. Her smile was quick, friendly, open. Her dress covered her from chin to wrists and ankles.

"Yes. Need some .45 rounds and some 10 gauge double-ought buck."

She picked items from below the counter and showed him a box of 30 .45 shells and another full of 20 rounds of double-ought buck. He looked at them and nodded. "I've seen a fabric belt that would hold shotgun shells, a kind of cartridge belt. You have any of those?"

"The pheasant hunters like them. We've had some now for a while. I think we have one left." She smiled again and bent low and brought out a brown canvas belt that had places for twenty shotgun shells. He tried one of the ten gauge rounds and it fit snugly so it wouldn't fall out.

"Good. How much for everything?"

She told him and he put down the money from what he had left after buying the clothes.

"You're new in town," the woman said.

"Yes, just passing through."

She held out her hand. "I'm Aggie Cump. I own the store here now. Good to have you in town."

Aggie felt her knees go weak when he took her hand and she put one hand down on the counter to steady herself. She hadn't felt this way since she was fourteen. This man was so handsome it made her ache.

He took her hand and shook it gently. "Ma'am, I'm Buckskin. Pleased to make your acquaintance.''

She shivered slowly realizing how strongly this man affected her. She managed a smile. "I'll wrap these up for you." She took the items to the back counter and wrapped them in brown paper and brought his change.

Twice she had to take deep breaths. It seemed like a whole lifetime of desires suddenly rushed over her all at once. Ridiculous. She hadn't felt this way since—well, since before Arthur had died. Three years ago. Oh, my, such a long time.

She got back to the gun counter and smiled and gave him the change.

"Ma'am, I'm looking for a man. He's got a white stripe down through his dark hair. Remember seeing anyone like that?"

"Goodness, that is unusual. No, I don't remember anyone. But we have so many new people here, off the train, you know."

She was prattling like a giddy girl. She looked up at him and saw his eyes were brown, a generous mouth and solid nose over a firm chin. So handsome it made her weak.

Aggie had an urge to invite him to dinner that night. Absolutely impossible. She could never do that. Why not? If he was married he'd tell her quickly. There was a chance. . . .

He turned to leave.

"Thanks a lot, come back for whatever you need," she said.

He turned and smiled. "Yes, ma'am, I'll probably just do that."

"We stay open until six."

"That's good."

"I think we have the best stock of any store in town. Even food and clothes."

"Good, I'll be back." He smiled as he left.

Aggie Cump leaned on the counter. She sighed.

Oh, damn! She had acted like a giddy young girl. She had wanted him to stay and so she had kept talking to him. He must think she was terrible. But what a handsome man, and such a tough lean body!

For just a moment she wondered what he would look like naked. She turned, almost blushed just thinking about it. Then she realized she was damp down between her legs. He was such an appealing man. She moved and knew she was more than damp. She hadn't felt that way in just years!

Aggie Cump did own the Laramie General Store. Her husband had been killed riding with a sheriff's posse three years ago when they rushed off after a pair of gunmen who robbed the bank. She had survived. They hadn't had any children, which was her fault she was sure. But it had helped not having babies at home and the store to run, too.

She had learned about the store in the three years that they had run it before her husband died. She dug in, developed it more, got in better merchandise, put in more things for women, and made a success of it.

Some men in town had said she couldn't do it. She'd fooled them! But now, suddenly, all of that success seemed not so important. She realized that she hadn't touched a man for three years. She had pushed down the occasional surges of desire. Now she couldn't push this one down.

She had refused to go out with men or let anyone come courting even after a year's mourning. Oh, god, what she was missing!

He said his name was Buckskin. What a strange name. But he was beautiful, and she knew he would look even more perfect naked. She let herself think about it and for just a moment she rubbed her breasts. They were full, larger than most women's, and her husband had loved to play with them.

"Oh, god!" she said softly. How she missed having a man. One way or the other she was going to do something about it, and soon. The next time he came in she would be ready.

Buck walked the town. It was time for him to report for work at the Emporium, but he wanted to check once more. He did not see the man with the white blaze in his hair anywhere on the street or in the stores. Eight saloons produced no sight of him either.

He checked the horses tied at the hitching rails as well. Then he saw the roan from the livery. A man rode the gelding down the street. Morgan walked out in front of the animal and held up his hand.

The rider stopped and looked down.

"Yes?"

"This your horse?"

"Is now, why?"

"How long you owned it?"

"About an hour. Bought him from a man in a saloon. He was offering a good horse at a good price. Paid twenty five but still a low price. Why, you want to buy him?"

"Who sold him?"

"Strange little man, maybe five-four. Had a black mole on his nose, shifty green eyes and a fresh haircut. Wondered if he'd stolen the horse but he had a bill of sale from over in Idaho. This guy couldn't count. A man with a white blaze in his hair counted the money for him. The little guy had a lisp when he talked and he was left handed. Looked like he spent a lot of time outdoors, sunburned and windburned."

Morgan believed the rider. This man in the

saddle couldn't have been a raider. He was all town man. Maybe he just wanted a horse to ride. Morgan touched his hat brim.

"Thanks for your help."

"This guy I bought from, he an outlaw or something?"

Morgan shrugged. "Getting hard to tell the outlaws from the townfolks these days."

"That's for damn sure," the man on the horse said and rode on past.

Morgan went on to the Emporium, stashed his hat in his room and put his package of ammunition there as well. He needed a carpetbag of some sort, and a second blanket for the trail. Never could tell when he might need them. Tomorrow he'd try to buy them.

The bar was quiet. Morgan got a deck of cards and played solitaire at a table with his back to the wall so he could see the whole place.

Lily came out and nodded. She had on a conservative dress that set her apart from the soiled doves. It was still attractive.

She smiled remembering that afternoon. "You missed supper. We eat here at four o'clock before the rush. Should be some good snacks at the table upstairs. Why don't you go up there and eat something before we get busy down here."

Morgan nodded, left the cards set up and Lily sat down and finished the solitaire hand. She lost.

The "spread" as the girls called it upstairs, was partly left over from the house supper, and partly made up specially by Gwen, the short little red head with almost no breasts at all but one of the most popular of the fancy ladies. She was good in bed and in front of a cookstove.

Tonight there were chicken legs, biscuits and honey, small slices of apple pie, apple juice and plenty of hot coffee.

Gwen was still putting food on the table when Morgan went upstairs. The girls all called him Buck as well now, and he rather enjoyed it. Reminded him of his father, William Frank "Buckskin" Leslie and the old family ranch at the Spade Bit, over by Boise, Idaho. Also it didn't give away his real identity in case any alert deputy sheriff or bounty hunter was listening.

Gwen looked up and gave him a tentative smile. "Buck, you ain't mad about the bathtub are you? We was just having some fun."

Buck took a bite of the still hot fried chicken leg and grinned. "How can I be mad when I got to see five pretty girls in various stages of undress? Anyway, I'm not that modest."

"Oh, I'm glad. Some of the girls thought you might not like it—being exposed that way."

He leaned in and kissed her cheek. "Hey, I've been exposed to a lot of nice ladies. Doesn't bother me, if it doesn't bother them."

They both laughed. "Try the pie, it's really good. I put lots of cinnamon in it this time." She took off her apron and came out from behind the table. She had on a typical low cut dance hall girl type dress except it was short. She had cut it off almost to her knees, and it showed a shocking stretch of shapely female leg.

"How do you like my new dress? I made it myself."

"Yeah, yeah!" Buck said. I'm glad you ran short of material. Within a week the other girls are going to cut off their skirts to that length, too."

Gwen ran up to Morgan and gave him a big hug. "Oh, such a nice man! I'm glad you came here. You're reminding me more and more of my very favorite big brother back in Indianapolis."

She pecked a kiss on his cheek and hurried along the hall to the steps that led to the big gambling hall downstairs.

"I think you made a friend," a voice said from the other direction.

When Morgan turned he saw a tall brunette he remembered from the bathroom. He had just taken another bite of chicken. The woman laughed. She still had on her robe.

"Hi, I'm Jody and you're Buck. I met you in the buff this afternoon. You've got a great body. That was our Little Miss Sunshine, Gwen, who always thinks the best of people. You'll get used to her. Damn good cook, though. Oh, just to even things up. . . ."

Jody opened her robe and held it wide to reveal her naked body. She was well constructed, slender waist, flaring hips and good sized breasts.

"Is that a long enough look?" Jody asked grinning.

"I never get a long enough look at a beautiful naked female," Morgan said.

Jody laughed and pulled the robe back and tied it. "I had to have one more of those chicken legs. From the looks at the crowd downstairs, I'll be working it off before the night is over."

She bit off some chicken and chewed it. "Yeah, good. Hey, you ever need any, you know, get really hard up. . . ." She shook her head. "Hell, I'd wager you never get hard up. Bet you a dollar you've never bought a woman in your life." She shrugged. "Hey, glad to have you working here. You're a thousand times better than that bastard Brock. He took us any time he wanted and never paid a dime."

She finished the chicken leg and wiped her fingers. "Hell, I better get dressed. Got to hold up my end of things around here, so to speak." She grinned, waved and went back down the hall to one of the rooms.

As he ate another chicken leg, Morgan remembered he hadn't had any breakfast or dinner. He tried a couple of the small sandwiches and then took a cup of coffee and went downstairs to his wall table. A new hand of solitaire was laid out and the game about half played.

He lost that one, too.

Things picked up from five to six, then tailed off until the main crowd of miners and cowboys and towners arrived about seven. He'd been back upstairs once to have two more pieces of chicken and a pair of sandwiches and then he put three of the small slices of pie on a plate and ate them. Delicious. That small girl, Gwen, could cook.

One man bumped another at the bar and loud words erupted. Morgan didn't seem to move fast but in a few smooth strides he was between the two men staring at them alternately. He was bigger than one, about the same size as the other one but heavier.

"What's the problem between you two gentlemen?" Morgan barked so he could be heard all over the saloon. Conversations quieted and half those inside watched. Lee knew a new man always gets tested. These two could be best of friends setting him up.

"Little bastard called me an asshole," one said.

"Are you?" Morgan asked him in a tone that allowed no room for question. He stared hard at the man.

"By damn, no. It was his fault."

"Spilled my beer," the smaller one said.

Morgan grabbed each of them by the shirts and pulled them together face to face. "All right, we'll settle it right here, an Apache knife fight on the end of a kerchief. Each hold one end of a regular kerchief in your mouth and fight to the death. You both agree?" He looked from one to the other.

"Well . . . maybe he didn't bump me that hard," the smaller man said meekly.

Morgan glared at the larger man. "You up to a knife fight and not let go of the kerchief with your teeth?"

"Hell no . . . I come in here for a friendly drink. . . ."

"Then keep it friendly, friend," Morgan said. He let loose of both their shirts, patted them back in place. He signalled the bartender who was there in an instant.

"A fresh beer for these two sports," Morgan said. "Put it on my tab. Any more trouble and you two will be spitting out teeth, understand?"

They both nodded. They took their new draft beers and moved away from each other, then glanced at Morgan who stood watching them.

The poker games continued, the chatter went on. One of the girls yelped when she got pinched. She turned and slapped the man and a moment later the two of them went up the stairs to her room.

Another night at the old Emporium Saloon, Morgan thought. He wouldn't be here long. He had three men to find, then he'd move on—in spite of the way Gwen could cook.

Chapter Four

The test of the new bouncer in town came a little after eleven that first night. Brock walked in, just drunk enough to fight good. He looked around, dropped a bottle of whiskey he carried and it broke all over the floor.

The swamper handy man ran for a bucket and a mop.

Two of the girls ran upstairs.

Half the drinkers and gamblers in the place stopped and watched the drama they knew was starting.

Lily walked up to Brock and slapped his face.

He grinned. "Wasn't I good enough in your bed, Lily?" Brock asked.

She slapped him again and turned. "Buck, throw this bum out of my saloon."

Morgan had been watching as well. He came toward Brock who scowled when he saw him.

"Sneaky punch!" Brock bellowed.

Morgan came forward, stopped an arm's length away. "The lady said you should go outside," Morgan said.

"What lady? You mean the whore, Lily."

Morgan hit him with a right fist in the nose so fast Brock didn't even know it was coming.

He growled. "Bastard!" Brock bellowed. He

felt of his nose and his fingers came away bloody. "Bastard!" He lunged ahead.

Morgan met him with a snap kick to his belly and then a hard right hand to the side of his jaw.

The kick in the stomach doubled Brock and the jaw blow put him on the floor. He looked up from his knees, fury twisting his face into an ugly mask.

He surged up and plowed into Morgan waist high. Morgan's raised knee caught Brock in the chest, absorbing much of the force, but slamming him back to the stand up bar. Morgan hit with his shoulders, spun both of them around and got a hand loose to smash down on the back of Brock's thick neck. He hit him again on the side of the head, then brought his knee up aimed at the invader's groin but Brock moved his legs protecting himself.

They spun apart. Brock grabbed a bottle off the bar half filled with whiskey. He swung it like a hammer.

Morgan danced away from the swings. On the third bottle swing by Brock, Morgan timed it just right, he followed in behind the bottle and smashed his fist twice into Brock's face. Brock dropped both arms. Morgan pounded a hard right into Brock's gut and he doubled over.

This time Morgan rammed up his knee and caught Brock's chin. His head snapped back and for a moment Morgan thought he'd broken the big man's thick neck. But there was no cracking sound.

Brock dropped to the floor on all fours, then slowly tipped on his side and spilled on his back, unconscious.

A cheer went up from the room. Morgan pointed to two men standing at the bar.

"You and you, drag him out to the street." The

men jumped to their task, taking Brock's hands and pulling him out the front door to the boardwalk.

Inside Morgan looked around at the faces.

"So now you know," he said. "It wasn't a lucky punch the first time. Anybody else?"

Men turned quickly back to card games, studied their drinks, or talked to the girls. Morgan grinned, went to the bar and held up four fingers.

The barkeep, Lewey, poured a glass half full of whiskey and handed it to Morgan who bolted down some of it, shook his head and then sipped. A man moved away from him and Lily stepped in beside him.

"Good work. You didn't even break up a chair."

"You knew he'd be coming back. I knew he'd be coming. Half the town must have figured it out."

"You put on a good show."

"Besides that, I was fighting for my life. He's a tough sonofabitch."

"True, but not as tough as you are. Thanks."

"My job. I got paid, now I've got to earn my wages."

She leaned close. "You more than earned your wages this afternoon," she said softly, then moved around him and to her office in back of the bar.

Morgan took the rest of the glass of whiskey to the side of the room and found an unused table next to the wall. He took out the deck of cards he had pocketed and laid out a seven card game of solitaire. There were dozens of ways to play this single card game, but he only knew one.

One of the girls screeched, but when he looked up he saw she was just teasing a man. A minute later she put his hand on her breasts and led him up the stairs. Three men at his table hooted at him.

"Do her once for me, Willy."

"Yeah, Willy. But tell her to be gentle with you, 'cause this is your first time." There were more hoots and cheers as the pair vanished up the open stairs.

Morgan settled down. He won the first game of solitaire and got a cold bottle of beer from the bar.

Just after midnight one poker game outlasted the others. There were six men around the table but one stood out. He was tall, thin, wore a light gray suit and a string tie over a white shirt. He had on a vest the same color as the suit with a fob and a heavy gold watch and chain.

He won a little, lost a little. Morgan moved over to watch the game. It ended shortly and the Englishman had won about twenty five dollars—a month's pay for a cowhand. He spotted Morgan and walked over.

"Could I sit down and talk, sir?" the Englisher asked.

Morgan nodded. The man sat, lit a long black cigar and stared at Morgan. He held out a thin hand. "My name is Bedford Harwich, I'm a visitor in your fine country. They call you Buck. I saw you flatten that big bruiser Brock in here tonight. It was quite the most excitement I've had here in town. You are a handy man to have around."

"Part of the job, here," Morgan said, shaking his hand.

"You're too modest, Buck. I like that in a man." He watched Buck a moment. "How would you like to come work for me? I need a—what to call him—an assistant? Someone who is good with his fists and his guns."

"I have a job right now."

"Quite, but what I'm offering would be more of a *position*. You wouldn't have to deal with these ruffians—except perhaps on occasion. There would be travel, some adventure perhaps."

"Sorry, Mr. Harwich. I've had about all the adventure I can stand."

"I really hope that you will reconsider my offer. I'm planning on opening a small ranch nearby and watch it grow. I'm prepared to invest a rather sizeable sum of money so I'll need someone on site to keep me informed, to sell the cattle that need to go to market, those sorts of things."

Morgan saw two hardcases come in, but they went to the bar for nickel beer and minded their own business.

"Mr. Harwich, if you're interested in hiring me, I can tell you I wouldn't consider moving from here for less than a hundred and fifty dollars a month."

"A hundred and—I see. Well, I'll contact my bookkeeper and see if our budget can cover that much. It is rather more than I had in mind."

"I'll be here," Morgan said. "Stop by anytime."

Morgan stood and wandered around the tables. The main crowd had left. The working men had to get some sleep. Two drunks were already asleep at the back table. Morgan roused them and led them out to the alley. They both probably would sleep there tonight.

Lily came in and smiled. "Well, how was your first day on the job?"

"The job isn't my favorite, but it pays good. The food upstairs was wonderful. The afternoon side benefits were outstanding."

Lily smiled. "I hoped that you would be

pleased. Let's start moving out the night owls and get closed up."

A half hour later they had removed the last drinker and Morgan threw the heavy oak plank across the iron brackets barring the door.

Lily had shooed everyone else out. She watched Morgan. "I think you'll do fine here. I just hope I can keep you around for a while. Oh, if you're a breakfast man, don't count on Gwen. We all sleep until noon. Best morning food is at the Wyoming Cafe down on First Street."

Morgan waved. "See you tomorrow. Seems like a year since I've had any sleep."

In his room, Morgan found the bed soft, and a bolt on the door. He threw it, and settled down in the bed. It was so warm he didn't even need the sheet. He slept better that night than he had for a long time.

The next morning, after breakfast at the Wyoming Cafe, Morgan watched along the streets for the man with the white streak in his hair. Down near the general store he saw a minstrel kind of man singing and playing guitar. The man was totally bald. He sang and played and then passed around a tin cup looking for contributions.

Morgan dropped in a nickel and watched the musician. Had he seen the man somewhere before? There was a nagging notion that he had, but he couldn't be sure. He worked down the block and back up the other side. An hour later he saw the bald headed singer again and this time Morgan decided to follow him.

He wondered what the man would look like with hair? How long had he been bald? He might have shaved it off. Morgan sauntered along, stared in windows and moved along slowly as the minstrel man worked his way down the street.

At the far end of the three block long main street, he slung the guitar across his back and walked toward some houses. Morgan moved faster now so he wouldn't lose sight of the man. The bald headed man didn't look to see if he was being followed, he just walked down two blocks and into a small house beside the church.

The parsonage?

Morgan went back downtown and asked who owned the small house next to the church. The first shopkeeper said it was the parsonage, but since they didn't have a full time preacher anymore, they rented it to somebody.

The shop owner of a small shoe repair shop, shook his head. "Ain't had much luck renting the house. Usually vacant. Then yesterday this guy comes along and pays for a week's rent."

Morgan hurried back to where he could see both the front and back doors of the house. He was across the street and half a block down beside a buggy repair shop. He sat down and hunkered back against a fence so he wasn't obvious. Morgan settled down to wait. He was good at waiting. The Indians had taught him that one summer.

Two hours later the same bald headed man came out. This time he didn't have his guitar and he wore a hat. The low crowned cowboy hat was trail worn, and looked a little large for the man.

When he was out of sight, Morgan hurried down the alley in back of the place and slipped in the unlocked rear door. He paused to listen. After two minutes he heard nothing. Morgan walked silently through the five rooms to be sure no one else was there.

The place was furnished for an itinerant preacher. Food dishes lay on the kitchen table. The room was a mess. He found what could be a saddle tramp's bedroll and a small satchel. He looked through the contents quickly. In the bed-roll in the middle of a carefully wrapped silk scarf he found a locket.

Morgan looked at it a moment then frowned. It was a gold locket on a heavy gold chain. He'd seen it before. He opened the locket and saw a small picture of Virginia. The bastard had killed her and stolen her locket. He was one of the four raiders at the ranch.

Morgan figured she had left it in the cabin and it had burned up with everything else. He took the locket and put it in his pocket. It was the only thing Virginia owned of any value. He squinted his eyes a moment, his face going hard. He'd found one of the men who'd killed Virginia and little Lewis.

Again Morgan settled down to wait. He had only his .45 Colt with him. It would have to do. He had visions of blowing each man's head off with the Meteor shotgun with the ten inch barrels. Maybe on the next one.

By two o'clock on Morgan's Waterbury pocket watch, the bald man had not returned. Doing some drinking and gambling, no doubt, or maybe up in one of the cribs. Morgan walked back to his small room in back of the saloon and picked up the Belgium made short barreled shotgun. He loaded the two rounds, then found a large paper and wrapped the weapon in it so it wouldn't be obvious.

Then Morgan pushed the 18 shotgun rounds in the canvas bandoleer and put it inside the wrapping. He had a sandwich in the small kitchen where Gwen was fixing their supper.

"You better stay, Buck," she said wiping her hands on her apron. "I'm fixing beef stew with six different vegetables. My old mama told me to feed my man plenty of vegetables and he would always treat me right."

"Sorry, I do have to be out for a while. I'll be back as soon as I can. Oh, you were right about that pie. Best apple pie I've tasted in years."

"Good." She smiled like a fourteen year old getting her first compliment. "Well, I'll save some supper for you. Keep it hot in a pan on the back of the stove. You come look when you get back, ya hear?"

"Yes ma'am," Morgan said and hurried out the door.

He knocked on the back door, but nobody answered at the parsonage. Lee eased himself in and made certain he was alone. Then he took out the Meteor, checked the loads and slung the bandoleer around his neck. He attached the snap on the leather strap to the top ring on the middle of the shotgun and adjusted the strap around his neck so the weapon hung at his waist.

Now he was ready for the damn rawhider. He'd find out where the other two were, then blow this bastard into mince meat. Only he'd do it a foot and a hand and an arm at a time. The bastard was going to pay!

Two hours later Morgan heard the front door open and then close. He was near a short hall that opened from the front door into the parlor. Morgan stood. Footsteps came his way. They sounded a bit unsteady.

The bald headed man came into the parlor and saw Morgan and the Meteor aimed at his chest.

"Not a damn word, woman-killer, or you're dead," Morgan whispered.

"What'n hell?"

Morgan slammed the butt of the small shotgun into the side of the man's head and he crumpled to the floor, unconscious. While he had been waiting, Morgan had found some tough cord in the parsonage kitchen. Now he tied the man's hands to the tops of the parlor table legs, stretching him tight in a sitting position.

Morgan threw a glass of cold water into his face and the outlaw came back to conscious sputtering.

"What in the hell?"

"Hello, woman killer," Morgan snarled. "You're one life light in this big poker pot and I'm here to see that you pay up."

Chapter Five

The bald man tied to the parlor table glared up at Morgan.

"Don't know what the hell you're talking about. I'm a singer. I saw you watching me on the street."

"You also kill defenseless women and little boys and steal gold chains and lockets." Morgan took the locket out of his pocket and dangled it.

"I bought that off some guy this morning," the tied man yelped. "Don't prove nothing."

"Maybe not in a court of law, but we're not in a court. I'm the judge, jury and executioner." Morgan drove his fist into the man's exposed stomach. The bald man gasped, gagged and almost threw up.

"Where are the other two who were on the raid with you? I found their horses, so they're still in town. Where are they hiding out and how can I find them?"

"Don't know."

Morgan punched him in the jaw and his head slammed sideways against the table.

"Chrissakes, stop it!"

Morgan hit him again jolting loose a tooth.

"You getting the idea, bad ass?"

The tied man glared at him. Morgan kicked the

man's legs apart where he sat on the floor and positioned his boot between the man's legs a foot from his crotch.

"You ever been kicked good and hard in the balls, tough guy?"

"You wouldn't!"

Morgan rammed his right foot forward, catching the man's crotch, slamming his balls upward against his pelvic bones until they crushed like grapes underfoot.

The bald man's long wail of pain lanced through the parsonage but no one outside was close enough to hear it. He drew his knees up to his chest to lessen the pain. When his wailing died to a whimper, Morgan slapped his face gently.

"Where are the other two?"

"Here in town somewhere. We figured we better split up, don't know where they are."

"You shave your head?"

He nodded.

"You have a white streak down your dark hair?"

"Yes."

"What are the names of the other two?"

The wailing came again as the man shifted his weight where he sat.

"The names!"

"Lars . . . Lars . . . Mars . . . Mars . . . Oh God!"

Morgan grabbed his face. "You shot the woman near the well, right?"

Slowly the man nodded. His eyes looked up, they were dead already.

"So damn cold in here. Why is it so cold?"

Morgan swung up the Meteor shotgun and aimed it at the man's face.

"It's cold because you're gonna die. Then you'll be hot in hell for eternity. You ready, you damn woman killer?"

The man's eyes closed slowly.

Morgan moved his aim and fired. The killer's whole right hand disintegrated from the rounds of double-ought buck and his wrist broke free as his handless arm swung down from the ropes to his side.

A piercing scream cut off suddenly as the raider's head fell forward and he passed out.

Morgan got a glass of water from a pitcher in the kitchen and threw the water in the man's face. He came back to reality slowly, stared at the stump of his wrist on his right arm and wailed, almost fainting again.

"Bastard!" the man said.

"Yeah. Now you know how it feels to get shot-gunned, and live."

Lee "Buckskin" Morgan turned the shotgun on the man's other tied hand and pulled the second trigger blowing his hand free of the twine, mangling and cutting off fingers in the blast.

The bald headed man fainted again, falling under the table. Blood poured from both wounds. The man would be dead in five minutes if Morgan let him bleed.

No! Morgan thought. The bastard had to know he was dying. He had to suffer a little more. He owed it to Virginia and little Lewis.

Morgan brought the pitcher of water and sloshed it in the man's face. Gradually he came back to consciousness. He looked at Morgan through dulled eyes.

"Bastard," he said.

Morgan broke open the scattergun and took out the two spent shells and pushed in two new ones from his bandoleer.

"Thought you would live forever, did you?" Morgan asked. "Thought you could run over anybody you wanted to. Take what you wanted. Steal and kill and make your own laws. Life don't work out that way. Now you're gonna die, you murdering fool. Think about that."

Morgan stood and swung the Meteor so the twin muzzles aimed at the man's face. His eyes widened in terror. Buckskin Morgan lowered the muzzles to the killer's chest and fired one round from four feet away.

Fifteen balls the size of a .32 pistol round blasted through the man's shirt and chopped up his heart and lungs into a bloody pulp. The force slammed the body under the table and against the wall.

The surge of emotion hit Morgan. He breathed fast and hard. The power, the mind blowing charge of a rush that could never be surpassed blasted through him like a charging freight train. He gasped and reached for the table to steady himself. Then it boiled past him and he shook his head and looked down and saw the dead man against the wall.

"Two down, Virginia. Two dead and two to go. I won't let them rest until they all are six feet under Kansas soil."

He went into the backyard, saw that there was no horse in the small shed, and walked quickly downtown. He stopped at the first hitching rail he saw, untied a horse and walked away with it. No one called after him.

Back at the rear door of the parsonage, he tied the horse. Inside, he brought out the body and balanced it over the saddle, head and feet down. He walked the horse down the alley next to Main Street, turned the animal toward the sheriff's office and whacked the sorrel on the flanks. The big horse walked down Main Street probably wondering what was happening.

Morgan crouched in the shadows of the alley waiting. When the horse was fifty feet down the street somebody yelled and hurried out to the animal, catching the reins.

"A dead body!" the finder called.

Morgan strolled that way with the others. A minute later a depty sheriff ran up and looked at the body.

"It's that bald headed street singer who's been around town," the depty said. "Somebody done him right mean with a shotgun, looks like."

Morgan hung back along the boardwalk, the Meteor short scattergun mostly concealed by his buckskin fringed vest. He watched the people. His hope was that somebody would get scared and run when they saw their buddy cut down.

He saw no one with an immediate panic. The Sheriff came and said the body should be displayed on a door outside the sheriff's office for the rest of the day hoping someone would identify him and pay for the funeral.

"Tired of laying out two dollars for a grave digger," the sheriff said.

Morgan moved down to the alley and toward the back door of the Emporium. He picked up his rifle and bedroll and the Quickloader and headed for the livery. He wanted to be ready in case some lowlife decided to make a run for it.

Buckskin took his time saddling up his mount, tying on the blanket roll and adjusting the leather boot to hold the Spencer. Nobody else seemed to be saddling up. He still carried the cut off shotgun on the short leather strap around his neck.

He rode out of town to a small rise and sat near some brush and watched the livery. It was a little after four-thirty. Would a runner wait until nightfall? Morgan doubted it. If his two buddies were still in town they would hear about the man with no hands. They would drift past the display and make sure it was their friend. Then panic could set in.

He waited a half hour.

Morgan checked the shotgun and reloaded the spent round. It was a beautiful, deadly weapon. Aim anywhere near the person you wanted to hit and he was dead.

By six, Morgan began feeling he should get over to the Emporium and earn his two dollars already paid.

Five minutes later, he was about to get up and go back to town when he saw a lone rider coming from the street nearest the livery. The man rode hard and kept looking back. He seemed like a good prospect for killer number three. Morgan hoped that he was.

Lee mounted and rode at an angle so he would cut across the man's trail. The stranger saw Morgan coming from 300 yards off and turned away from him, galloping flat out on his gray horse.

Morgan grinned. The man was afraid of something. Morgan let the man race ahead. His horse wouldn't last long at that pace. A half mile later the man eased off and angled to the west and south toward the Medicine Bow Mountains.

Be interesting to find out why the man was in such a hurry. Ahead, Morgan saw a creek fed line of brush that wound in the same direction, but would put him out of sight of the other man. He rode into the brush, past it to the other side of the creek and picked up his pace.

Every quarter mile he made sure the runner was on the same course. Slowly he closed the distance. A half hour later he was ahead of the man and now he walked his mount out of the brush and directly at the stranger who was 300 yards away.

The man had no idea that his pursuer could be ahead of him.

Morgan kept his right hand free as he rode up to the man astride the big, strong gray. Lee nodded, then stopped a dozen feet away. "What's the next town?" he asked.

The man was of average height, and sported a new haircut leaving a white strip of untanned skin around the back of his neck. His clothes looked new. Morgan would take no chance on killing the wrong man. He had to know damn sure this was one of the men who slaughtered Virginia and her son.

"Back there aways is Laramie. What's ahead?"

"Nothing for a hell of a long ways. Rawlins, next good sized place."

Morgan paused. "Horse looks heated up a bit, should be walked out and wiped down."

"She'll be all right. Got to see my mother. She's sick in Rock Springs, and it's to hell and gone over this way. Want to get there before she dies."

"Yeah. I heard a man got his thieving hands shot off in Laramie, that right?"

"Could be. I just passed through."

The man shrugged, then his hand came out of his shirt with a hidden belly gun and he blazed a shot at Morgan. He missed. Morgan's horse shied, spinning him around. By the time he got turned around he swung up the shotgun and fired a shot at the spurred horse, but already it was out of range.

Morgan rode after him. Now he had his target. He had to be one of the killers or he wouldn't have tried a first shot. The chase was on.

Morgan pulled the Spencer out of the boot and rode hard after the other man. A moment later he had a shot and he led the horse and fired, but missed. The man leaned down around the horse and flashed down a small water course toward a small stream that flowed toward them from the hills.

The Wyoming landscape was flat here across the rest of the Laramie River valley, then lifted into foothills before coming to the Medicine Bow Mountains another 30 miles away. Morgan dodged a lush growth of sagebrush, lost sight of the man and then found him again as he surged into the brushy line that meandered along the stream.

He charged his roan down the slight incline, splashed across the stream and made sure the killer was not riding away past the screen of brush. When he was sure the man was still in the cover of the stream, Morgan rode hard west, downstream, hoping to pass the man and cut off his retreat.

As he surged along 50 yards from the trees he saw some slight movement ahead. He flattened out against the horse and cut away just as a rifle round slammed over his head. He kept going another 100 yards and cut into the brush. Morgan stopped the mare and tried to listen. He heard nothing from the other horse or rider.

Slowly he began working his way upstream toward where the man had last been. He stopped only partway there and listened. Wrong. The man would not be waiting for him. He was running. Morgan rode out to the edge of the brush and looked downstream on the far side of the creek.

He saw the rider on the gray well up a slight rise to the west. Damn, almost lost him.

Buckskin Morgan was moving again, riding hard up the slope. At the top he saw his quarry far down the other side. The killer was good, a

real outdoorsman. The last thought that this
would be a quick execution faded from Morgan's
plans.

Morgan pushed the roan hard for 20 minutes.
He had gained on the other man but the light was
starting to fade. He had wanted to close this out
before dark, but no chance now. If he didn't get
the guy slowed down he'd be out of the territory
by morning.

Buckskin rode hard, came to a spot where he
had a 30 yard place to watch the killer before he
would swing back behind the brush. Morgan took
out the Spencer and aimed in carefully, allowed
for the distance and fired. He rammed the lever
and fired five more times. The fourth round hit
the horse in the head and she went down.

Maybe he could kill the man before darkness,
after all, now that he was unhorsed. Morgan
spurred his mount and rushed forward. He kept
as hidden as he could. The man out there still had
a rifle and a six-gun. Morgan made a wide circle
around the dead horse. He knew the gunman
wasn't there any longer, but cautious gunmen
live longer.

He had rushed into the trees as soon as the
horse went down.

Damn! Cat and mouse. Morgan hated this. He'd
much rather get things out in the open and settle
it. One way or the other.

Lee hit the brush along the small creek in a line
west from where he had seen the killer enter. He
listened, heard nothing, then dismounted and
walked across the line of hoped for travel. On the
third crossing he found the footprints. Boots,
heavy heels, tapered toes, cowboy boots.

The heels sank into the ground deeper than the
toe, and there was no fast push off. The man was

tired but still moving forward.

Draw his fire? Yes.

Morgan mounted up, took a sighting ahead and stormed out of the trees and headed west. He generally followed the creek but headed a little away from it and then came back. When he figured he was two miles ahead of the spot where he had lost the killer, Morgan pulled into a heavy bit of brush on the bank of the stream and set up his "camp."

He built a small fire ring with rocks, made a fire, and set out a battered coffee cup he had in his saddlebags. He built up the fire so it would burn for two hours. Then he took off his blanket roll and covered some brush he cut to form the semblance of a body curled up and sleeping near the fire. He put his hat where the head would be. Yes, it would pass.

Morgan tied up his horse in heavy brush 20 yards from the fire. He moved further west, found a good site and settled in with an excellent field of fire on the little campsite. The killer had to come.

Morgan waited.

He was about 40 yards from the fire, on a slight rise in a sparsely wooded area. A fringe of pine trees had marched down toward the creek in some long ago chance seeding. He checked the wind. Yes, the fire was up wind from the killer. Even if the man was not an experienced woodsman, he should be able to smell an outdoor fire with smoke blowing in his face.

That was the lure, hoping that the man would bust in and shoot up the dummy below. At that point Morgan had only to wound the man, get his weapons and make sure he was one of the four killers at the ranch. Easy.

If it worked.

He waited for an hour. Darkness began to close in. A shadow darted through the gloom and for a moment silhouetted across the fire.

Morgan fired the Spencer, levered in another round and tried to determine what he had seen around the fire. He had no way of knowing if he had hit the man or not. A moment later he heard his horse wicker and a low human voice, then a pistol cracked in the darkness and a horse screamed in fear and agony. A second shot thundered through the night and then all was quiet.

Morgan shifted his aim at the place he had left his horse and fired his last six shots, but it wouuld be a miracle if he had hit the killer.

Now they both were on foot, and Morgan was angry that his plan had not worked. What in hell should he do next? Would the man keep running? Damn certain. Track him in the dark and take a chance with a torch now and then? Or was that setting himself up as a target?

Morgan lay there trying to figure out the best move.

Chapter Six

He listened. The gunman wasn't more than 30 yards from him.

"You killed Virginia and her son, you coward, and I'm gonna kill you."

Morgan waited hoping the man would reply out of anger.

"Coward? No bastard calls me a coward. At least I didn't shoot Elroy's hands off. Takes a real low down snake who ain't even a man to do that."

"I bet you're the one who shotgunned the little boy. Blew his head off, didn't you?"

"Hell, by then it was a war. You was shooting, too."

Morgan moved forward, slowly, quietly. He talked softer to make himself sound farther away.

"It wasn't a war . . . it was a damn sneak attack! I've killed two of you, just two more to go."

Morgan turned his ear in the direction of the man's voice. He heard a faint rustling. Buckskin had inserted a new tube of rounds in the Spencer, had six rounds in his Peacemaker and now moved forward cautiously.

Ahead he heard the brush cracking as the man ran. Morgan was right behind him. Another 20 yards and he stopped. No more sounds. The killer was out of the brush into the high valley, running across the dry countryside.

Morgan beat his way out of the brush and listened again. He heard someone panting ahead, to the left, out in the open. He pulled his six-gun and sent one round toward the sound, then jumped six feet to the left.

A flash of light and a gunshot ahead and Morgan emptied his revolver at the point of light. A scream shattered the night after the gunfire rolled away.

Morgan had hit him or the bastard was playing the old wounded duck game. Morgan kept moving up slowly, cautiously. Then he heard boots hitting the dirt again, fast and hard, and the quarry ran.

Morgan holstered the six-gun after he loaded it on the run, and pulled up the scattergun. He stopped, listened for the sound, zeroed in on it and fired both barrels, one after the other.

As the sound died he listened.

"Goddamn shotgun!" the same man screamed. "You and your damn shotgun!"

Morgan moved ahead but the voice sounded strange, as if it was muffled somehow. Behind something?

The handful of clouds blew away from the third-quarter moon and bathed the prairie in a faint glow. Ahead 40 yards, Morgan could see a boulder three feet high. Faint sounds came from behind it.

Morgan swung to the left and moved ahead, Indian walking and crouched so he made no noise and offered the smallest possible target. His foot hit a small rock. Morgan picked it up and threw it just behind the man's protective boulder.

The thud brought an immediate .44 blast from the killer toward the sound.

Yeah, he was behind the boulder. Morgan knew for sure now. He found another rock and threw it a little closer to the boulder but still on the far side. This time a pair of pistol shots sounded in the soft Wyoming night.

Morgan was through playing games with this killer. He moved carefully around the rock 20 yards away and threw one more stone to draw fire away from him.

The Meteor Belgium blasted twice one barrel after another at the pin point of revolver fire near the boulder. Then he dove and rolled away from his point of firing in case of return rounds from the killer.

Nothing happened for several moments. Then from some 500 to 100 feet away he heard a laugh. "Missed me, you bastard with the scattergun. You'll have to do better than that."

"Don't worry, I will. You're a dead man, you just don't know it yet."

Morgan ran toward the voice, then stopped. He could hear movement. He crept forward. It would be this way until daylight. An hour later they were still moving. Now and then the moon peeked through the clouds and they took a shot, but nothing close.

Then the man stopped running. He had found some kind of a defensive position. Morgan couldn't see it clearly, but it was a small cliff next to a stream. They had reached the first small foothills. Some timber dotted the landscape now, pine, Morgan guessed.

The killer had forted up behind the rocks and he wasn't moving. Morgan called to him twice but the man did not respond. From the sounds

Morgan knew the man had not left the place. He put two rifle rounds into the rocks below the cliff and settled down to wait.

There was no chance Morgan could sleep. But the killer couldn't either. It was a standoff, until daylight.

Morgan sat against a small pine and dozed, came awake, listened to the night sounds and then soon dozed again. He came fully awake just as the first false dawn tinged the eastern sky. Morgan moved so he had protection from the front, wedging behind his pine tree and a three foot tall boulder left over from some ancient eruption.

Ten minutes later it was light enough to see and the splash of rocks ahead took on the look of a real fortress. Morgan sensed at once that the talking was over. The killer wouldn't give away his position by shouting and neither would Morgan. He waited and watched. His Indian lessons in patience came into good stead for him now.

Morgan laid behind the rock for an hour without moving a muscle. He had a clear sight of the jumble of rocks ahead. There was no way out of it without coming into view.

A half hour later the sun was up and burning down into the rock pile. Morgan lay in partial shade. He heard a muttered oath, then a boot scraping on a rock. Morgan figured the range at about 40 yards. Too far to be sure with the shotgun. He lifted the Spencer repeater and waited.

A sun flash came off metal in the rocks. The rawhider was moving around. Morgan picked the best spot for him to come charging out, sighted in and waited.

Another half hour. The sun was out hot now

pan frying anyone in the rocks.

With a roar the killer charged from the rocks. He had ten yards to get across to the closest cover. Morgan fired twice, the second rifle round slamming into the runner's left leg, smashing him into the dirt. He rolled, and got up and crawled behind a rock before Morgan could fire again.

The killer didn't have his rifle with him when he ran. That helped out on the odds. He either forgot it or lost it in the dark. Good.

Morgan moved up, running hard. He was 50 feet from the rock when he at last saw the killer. A revolver fired but the round kicked up dirt ten feet in front of Morgan. A small cloud of blue smoke from the killer's pistol round rose from behind a rock. Morgan sent a rifle round just over the top of the rock, splattering into the granite behind it.

Lee crouched behind a small sagebrush bush to make as small a target as possible. Now was no time for a lucky shot from the killer's six-gun. He aimed another shot and then froze. A three foot long rattlesnake as big around as his wrist crawled directly for him.

The triangular head of the snake lifted and its forked tongue darted out to taste the situation. Danger? The snake's black eyes checked this long thing lying in its path. Morgan lowered the rifle slowly, then jolted it down pinning the snake's head to the ground.

Just at this time the killer lifted up and crawled around the rock he had hidden behind. He dragged one leg and was soon out of sight again. Morgan swore, took his pistol and blew the snake's head off with one shot. Then he lifted up and ran forward to see around the rock formation.

The killer was gone. Behind the rocks the small stream splashed down the gentle foothills. It mothered a lot of green brush and small trees. Upstream it led a half mile to heavy pine timber.

Morgan was starting to feel frustrated. How did he nail this guy? He listened again, more sounds of movement upstream. He ran ahead 30 yards and paused. He saw something ahead. A shirt sleeve. He sighted in, but didn't fire. The sleeve didn't move. It was a trap. The man had taken his shirt off and draped it over a bush.

Morgan studied it and then a figure, bare to the waist, flashed out of the brush beside him, six-gun blazing. Morgan's revolver came up in a reflex and fired. The bullet struck the other man's six-gun and blasted it from his hand. He was almost on top of Morgan. Then he was there crashing into him, knocking the pistol from his hand.

They slammed to the ground. There was no time to pull a knife, no time to lift the sawed off shotgun and blast the killer. Hand to hand combat.

Morgan slugged the face in front of him with a fist, took a clawing scrape of fingernails on his cheek, then got his knee into the man's chest as they rolled on the ground.

"Bastard!" the man screamed as he lifted a rock to smash down on Morgan. The buckskin clad man twisted out of the way and rammed his fist into the unprotected belly bringing a grunt of pain from the killer.

They rolled again and Morgan stayed on top, his hands clawing for the enemy's throat. He slammed a fist into his jaw, then again, and for a moment the killer sagged. Suddenly, he reared up and bucked Morgan off, kicking him in the side. Morgan dove on the man, pinned him to the green floor near the river. But he only had one hand free, the other was caught under their bodies.

His hand squeezed on the man's throat until he gagged. Then Morgan used a weapon a strange little man from Japan had taught him in San Francisco one night. Morgan squeezed his first two fingers together into a stiff lance and drove them with all his might into the side of the killer's throat. His stiff fingers penetrated the skin and knifed into flesh.

He bent the ends of his fingers into a hook and clawed sideways until he felt the pulsating carotid artery. His fingers slipped under the vital blood line and he jerked viciously outward. The carotid artery stretched, then broke and blood spurted ten feet through the air as the killer's heart pumped furiously.

Morgan rolled away, splattered by blood. He panted as he lay there in the grass. The killer stared at him a second, then his eyes went glassy as his brain ran out of blood and in 30 seconds he was unconscious. He would be dead in two minutes.

Lee Morgan sat up slowly. He shivered, watched the rawhider die, then stood and went to the small creek and washed the blood off his hands and shirt and the buckskin vest. He found the two six-guns and pushed them into his holster and belt, then caught up the Spencer where he had dropped it when the dead man rushed him.

Three down, he said to himself. Three down and one to go. He wondered who the last one was. Lars or Mars. It was a place to start. He turned back to the stream and washed off his face and then took a big drink.

He had a long walk back to town. Five, six,

maybe seven miles. Two hours. He could do an Indian trot and cover five miles in an hour. No. He felt drained.

Damn! He had done it. He had used the little Japanese man's finger stab and claw . . . and he had killed the man. With only his two fingers. Morgan shivered again. It was not his favorite method to kill a man. But it had worked. A professional uses what works when he needs it.

Buckskin felt the sun drying out his vest and shirt. Only a few blood spots showed on his pants. He pushed out a little faster, the Spencer over his shoulder, his left arm swinging as he walked downhill toward the valley and Laramie.

He would be glad to see the little town, to have a good meal and then about six hours of sleep. He hadn't been this tired for a long time.

As he walked, he was wondering who the fourth man was. Where he was hiding? What he did? Had Morgan already seen him in town and didn't know it?

He smiled for a moment thinking about Aggie Cump. She was a most satisfying and comfortable woman. Not exciting, but steady and honest. He would see her again—after this was all cleared up. Yes, later.

Morgan stopped thinking and put his energy into walking. That was the task at hand.

Chapter Seven

It was slightly before noon when Buckskin trudged slowly up the alley behind the Emporium and went in the back door. He walked to his room and dropped the weapons, washed the rest of the blood off his pants and scrubbed his hands and face, then shaved.

He found Gwen in the kitchen.

"You're lost, Buck," she said.

"You found me, Gwen. I'm hungry as a she bear with six cubs, got anything to eat?"

"How about two big roast beef sandwiches, with dill pickles and some potato salad I'm making for tonight. She poured him a cup of coffee and set out two big donuts for him to work on while she made the sandwiches.

"Chew on those until I do the sandwiches. Mustard and horseradish and lettuce?"

He nodded. "You could start up your own restaurant almost anywhere," Morgan said. "You make any food taste so damn good. Ever think about a cafe?"

"Thought about it. But I'd need at least five hundred dollars, and that's like hooting at the moon. At least here I'm a *partner*, not just another whore."

"You don't mind that word?"

"No, it's what I am. If I ever get to be something else, then I won't like the word." She looked at him levelly. "I hear you're a killer. You mind that word?"

"Depends on who I kill. If the man deserves it, then I feel good."

"Oh. Yeah, I see. We're a lot the same." She put the big sandwiches in front of him.

The home made bread was eight inches across and half an inch thick. The wafer thin sliced roast beef had been piled high between the bread. He took a bite and growled when the horseradish bit him back.

"Yeah!" he said.

After the meal he thanked Gwen again, then went into his room, locked the door and slept.

It was after seven when he got up. He had a cup of coffee from Gwen's bottomless pot and wandered out to the saloon. It was too late today to find out much about killer number four. Tomorrow, with a clear head, he'd turn the damn town upside down and dig out the bastard.

Lily sat down beside him where he perched at his usual wall table.

"Missed you," she said. "You all right?"

"Yeah. I found one of the men I was hunting and we took a ride into the hills. Lasted all night."

"Just one of you came back?"

"Yeah, walking."

"Ouch. Oh, we have a big game on tonight in the side room. Nobody gets in there without a hundred dollars to spend. It's where the towners who don't want to be seen at the tables do their gambling. We've got five ready for tonight, including your friend that Englishman. What's his name—Harwich."

"You want me in the room to be sure nothing

happens?"

"Right, and pat them down. I don't want any weapons on the players. The Englishman will have his new bodyguard with him. He has to be clean, too."

"What time?"

"About nine."

Morgan finished his coffee. "I'll be there. Any trouble last night?"

"Smooth as turkey gravy."

"Good." He took the cup back to the kitchen and filled it. This was going to be a long night. He found a cardboard box and took it into the side room. The poker table was set up for six. There were two additional tables and a side table for drinks. He left the box and went out to the saloon. Nothing happened to disrupt the usual flow of commercial drinking until nine o'clock.

At the door of the back room, Morgan took weapons from the players, then patted their sleeves and chests and backs, but found no hideout guns.

The Englishman was not pleased.

"We're all gentlemen here, sir," he said. "Is this quite necessary?"

"House rules, Mr. Harwich. Be surprised how many 'gentlemen' I've seen draw a belly gun and shoot somebody right between the eyes."

The Englishman's bodyguard came in, growled when Morgan held out his hand for the man's six-gun. He permitted himself to be patted down with a snarl. He didn't look fast. His holster wasn't tied down right. Morgan shrugged. He had no teeth now anyway.

The game soon got underway. Beside the Englishman they had the vice-president of the town's ony bank, Jared Reynolds. He looked about 45, short and round, with ruddy cheeks and thinning brown hair. He had a passion for gambling and Morgan knew right away he would lose. He was too anxious, too sure that he would win.

Also at the table was Willis Jerome, the town's best lawyer from comments around the table. He was about 40, quick, alert with a couldn't-care-less attitude which meant he had a good chance of winning.

A big rancher from outside of town named Kay Smith sat in. He was rugged and square and probably planned on losing his hundred for the sport of it.

To Morgan's surprise Lily sat in. She was good at poker he soon found. There was no percentage to the house here and they played with real money, not house chips.

"Table stakes, gentlemen," Lily said. "Let's not see anyone trying to up their stakes after we get started. Is everyone satisfied with their playing money?"

The game got underway with Lily breaking the seal on a new deck of cards and dealing.

An hour later the barkeep brought in another bottle of the good whiskey and a dozen bottles of cold beer.

Lily was slightly ahead. The lawyer was the big winner and the rancher lost steadily but didn't mind. He was the talker in the group and once in a while somebody told him to quiet down. He didn't object.

The banker, Reynolds, won the first two hands, then lost the next four. He was down to about $25. The next game was seven card stud.

Reynolds had a good feeling. His two down cards were aces! He tried not to let it show on his face. He'd never been very good at a poker face. His first card up was a king of hearts. Not bad.

He had an ace of hearts. His king showing on the table was high. He bet five dollars and nobody raised. The next card he got was a queen of hearts. Three legs of a perfect royal flush!

He swallowed. Lily had a pair of sixes and was high on the table. She bet ten dollars. He put in the ten dollars and stayed in the game. He had to stretch his available money to see that last card.

His next card came up a jack of clubs. Damn. He had four parts of a Ace high straight. Not bad. Lily's pair of sixes was still high. She bet five dollars this time. It would cost him five to see his last card. No, the lawyer raised the five to fifteen. It would cost him ten dollars.

Reynolds sweated. He wiped his forehead. The bet was back to him to stay in at ten dollars.

"Can I stay in and be five dollars light?" he asked the table. Everyone but Lily nodded. She frowned, then shrugged. He put in his five, then pulled it back and put a gold piece on top of it. Light.

The cards went around. The lawyer with a pair of fours got his third. His fourth four was showing on the table in another hand. No aces were up. No tens were showing. Damn good chance for an ace or a ten. Four tens in the deck. Any one of them would probably win the hand. Just one ten and he would get healthy again!

The card came down to the next player. Lily picked up two pair on the table. Reynolds' turn. The card sailed out. An ace. Oh, damn. He wilted. So damn close. He had three aces.

Lily's two pair was high on the table. She looked around. Two pair or three of a kind in a game of seven card was not a good hand. He watched Lily. If she didn't go too high he might go light. Hell, he could at least see what the bet was.

Lily scowled.

"That full house you have, Lily, isn't good enough to take our money," the rancher said.

"Hell, what a bad spot I'm in," Lily said. "If I bet 50 bucks, everybody will blow out. If I bet five you'll think I'm bluffing and everyone will raise me. Hell. Ten bucks is the best way to bet."

Reynolds slowly dropped his cards face down and shoved his hand into the pot.

One damn ten away from a straight. Damn. He watched the game. Two times it raised, then the lawyer was the last one in the pot with the two pair showing in Lily's hand. The lawyer called.

"Full house, queens over sixes," Lily said.

"Damned good hand," the lawyer admitted. He started to fold his hand. Then spread it out. "But it doesn't beat my four little sevens."

"Be damned," Lily said. "You were in the ideal spot of not having to bid."

Reynolds grunted. He'd been right on the final outcome at least. He stood, pulled his wallet and took out a five dollar bill which he handed to the lawyer.

"Hell, I'm busted for tonight. Next week I'm gonna clean out some clocks around this game. You all be sure and be here." He scowled at all of them, nodded at Lily and walked out the door and to the front of the saloon.

On the way out he talked to one of the girls in the saloon. She shook her head and he left. Down the street he went into a second bar and talked to the first girl he saw. He slipped her two dollars and she grinned.

Jared Reynolds was furious. He had lost another three hundred dollars. A whole damn year's pay for a bookkeeper in the bank. He just couldn't seem to win. He went in the side door of the bank when no one saw him and dug out account books and looked through them. It was getting harder and harder.

At last he found an account that had not been used for almost two years. It had $600 in it. He made a withdrawal of $200, and found another account he could tap for $100. That made up his loss for tonight.

He made a quick mental calculation. He was up to over $3,000 now. He had lost that much in the past two years. It didn't seem possible. Three thousand! He only got paid a little over $600 a year. Five years pay!

Sweat beaded his face as he thought about it, making his cheeks redder than ever.

A knock sounded on the side door and he hurried there, opened it a crack, then threw it wide and pulled the girl into the room.

"I'm Sunny. You all ready?" She put her arms around his neck and kissed him, pushing her breasts against him. "I've never had a banker before, are you good?"

"Best you've ever had. I'll show you why." He took her into the main bank vault and took out a drawer full of twenty dollar bills. In the back room he lit a small lamp and scattered the bills on a couch.

"You ever been poked real good laying on a mattress of two thousand dollars?" he asked her.

Sunny squealed. She dropped down on the bills and wiggled her bottom against them. "That feels soooooooo good!" She stood up and stripped quickly. "I want my bare bottom on them. Ohhhhhh that's just wonderful!"

Reynolds watched her for a minute, then pulled open the fly on his pants and jerked out his penis.

"Work time, little pussy. Spread them and give me that two thousand dollar poke."

"Oh, yes! Wait until I tell the girls!"

He slapped her. "No! You don't tell nobody you was even here tonight. You can't say a word about it. I'll give you five dollars."

"Yeah, yeah, okay. So get it in me!"

He bent and lifted her legs and jammed at her spot until he hit it and sank in.

"Damn, you found the right hole. Remember, this is my first two thousand dollar mattress poke, so I want it to be a wonderful one."

Reynolds didn't have a lot of staying power. He pounded a half dozen times, then realized he had lost control and slammed into her eight more times and pushed her up the couch on the slippery paper bills.

Sunny squealed as Reynolds climaxed and tried to fake her own passion, but she couldn't.

"Now if all that two thousand dollars was mine, I could really show you a great time," Sunny said.

Reynolds was panting then, trying to recover. He fell on top of Sunny and she squirmed a minute, then stopped and tried to figure out how she could slip a couple of those twenties into her mouth so he couldn't find them.

A moment later Reynolds was crying. Tears streamed down his face and he blubbered into her shoulder.

"Hey, Jared, Honey. What's the matter? Didn't you like your two thousand dollar poke?"

He wiped his eyes. "No, no, you were fine, Sunny. I've just got troubles, that's all."

"With a two thousand dollar bed you got problems? What kind of problems?"

"See, I like to gamble a little, play poker, the back room where nobody can see."

"Oh, damn. High stakes?"

"Higher than I can afford. I—I borrowed some

money from the bank."

"And the President doesn't know about it?"

"Yeah. Something like that."

"How much, Jared? How much you steal?"

"Over three thousand."

"Holy Christ in a basket. Three thousand . . . dollars?"

He nodded.

"You're in deep shit. Christ, three thousand!"

"I don't know what to do. I could confess and go to prison. Or I could shoot myself. That might be better."

"Hey, baby. Don't do that. You've got nothing to worry about at all. I got the answer to all your problems."

He pushed up and sat on the bed.

She sat beside him. "Yeah, there ain't no problem Sunny can't fix."

"What? What can I do?"

"Friday night you and me meet here and we clean out the safe of every dollar in the place and then we take off for San Francisco. We ride out of town and catch the west bound train and nobody ever sees us again!"

"I don't know."

"Hell of a lot better than killing yourself."

"Yes, I admit that. But to steal. . . ."

"Hell, you already stole over three thousand. How much cash is here on a weekend?"

"Ten, maybe eleven thousand dollars."

"In cash?"

"Yes."

"So what's the problem? We come about midnight, clean out the safe and put it in a bag, take a buggy and ride west. We put the buggy on the tracks to stop the train and tell them we're eloping and don't want nobody to know. We get away free and clear. We'll disguise both of us. . . ."

He grabbed her and kissed her lips. He'd never kissed a whore before in his life.

"Sunny! Let's do it. Yes! That's a way out. I've been trying to figure it out for weeks. Don't tell anybody anything. There's to be a shipment of Federal bank money on Friday. We'll take it with us. Yes!"

She put her hands down to his crotch and began working him hard again.

"This is going to cost you. Right now I want forty dollars to get some nicer clothes, and then I want you to pleasure me. I'll show you where, your hand right down here, this little button. You twang it like a guitar string and then I'll show you what to do next. This is one time the whore is gonna get her rocks off for a change." She wiggled around on the twenty dollar bills.

"Oh, it feels so good on money!"

Later she stared up at him.

"Friday night. Don't come see me before then. Two days. You get ready. Rent a buggy we can get down the tracks about ten miles or so, and have two stout bags we can carry the money in. We might not take all the gold, it's so heavy."

"Let's go tomorrow night," Reynolds said.

"Hell, no," Sunny snapped. "We go Friday night and then nobody comes into the bank until Monday morning so nobody knows the money or us are missing. We have a two day head start on them when they start to look for us."

"Yeah, you're right, Sunny. Damn, seems like you're right most of the time."

"Now, sweetheart, you pleasure me again," Sunny said. She could make this dope do just about what she wanted him to do. Once they got on that train and away, the little man would take a fast dive off the train somewhere.

As Reynolds moved his hand to her crotch, she folded four of the twenty dollar bills and put them in the pocket in her long skirt that lay across the cot.

"Oh, yeah," she said gently. "Soon, baby, both of us are going to be rich!"

Chapter Eight

Morgan stayed with the poker game until a little after one. It closed down when the rancher lost his table stakes and everyone decided it was time to close up. Only Lily and the lawyer were still ahead in the game. Both won more than enough to make it worth their while.

Morgan flushed one drunk out of the saloon and barred the front door. The apron finished cleaning up at the bar and went out the back door.

Lily sat at a table and watched Morgan.

"A worthwhile day, all in all. I scored tonight, and I hear you did some good this morning."

"True. I found one more of them."

"I'm not asking about it, but I'm happy for you. Oh, the girls tell me my taste in men is improving. They like having you around, especially Gwen. She wants to keep you here as a permanent fixture."

"You should set up Gwen in her own small cafe. She could make ten times what she makes for your business now."

Lily frowned. "You really think so?"

"True. She has a touch with food. She loves to cook. Why don't you loan her $500 and let her pay it back when she can. The two of you split the profits until you're paid back."

"Yeah, you might just have an idea there. I'd never thought much about it. Gwen's popular here as a soiled dove. Would we need to put her in another town?"

"Hell, no. In a year most people will forget she evere worked in here."

"It's a good idea." Lily smiled at him. "You have any special plans for the rest of the night?"

"Just some sleep. I'm not fighting at full steam. I wouldn't be much good for you tonight."

"Yeah. And I can't get used to having it regularly again." She stood and started for the stairs. "Sleep well, Buckskin."

He did.

Morgan got up at seven, shaved and took a bath in the tub and was at the cafe for breakfast at eight. Then he began working on his last man. How to smoke him out? All he had were the partial names, or sound like words. Lars . . . stars . . . It could mean anything, be anybody.

The idea hit him solidly and he left the rest of his coffee and hurried over to the Laramie General Store. Aggie Cump was just opening up.

She smiled. "Missed you last couple of days," she said.

"Two days ago I was chasing around up in the hills. Yesterday I was catching up. There's something you can help me with though." He told her about the two partial names he had. "Could they be anybody you know in town?"

Aggie listened to the names and knew she had to concentrate. She had been staring at his wonderful body and in only two or three minutes she was getting all damp down below. She shook her head and thought again.

"Yes. Star could be Larry Starley, he's lived here for years. Or it might be Paul Starwell the barber and preacher. The other one, Lars, could be Bill Larson, he's the livery man."

"Mrs. Cump, I was thinking more of somebody brand new in town who stopped in recently maybe looking for general delivery mail or waiting for some mail."

"That's easy, I'll just check my book. I always write down those asking about general delivery mail. Regulations." They went to the little post office desk and she opened a ledger.

"Oh, yes, I'd forgot about him. I do have a name that might fit. Came in three or four days ago. His name is Paul Larston. I can't remember what he looks like."

By now it was all Aggie Cump could do to keep her hands off the handsome man. She felt he was almost ready to leave.

"Well, thanks a lot. Now at least I have a name to check out, whether it's my man or not. Thanks again, Mrs. Cump."

"Oh, quite all right, just part of the job. I hesitate to ask you, but I wonder if you could help me for a minute. Something I need moved in the back, a keg of nails, and it's so heavy."

"Sure, I can help. Where is it?"

"Right back here, in the storage room." Oh, glory! She could feel wetness running down her leg! "There are two of them, actually, six penny and eight penny, the most popular sizes."

She led him through a door into the storage room and showed him two raw wood nail kegs. A hammer lay near by. He hit the top of the keg until the thin wood top broke and he picked out the pieces of wood exposing the one hundred and twenty pounds of new nails.

"Can I dump them in a bin for you?"

"Oh, no, I'll take them out a few at a time. I want to thank you," she plunged ahead. Aggie walked up to Lee Morgan and kissed him on the cheek. Then she grabbed his arms and kissed his lips, a hot demanding kiss. She leaned in against his chest.

"I've wanted to do that since the first day I saw you. Lordy, I didn't think I'd ever have nerve enough." She leaned back, saw a soft smile on his face and took his head in her hands and reached up and kissed him again.

"So good!" she said softly as she let go of him. Then she caught his hand and put it over her breast. He bent and kissed her lightly, then caressed her breast. She ripped her bodice open and moved his hand inside, under the chemise, directly on her hot breast.

"Buck, this is the real favor I want you to do for me. I . . . I haven't let a man touch me for almost three years now . . ."

He kissed her again, his fingers playing with her extended, hot nipple. She brought his head down to her breasts and pushed the cloth aside. Morgan licked the orb, then chewed lightly on the sparking nipple before he sucked her breast into his mouth.

"Oh, the front door is open!" she said. She pushed him away, arranged her dress to cover herself and hurried out to the front door where she locked it and quickly returned to where Morgan waited for her.

"Right here?" Morgan asked. She caught his hand and led him around a stack of buckets to a big box filled with new blankets. He took out half a dozen and spread them on the floor and sat down.

She dropped beside him, and he kissed her. Then he found her breasts and she moaned and lay on the blankets on her back.

"I usually don't do this. I mean, I haven't had a

man since my husband died. But I couldn't let you get away."

He rubbed her breasts until they felt like they were on fire, then lifted her dress over her head. She undid three petticoats and took them off; then some soft, white, cotton underthings and sat there naked.

She undressed him, making little sounds and yelping in delight when she took off his shirt and found his hairy chest. She nuzzled in it, then let him take off his boots and helped him with his pants. When she pulled down his short summer underwear she put her hand to her mouth.

"My god, they are that huge. I'd forgotten." She bent and kissed his lance, then stroked it back and forth with her hand. She brought her breasts to his mouth for his ministrations and at last lay down on the blankets.

"Now, sweet man," she said. "Make love to me now, soft and sweet and gentle. I don't think I've forgotten how."

She lifted her knees and spread them and Morgan moved into position and entered her gently. She was moist and open and ready and he eased in until his pelvic bones clashed with hers.

"Oh, my, yes!" Aggie said. "It's been so long. Don't be too fast."

He reached down and found her soft node and rubbed it back and forth. He smiled as her breathing raced and she began humping up at him. In a moment she boiled into a surging climax that rattled her and sent her body into six hard spasms that ended with little yelps of delight.

She opened her eyes and stared. "Lordy, not in all the times have I come so hard. Wonderful."

She began moving her hips in a circular motion. It set Morgan on fire. He snorted and humped and in a dozen hard strokes he was so ready he couldn't stop.

"You next," she said.

Morgan grunted and moaned as he slammed into her six times, jetting his seed hard and deep as her hips rose to meet him to gain the deepest possible penetration.

She climaxed again as he peaked and together they thrashed on the blankets until both collapsed, sweating and panting like a pair of steam engines. They rested for a few minutes, then he leaned up and looked down at her.

"You are a terribly sexy lady," he said.

"And you are a terrific lover. The best of the two men who have ever entered me. You have a slave for life."

She sat up and her breasts bounced and jiggled. Morgan captured one with each hand.

"I wonder if you know how good that feels after they have been touched by no one but me for such a long, long time. Your hands are like the touch of passion all over again." She caught his soft tool and began urging him back into action.

"You've rested long enough, come on." Gently she caught his scrotum and massaged his balls. He hardened almost at once and she kissed the purple head as it emerged into full, hard readiness again.

She pushed Morgan down on the blankets and sat on his stomach. Then she slid lower and whispered in his ear.

"May I be on top? Can I ride you like a pinto pony in heat? I really love it that way."

He nodded and helped her lift and position herself. Then she lowered onto his staff and squealed in joy and rapture as he lanced upward into her higher and higher until he touched the tip of her uterus and she yelped in surprise.

She rested on her hands and leaned down and kissed him.

"This is so good. It makes me think back to when I was married, and every couple of nights we'd figure out some new way to get together. Lots of them wouldn't work, but we'd keep at it until we found a way we could . . . could do it. The pony is my all time favorite."

She began moving up and down and then back and forth. Soon her hands found the right spot on the floor beside him and she galloped back and forth across him like a mare in heat. She climaxed quickly, wheezing and moaning and then shaking with such great spasms he was afraid for her. Her face contorted and she wailed and then gasped at the end of it.

She rode him again and a minute later tore into another long climax that left her breathless.

The third time she rode him Morgan complicated it by not being able to hold back any more and humped her white bottom high in the air as he surged seven times shooting hot fluid into her still spasming vagina.

They both collapsed and he held her tightly to him, her big breasts squashed against his chest.

Aggie had a smile on her face that might give her away if it lasted. They lay there for ten minutes, then Aggie laughed softly and looked up.

Somebody knocked on the front door.

Aggie scowled. "Oh, damn! I guess that's the end of it for today. Will you come back? Will you come to the house tonight after your work? I can't just let you go after this. I know I was a forward hussy, and I tried to seduce you, but I really want to see you again."

"I'll be in town, don't worry, I'll see you again.

Right now maybe you should get dressed before your customers break down your front door."

Morgan sat there naked and watched her dress. It was one of the joys of life, watching a woman put on her clothes. When she was prim and proper, she stuck her tongue out at him, bent and patted his soft penis and hurried out into the store.

Now Morgan hurried and dressed before some customer wandered into the back of the store and found him all naked.

He dressed as quickly as he could, waited until there was no one in the store and went out front. Aggie met him by the cash drawer and put his hands on her breasts.

"That just feels so *damn* good!" she said. She giggled. Aggie Cump hadn't giggled in years. "Look at me," she commanded. "This smile on my face, is it a giveaway? Does it tell anyone who looks that this lady just made love?"

"No, I don't think so. It shows a woman who is happy, and for the moment satisfied, and who knows that there will be more times she can count on."

"Oh, yes, there must be a god." She surged up and kissed him. She was standing behind the counter and she caught one of his hands and put it between her legs. Her legs had parted and he could feel the damp spot on her underthings.

"Oh, damn! I want you again right now! When did I become such a sex starved woman?"

A small bell over the front door jangled.

"You better get out of here. If that's a woman, she'll know for damn sure we just made love."

Morgan chuckled and stepped back. Aggie arranged her dress and walked toward the customer. It was a man, who needed some eight penny nails.

"Yes, I just opened up a new keg this morning, how many pounds do you need?"

Morgan waved at her as he walked toward the front door and outside.

Yes, yes! The glories of the ladies. But first he had another job. John Larston.

The hotels would be his first try. There were two hotels in Laramie right then. It cost him a quarter at each of them to take a quick look at the register. No one by that name had registered at either hotel during the past week.

There was nowhere else in town where a man needed to use his name. How else could he trace him? He tried the livery, but the man there said he had nobody he knew of by that name.

"Course half a dozen men a day leave horses here. I didn't ask you your name when you was in, did I? Sometimes I do, sometimes they tell me to be sure I treat their animal right. But I don't recollect any name like that in the last few days."

Morgan thanked him and began wandering down the street and in and out of the stores. He asked several of the store owners and proprietors, but again drew a blank on the name.

He had to be new in town, and if he asked about General Delivery that would mean he had planned on being here and told someone who might write him a postal letter here. It was all too vague and flimsy.

One more man to go and this could be him. Only how could he find the bastard?

He wanted to see Lily. She wasn't up yet, he knew that. The Emporium wouldn't open until at least ten o'clock. He took a deep breath and cursed silently, then wandered down the block.

For twenty minutes he leaned against the Demorest Home Restaurant, and watched the men passing by. Then he snorted and closed his eyes in disgust. He didn't have the slightest idea what the man he was searching for even looked like.

Chapter Nine

As Morgan leaned against the wall in the morning Wyoming sun, he thought of a new approach. The ranches! Men had to give a name when they signed on at a ranch. At least some name. He kicked away from the warm store front and walked to the livery.

He rented a horse and saddle and got directions to the biggest and closest ranch. It belonged to the same man he had watched play poker last night. Kay Smith. His spread was about six miles north of town on the Laramie. Morgan was a quarter of a mile out of town when he turned west.

In his current financial condition he had to go out and bring in his saddle. In fact, there were two saddles out there. He could use one and sell one. The rawhider wouldn't mind. He found the first saddle easily, made a wrong turn and wasted an hour in the brush before he found the second one. He checked the contents of the killer's saddlebags and was surprised.

It held ten twenty dollar gold pieces, a good pocket watch and a few letters. He tied one saddle on his horse behind his own, and slung the other one over his back. His arm was ready to fall off when he got back to the livery.

After dumping the saddles and telling the stable boy to hold them for him, he rode out again. This time he made it to the Smith spread.

It was big. Large ranch house, a dozen buildings, thirty or forty hands working the pens and corrals getting ready to go out on a sweep of some distant range.

Kay Smith met him at the kitchen door.

"You lost way out here in the wilderness, Morgan?"

"Mostly. Looking for a varmint by the handle of John Larston. Did you hire on anybody by that name in the last week?"

"Afraid not. Fact is, ain't hired on anybody for near a month now. Come in for a cold beer and set a spell."

Inside it was large and cool. A woman flashed through the edge of the room, smiled and waved and was gone.

"That's my wife, Ella. She's a mite shy with strangers." Smith tipped the cold bottle of beer and drank, then eyed Morgan. "This Larston, he wanted by the law?"

"Probably. Should be if he isn't. He and three others shot down a woman and a four year old a week back out to the east. I come to pay my respects with double-ought buck."

Smith belched and grinned. "Know what you mean. Shotgun is a fine way to settle things quick."

"I'd be grateful if you hear that name, you give me a nod."

"Right, I'll do that."

Morgan stood and they went outside.

"Long ride for so little," Smith said.

"Not so," Morgan said. "I got a free beer." He mounted up, waved and rode back toward town.

Riding time was thinking time. His financial

situation was suddenly bettered. The $200 was found money. It would pay for a new horse to replace the one the killer had destroyed and give him some breathing room.

Now, just where the hell to find that bastard Larston—if he really was the right man. John Larston could have been someone going through town on the train.

Morgan scowled for the next four miles trying to figure out a sure fire way to scare the other killer into the open. Scare him or dig him out, he didn't care which.

When he made it back to town he settled up with the livery stable man on the rental, then bargained with the man. First he sold him the saddle and saddlebags for twenty-two dollars. It was a good western saddle, finely made, worth half again that much, but Morgan already had one he liked.

"Now I need to buy a horse," Morgan said. "What do you have with a little stamina, some drive and deep chested?"

They looked at three in the corral. Morgan liked one, a big gray mare with a stride that would eat up the miles. She watched Morgan as soon as he came in the corral. At first she stayed away, but when he flipped a noose around her long gray neck she walked up to him obediently.

Morgan liked that. He looked in the big brown eyes and still liked her. Her teeth were not too long, maybe eight or nine years old. He saddled her and rode around the corral, then signaled for the gate to be opened and he took her for a ride into the open country.

She moved like a surging river current, smooth, even and with a confident sense of power. Then they walked. She still had a stride that would leave normal horses behind. Morgan tried some sudden turns and he soon found out she'd had training as a cutting horse. Once he almost lost his seat.

Ten minutes later back at the livery he began to tell the livery man what he didn't like about the horse. The livery man just grinned.

"Best damn horse I've had in here in five years. A hundred and twenty dollars and she's yours. I'll throw in a new bridle and reins."

They haggled for half an hour. Morgan wound up paying $85 cash. She was a mount worth at least $150.

All the haggling made him hungry. When he checked his new watch it was almost four in the afternoon.

He walked into the small dining room of the Emporium Saloon beside the kitchen and his mouth began to water.

"Early," Gwen said wiping a line of sweat off her forehead. "You know how to mash potatoes?"

He did.

The girls straggled in, but by four on the dot all were there including Lily.

"Finally get hungry?" Lily asked.

"I'm thinking about opening a restaurant, and I'm hunting the best cook in town," Morgan said.

Gwen looked up, smiled and then continued forking small steaks onto a platter. One steak was twice as big as the others. She put it on a separate plate and carried it to Morgan.

"Hey, I wanted that one!" Jody yelped.

"Jody, you get any fatter and I'll be able to charge twice for you, once going and once coming," Lily growled. "Now hush up. We want Buck to at least think that you're a refined lady."

"Damn right, you're all ladies," Buck said. "I have a question. Has any of you heard the name

John Larston? Would be in the last week or so."

"I never want to know names," Phyllis said. She was small but big busted and now her robe slipped a little and a nipple winked at Morgan.

The others shook their heads.

"We're not real big on names, Buck," Lily said. "But I'll keep my ears open around the gamblers."

Then the food came. Besides the man sized steak for Morgan there were his own mashed potatoes with lots of salt and butter mixed in, a pot of new brown gravy, fresh green peas and carrots, huge slabs of fresh bread still warm from the oven, home made gooseberry jam, and lemon cream pie for desert. Morgan had another cup of coffee. The girls wandered off to their rooms and Morgan sat with Lily.

"I been thinking about that cafe idea. The man running one in town now wants to move to San Francisco. He tried to get me to buy it six months ago for seven hundred dollars."

"Sounds interesting. You'll become owner of half the town in ten years."

"My hope. I'll offer him six hundred. He'll probably jump at it. He can't cook worth sour beans."

"Talked to Gwen about it?"

"Not yet, think I should?"

"Give her something to think about, look forward to. Yeah, I'd tell her if it was me."

"You're not really a bear, Buckskin, you're a pussycat," Lily said watching him.

"Everybody's got more than one expression. You ever see me really angry?"

"Don't figure I want to."

"You figure right, lady." He stood, then bent and kissed her cheek. "Got to get out and plow the farm, see who I can turn up in a deep furrow."

"Good luck. Don't forget to turn over a few rocks. Surprising what's down there sometimes."

Sunny sat in her crib that afternoon three doors down from the Emporium Saloon, thinking. She'd begged off dinner, telling the man with the whip that she was feeling sick. That would get her out of regular work tonight. She could slip out early, about ten they had figured.

Sunny stared at the small bag she would pack to take along. Just some essentials, some underwear and an extra pair of shoes. She'd wear a pair of jeans she had cut down for the riding. They might not get on the train. She wanted to be able to ride a horse if she had to.

Sunny grinned. If it went off the way it looked right now, she'd never have to work another night in her life. She didn't give Jared Reynolds a second thought. As soon as they were away clean, she would get rid of him. Pushing him off the train would be easiest, kill him and get rid of the body all in one hard push. Then all that bank money would be hers!

If that didn't work, she had the derringer. A twin shot .45 can put a lot of scare into most men, and it had killed a man before. He was getting nasty and cutting her with his big knife, so she shot him. They had dumped his body into the alley and the sheriff said he wasn't surprised. The crazy man had been asking to be killed for years.

She grinned when she looked at the four folded twenty dollar bills. She had some money coming from the fund the boss kept for each girl. He was good that way at least. Saved a couple of dollars a week so if one wanted to move on, she'd have some cash to at least buy her ticket.

Sunny thought how much money twelve thousand dollars was. In one dollar bills it would make a hell of a big suitcase full. But if they were all twenties it wouldn't be so big. She could carry that much in paper twenty dollar notes.

She'd let Jared carry the gold. If he took any. Somebody told her once that there were sixteen double eagles to a pound. That would be three hundred and twenty dollars a pound. They could take maybe ten pounds. . . . three thousand, two hundred dollars! Yeah, she would even carry it.

Sunny made sure that the derringer was safely tucked into the holster on the band around her thigh. She wore it most of the time now. Had since two days ago when Jared had picked her out at random among the girls. What a great moment that was! Otherwise she'd be here waiting for the cowboys to come in and jam into her, and some other girl would be going with Jared.

No, not so, it had been *her idea* to rob the bank and run away. Jared never would have thought of it himself.

Sunny went to the mirror and combed her hair, then brushed it. She scrubbed her face until it shone with her good health. From now on she'd pay more attention to how she looked, and dressed. Yes, she was going to spend three hundred dollars on clothes at the first big town they came to!

For a minute she wondered what a fifty dollar bill looked like. She'd never seen one. Or even a hundred! She wanted a hundred dollar bill that she could hold in her hand and maybe put in that little secret compartment in that fancy girdle she bought once. One little old hundred dollar bill wasn't much to want, since this whole thing had been her idea.

She was sure that Jared would give her the hundred dollar bill. If he didn't, she might kill him quicker than she had intended to.

Morgan stayed at the Emporium that evening. He figured he owed it to the management. Nothing much happened. He got bored and played a game of penny ante poker with two old timers. They ran the barkeep out of pennies. Morgan lost thirty cents before he realized the old buzzards were cheating.

He began cheating and won six pots in a row, then explained to them that cheating wasn't allowed in the Emporium, even at the penny ante table. They grinned, said it took him a long time to catch on. He bought them each a beer and circulated.

There was no game in the back room.

The trouble came when a man who looked half Mexican drove his knife an inch into the table and demanded to see a "layout" of the cards in the deck. The dealer refused. Morgan's knife point touched the dealer's wrist before he could move the deck.

"I think the gentleman is corect, dealer," Morgan said softly. "Any player has a right to count the cards and ask for a layout at any time. Everyone around the table please stand up, now!" The four men stood.

Morgan counted the cards.

"Fifty four!" the Mexican man hissed.

"True," Morgan said. He laid out the cards by suits and soon found two extra aces. Buck turned to the dealer. "Would you care to explain this?"

"I just got the deck."

"The deck is the dealer's responsibility." He put the cards in the middle of the table. "Any losers at this table?"

Two men nodded. One was down nearly twenty dollars, the other had lost ten. Morgan took fifteen dollars from each of the two winning men's stacks of money and paid off the losers.

"Now, it's ended." He pointed at the winners. "You two are excused. You go out the alley door. I don't want to see you in here again."

When they went, furious with themselves for getting caught and with Morgan for dealing with them, Morgan turned to the other two men.

"Sorry, it happens. Watch out for card sharks. If you're going to play, have someone teach you how other men cheat at cards. Now, you two, go out the front door." He watched the Mexican man a moment.

"Señor, I've seen men killed for calling a cheater. Be damn careful next time."

Lily came up and looked at the cards. She pulled out the two offending aces and ripped them in half. Then she pocketed the deck in one of the pockets in her big skirt and put a sealed deck on the table.

"Excitement is over, folks, let's get back to business." Lily said.

They closed up just after twelve.

Morgan slipped out and found the widow Cump's small house off First Street. It was painted white with a brown trim and had a new shingle roof that should last for five years yet. There was no grass in the yard, but few houses had any grass. A pair of spindly rose bushes fought against the cold of winter and the blistering hot summers.

He saw lights on in the front room, so he went up the steps and knocked on the front door. Steps sounded at once and soon the door opened.

"Yes?"

"Aggie, it's Buck."

"Good, come in." She closed the door quickly and looked at him, suddenly feeling shy and unsure of herself.

"I'm glad you came."

"I said I would. Are you all right?"

She smiled. "I've been just fine ever since this morning. That was brazen of me, I know. But somehow, I just couldn't let you walk away without letting you know how I felt."

"I'm glad you did." He caught her hand and they walked into the living room where the blinds were drawn. She steered him to a couch with needlepoint pillows on both ends. They sat down close together and she kept holding his hand.

"Can you stay a while?"

He nodded.

"Can—can you stay all night?"

"I'd like to."

"Good, then we don't need to rush. I usually like things soft and gentle and slow. Does that bother you?"

"Whatever you want."

She jumped up and left the room and came back with a tray that had been fixed before he arrived. On it was a half full bottle of whiskey and a small pitcher of water and two glasses.

"I thought you might like a drink. I know I would." She took a glass and poured it half full of whiskey and handed it to him. Her own glass she filled half full of water and added a dash or two of the amber whiskey.

"I'm not a big drinker," she said.

Later they sat on the bed and she smiled. "No man but my former husband has ever sat on this bed," she said. "I wanted you to know that."

"I understand. Aggie, I don't think that you're

a loose woman. I think that you're a loving person, who has been true to your former husband for three years. Now, it's time for you to get on with the rest of your life. You should marry again. Don't think it will just happen. You should search out the right man to help you run the store, and let him know your feelings."

Aggie grinned. "I guess I learned how to show that down at the store today."

"That might scare off some men," he said. "At least invite them over here once or twice before you seduce them."

They both laughed.

"How is it, being married?"

"It's the best. A woman feels wanted and protected, loved. My husband said he felt satisfied, loved. Said he didn't have to worry about where he was going to satisfy himself when that urge hit him. He knew I was here and wanted him anytime he needed me."

"Every night?" Morgan asked.

"No, silly. Once a week, sometimes twice a week. Sometimes, the longer a couple is married the longer the interval. A couple in their sixties might make love once a month and be gloriously satisfied.

"I like twice a night better," Morgan said. He pushed her down gently on the bed and then bent and kissed her surging breasts through the fabric.

"Oh, yes, Mr. Morgan, but I do like it when you do that." She smiled. "Would you let me have my way the first time?"

"Sure."

"Both of us with all of our clothes on. You just open things or tear a hole anywhere you want to."

"You're crazy," Morgan said gently.

"Not crazy, I'm falling in love with you."

"You know I can't stay here."

"I know. But I can love you for a few hours or a few days, and I'll consider myself lucky."

Morgan kissed her.

Chapter Ten

Aggie was gone when Morgan got up. There was a note pinned to his shirt:

"Buckskin Morgan: I've gone to work. Couldn't bear to wake you. Hot coffee on the stove. Eggs and bacon on table. See me this morning. Love you. Aggie."

He folded the piece of paper and pushed it into his pocket. He dressed, cooked the eggs and bacon, spread jam on bread and had two cups of coffee.

Today he was going to find the fourth killer. He had a feeling. It was about nine in the morning when he began walking the town, asking everyone he saw if they knew a man called John Larston. Not a person had ever heard the name.

About eleven he went in the Laramie General Store and waited until Aggie finished with a customer. She reached out and held Morgan's hand. Tears came to her eyes.

"It's been so terribly long since I wanted to hold somebody's hand this way. Sorry, I shouldn't be crying."

"Cry a little. A doctor friend of mine says it's good for us to let our emotions out." He put his arms around her and hugged her, then stepped away when he heard someone at the front door.

Aggie dried her eyes and sniffed. She grinned. "I'm acting like I'm sixteen again."

"When you smile that way you look sixteen," he said. "Before that customer gets surly, heard anything from John Larston?"

"He hasn't asked about any mail, and I don't have anything for him."

"Damn! I was hoping. Well, I'll keep looking. I'll be back." He touched her shoulder and she smiled, then went to wait on the customer.

Out of frustration more than anything, he went to the livery and saddled his big gray lady and rode into the alley behind the Emporium Saloon. Inside he picked up his short shotgun and the bandoleer of shells and rode straight north along the river and into the flatlands.

He grinned when he opened up the big gray and let her run. She laid her ears back and her salt and pepper mane blew in the wind as she raced along the road north for a quarter of a mile. He eased her off and patted her neck. She turned and one big brown eye looked back at him as if to say 'told you I could run.'

He was more than pleased with his new mount. Morgan stopped near the river and threw small sticks into the swiftly running stream and shot at them with his Peacemaker as they floated by. He put a dozen rounds through the revolver, then reloaded the cylinders and pushed it back into leather.

The Belgium Meteor lay against his waist where it hung on the leather strap around his neck. He practiced lifting it with one hand and firing it. It was much more natural with his right than with his left hand.

He fired one handed, then shifted to a more deliberate left: aim from the waist for a two handed shot. He was much more effective with both hands. But at ten to fifteen feet the spread pattern of the shot from the ten inch barrel was amazing—sometimes as much as six feet wide.

A ground squirrel 30 yards away popped up to see what the racket was. Morgan turned and fired the Meteor. The squirrel sat in the opening of his hole untouched as hot lead rammed into the ground all around him. The dispersal at that range made it ineffective.

Morgan put the Meteor in the big rifle boot where it was swallowed up, and rode another three miles up stream, getting used to the easy stride of the big gray. Then he turned and rode back to the livery at a canter that chewed up the ground at a pleasingly fast rate.

A few minutes later Morgan knocked on the door to Lily's office and went inside. She looked up from where she was cleaning her fingernails.

"Ah, the man returns. Enjoy yourself last night?"

"I try always to enjoy myself."

"Did the lady find you enjoyable?"

"You'll have to ask her about that," Morgan said with a grin. "You don't miss one hell of a lot, do you?"

"Not in my own back yard. Found the killer yet?"

"Not so you could notice."

Lily wore a loose fitting purple dress that covered her in the latest style. She frowned at him.

"I talked to that man with the cafe. He told me now he wants nine hundred. I offered him five. We'll probably agree to something around seven. You still think it's a good idea?"

"Yes. So some of the uppity women won't go in there, they aren't the main customers, anyway. Most single men like to get a good meal now and then. They will make the place. Buy it. I'd buy it if I had the cash."

"And give it to Gwen?"

"You've never tasted any of my cooking. Even I get tired of it after a while. Money easy made, easy spent."

"I wouldn't know, mine all came hard."

Morgan nodded and said goodbye, then took another tour of the town asking everyone he talked to about the man's name. He still found no one who had heard of him.

At four he came back to the saloon to eat with the girls. They were all dressed this time and seemed subdued. Gwen grinned at Morgan and pulled him aside before dinner started.

"You talked to Lily about the cafe?"

"Yep."

She brushed back tears. "How can I thank you?"

"Just run the best eatery in town, that's all. Now, what are we eating tonight?"

They had fried chicken, mashed potatoes and chicken giblet gravy and three vegetables. Gwen brought in her specialty for desert, gooseberry pie.

Friday night was uneventful at the Emporium Saloon. No gunfights, no arguments, and not a large clientele. Morgan won two games of solitaire, talked with a man who was wondering what the riding trail was like going east.

"If I sell my horse and buy a railroad ticket, I got no horse when I get back to Nebraska," the man said. "Least this way I won't be walking. You know how a cowboy hates to walk anywhere but to the chuck wagon or a saloon."

Morgan knew.

By ten o'clock all was still calm and easy drinking around the saloon. Morgan relaxed in the far corner and let his hat slip down over his eyes for a moment.

At ten o'clock, Jared Reynolds stood waiting on the corner of the alley that came out at First Street. He was in the shadows and hoping no one saw him. Two men walked down the other side of the street but didn't see him.

He heard something in the alley and looked carefully. When he listened he heard someone puffing. A moment later Sunny came into sight lugging a big suitcase.

He ran to her and lifted it away from her. "You said you'd bring just a small bag."

"I know," Sunny said. "But I couldn't bear to leave things I thought I could. It isn't so much." Sunny wore a floppy man's hat, a pair of jeans, and a shirt too big for her that hung outside the jeans. She would be mistaken for a man by almost anyone in the dark since her brown hair had been pushed under the hat.

Reynolds wore his black suit, white tie and cravat as usual. He didn't want anything to look out of the ordinary if anyone saw him.

They paused at the exit of the alley, watched both ways, then walked down toward Main Street and in the side door of the bank.

He lit a lamp that wouldn't show outside and then at last Reynolds relaxed. "Yes, the hardest part is over. I've got a small buggy sitting across the street. We take what we want, and drive away. Easy."

"So open the vault," Sunny said.

Reynolds looked at her. "The other, stealing from the accounts, I could get away with and go on as if I wasn't a thief. You know that once I take cash from the vault, I'll be making a major change in my life. I won't be able to hold up my head and even pretend to be an honest man."

Sunny slapped him. "Get over that stuff. You're a crook, an outlaw, when you stole the money for gambling. Don't fool yourself, you're still a crook. Let's get the money and run."

Reynolds shook his head. "Yeah, I guess you're right. I've been fooling myself too long." He opened the vault and took down two canvas bags from the shelves. Quickly he pulled the drawers open and dumped the carefully stacked paper bills into one bag. They filled it.

"What about the gold?"

"We don't have much, maybe a thousand dollars worth. Everybody wants the paper money now."

"So let's take the gold, too."

Reynolds moved to another drawer in the walk-in vault and pulled it open. He pushed the stacks of double eagle, eagle and half eagle gold coins into the second canvas bag.

"Didn't you get that federal bank money?" Sunny asked.

Reynolds laughed. "Yeah, I almost forgot. It's still in the fancy wrappers."

It was stacked on the shelf nearest the door. Sunny grabbed the stacks, and dropped them in the gold bag.

"We have any hundreds?" she asked.

Reynolds reached to the back of the shelf and brought out a bundle of fifty one-hundred dollar bills.

"Five thousand dollars, right there," he said. Sunny took the bundle and pushed it into the pocket in the heavy shirt she wore and buttoned it.

"You want to carry that?"

"Damned right. Remember, this was my idea. I gave you the way out of your mess. Right?"

He nodded. "All right. Let's get it all."

Two minutes later he had cleaned the vault of every bit of cash except the silver coins. They were too heavy to carry. He strapped the bags together and hefted them.

"Lighter than I figured," he said. He took her heavy bag, let her carry one of the canvas bags and they went to the bank door.

Reynolds paused. "Oh, damn, almost forgot the note."

"Note?" Sunny asked.

"Yes. When they find the money gone Monday, and me with it, I need some excuse. So I wrote a note saying four men held me up and tortured me until I opened the safe for them. They are stealing the money and will take me with them. If anybody follows them to the east, the men will kill me. Please don't give them an excuse to shoot me. They are inhuman. They already broke one of my arms and cut me with knives."

"Will people believe that?" Sunny asked.

"Of course. I'm an upstanding citizen here in Laramie. Everyone will believe the note. The sheriff will send a posse toward the east and they will watch the east bound train for five men getting on board."

"Yes, it's brilliant. While they took to the east, we'll be tearing along to the west!" She kissed him and rubbed his crotch. "First chance we get I'm gonna service you just so good you'll be limp for a week. What's next?"

"Next, I check to see if anyone is watching. If they aren't, we walk outside and across the street. I put the bags in the back of the buggy and we drive away out of town to the west. The train doesn't come through town until about ten in the morning.

"We should be eight or ten miles to the west of

town by then and about eleven it will stop for us."

He checked outside.

"Now, slowly. We step outside, I lock the door and we walk across the street. Easy. Here we go."

It went fine as they crossed the dark, deserted street, and climbed into the buggy. As far as he could tell, no one saw them. He turned the buggy around and went due west. There was a trail of sorts along the tracks. Not a road really but it was getting used more and more.

The tracks were a known landmark and tended to funnel riders going across country into towns. If you were lost and hit the tracks you could go in either direction and sooner or later you would find a town.

The buggy moved along easily in the darkness. The horse eager to get out for a run. It was a light load.

"How we gonna stop the train?" Sunny asked. She had taken the packet of one hundred dollar bills from her pocket and riffled through them. *Five-thousand dollars, god!*

"Easy. I drive the buggy onto the tracks with the horse staring at the oncoming train. The engineer will have no choice but to stop. I'll do it on an open place where there's lots of time to see the rig and stop. Then we get on the train, pay our fare and ride on west wherever we want to go!"

"Yeah, we got the money. Hell, we can ride all the way to Sacramento if we want to!"

Reynolds relaxed a little. The worst was over. "Damn right, all the way to California and then over to San Francisco."

"Yeah! I want to see San Francisco. I hear they got some whore houses there that look like palaces."

"Sunny, you'll never have to work on your back another night of your life. I'm the only one who'll be poking that hot little pussy of yours. Get used to it."

They rode along for three miles, then the buggy lurched to one side as they hit a rock in the trail. There was a grinding crunch, then the buggy tilted down on the back wheel and stopped.

"What the hell happened?" Sunny asked coming up from where she had been sleeping on his shoulder.

"Trouble. We might have broken a wheel. Damn!"

"So we have to walk?"

"And carry the three bags? There's a water stop about ten miles out of town, but we can't be more than four miles away from town now."

"So we drive the damned broken rig onto the tracks here and wait for the train," Sunny said sourly. "Only goddamned thing we can do."

"No, there is an alternative," banker Reynolds said. "We can unhitch the horse and ride her."

"All the fucking way to San Francisco? Use your head, Jared. We keep the horse on the tracks with the buggy and stop the damned train in the morning. Between now and then we take the seat cushions out of the buggy and make ourselves a bed."

Reynolds watched her in the faint light. "Hell, I guess you're right. First we take out the money, then your bag and mine and then we get the cushions. We can make a little camp right down there, we'll be out of the wind."

They carried the bags to a spot just below the tracks and spread out the seat cushions. It made only a one person wide padding.

"Now, get the horse and buggy up on the

tracks," Sunny snapped.

Reynolds looked at her quickly. He wouldn't have to bother with her much longer. In fact, he might even take care of her tonight if she kept being so bitchy. But he led the horse, tugging it to come up the incline of the tracks and then down across the ties until the horse had dragged the buggy in position. The broken wheel had left a deep scar across the ground but no one would mind. He took the reins, cut them off, tied them around the horse collar and then tied them to the tracks so the horse couldn't bolt away in the night.

Down at their little camp, he found Sunny stretched out on the padding.

"Comfortable?"

"Sure."

"Good. Now take off your pants. You've been so snotty tonight it's time you learned who is boss on this little outing. I'm gonna ram it up you proper so you'll remember."

"Cost you a hundred dollars."

"Sunny, no," he said softly, holding her face in his hands. "You're not a whore any more. It's different. When a gentleman sleeps with a lady, he brings her presents. Now you're a lady, I said so. So now I'll bring you presents. Like dresses and jewelry. You get presents, not a whore's fee."

"Hell, I don't see no difference."

"There's a big difference. Genteel ladies don't sell their cunts. Instead they permit themselves to be seduced and get presents. Try to figure it out. Now get out of your pants."

She started to pull them off reluctantly.

"I still don't see the difference. You'll buy me a hundred dollars worth of dresses and clothes?"

"Yes, just as soon as we get to a proper town."

"Oh, okay. That's fine by me. Always did want

to get a hundred dollars for a one night job. Damn, I made it."

He jerked the pants off her and some flimsy underwear and took her hard and fast, not even taking off his own pants. She whooped and yelled and made fun of him while he was working and then as he came she settled down.

"I always wanted to do that sometime. Couldn't working in the damn saloon. You understand?"

He didn't, but he nodded. It did start him thinking. She might carry a derringer. Lots of the whores did. She could kill him in the night and get on the train in the morning and leave him rotting there in the sun and take all the money with her!

An hour later when she snored softly beside him, Jared Reynolds couldn't get the idea out of his head. She might push him off the train. She was a bitch, a tough little whore who would do anything for money.

Jared took his .32 revolver from his inside coat pocket and put the muzzle against Sunny's head where she lay sleeping. His finger tightened on the trigger.

Sweat broke out on his forehead. He had never killed another human being. Not ever. He hadn't been in the big war. But he had to shoot Sunny right now! It was shoot her or she would kill him. His finger tightened again, then he shook his head and put away the gun.

He might regret it, but he just couldn't kill her this way in cold blood.

Chapter Eleven

Saturday morning before eight o'clock, Harry Fenwick hurried into his bank. The Laramic Home Bank would be closed today and it would give him a good chance to check the gold coins. He was a coin collector and had almost a perfect set of all the U.S. gold coins issued. He was missing a few of the early three dollar gold coins minted in 1854.

His dream was that he could have a complete, perfect set of almost mint new gold coins to give to his grandson on his 16th birthday. He heard there was a new magazine put out just for coin collectors. He'd have to try and see where it was published.

Harry wanted to check the three dollar coins and perhaps the quarter eagles as well for three dates, then he would slip away to the river for some quiet fishing. The fishing wasn't too good this year, but the relaxation was wonderful.

The first thing he saw when he went in the Bank's front door was that the vault was open.

"Damn, did Reynolds forget to lock it again?" It had happened twice before, but at least those times the big door had been closed.

He saw the note taped to the open door and stared at it for a moment before charging inside.

Cleaned out! Only a few silver coins left!

He grabbed the note and read it.

Harry staggered against the wall. Robbers! the most dreaded word in the banking world. There was no protection against them. He and everyone in town would lose.

"The sheriff!" he said out loud, then ran to the front door, the note in his hand as he rushed down the street to the court house and the sheriff's office.

Ten minutes later the sheriff sent two of his deputies out the east road. They came back with a report that they could find no set of five tracks heading east.

Buckskin had been to breakfast and came past the sheriff's office when he saw the general excitement. Somebody told him what had happened.

Lily was up when he slipped into the back door of the Emporium Saloon.

"I heard about the robbery," she blurted. Her face was splotchy and her hair was in papers. She wore a robe and didn't notice when it slid open and one breast came out.

"Buck, I've got three thousand dollars in that bank. If the robbers get away I'll be wiped out. You've got to find them and bring back the money."

"There are five of them," Morgan said.

"Don't matter, you can take them. You've got to go find them."

Morgan sighed. "I'll take a look. Promising nothing." He went to the livery and saddled the gray. The note said the robbers were heading out east. Now why would they say that? It might mean they went west.

Morgan went past the bank and sat on his horse across the street. It was a not much used

side street that went down along the side of the
bank. He was just across from the bank and
noticed that directly in front of him were horse
droppings, not more than 12 hours old. That
would mean they were left there from ten to midnight last night.

Why would a horse stand there that long? He
checked the ground and found the buggy tracks.
He dismounted and looked for footprints. Easy.
In the dust of the street he could stand on one
side and see two sets of foot prints coming from
one side to the other. The toes all pointed this
way.

There were sturdy town shoes on one, a man's
from the size, and smaller prints made with open
heels and pointed toes. A woman's boot?
Curious. They seemed to vanish near where the
rig had been parked.

He began to follow the buggy tracks. In places
the hoof prints of the one horse were cut into by
the buggy wheels. The rig had turned away from
Main, did a U turn and headed back the opposite
way. Interesting. He followed the tracks. There
were almost no prints or wagon tracks over
these, which meant they had to be made late last
night or extremely early this morning.

The buggy went down two blocks to the
residential area and turned west. Tell them east
and go west, good plan. It's what he might have
done. Yes. He picked up speed and followed the
tracks easily now. They crossed the tracks to the
trail that followed the steel rails westward.

Nothing interfered with the plain buggy tracks
here. Morgan stretched out the gray and let her
run, slowed now and then to check the tracks,
then began watching ahead. No telling how far
ahead they were, or why they came this way.

There certainly were not five horsemen. A man

and a woman in the buggy, late at night. Possible. Worth a small ride to see what turned up.

The train tracks ran straight and smooth, with small dips filled in to make them as level as possible. At one of these dips, Morgan found the trail going down sharply and then up to a slight rise that gave him a view ahead.

In the morning light he thought he saw something standing directly on the tracks maybe a half mile ahead. Morgan left the trail and circled to the north a half mile from the steel rails, then moved up toward whatever stood on the tracks. It certainly was not a railroad engine, he could tell that.

He was a quarter of a mile away in the flat country, working along a slight depression when he came to a rise that gave him a good look at the tracks.

There it was, a buggy with horse hitched standing on the tracks. One side of the rig slanted down alarmingly as if it had a broken axle or a lost wheel. Yes, that would stop almost any buggy.

Morgan tied his gray to a small sage and took the shotgun with him. He moved ahead toward the buggy. He worked up slowly, staying low and out of sight. Soon he could tell there was no one inside the tilted buggy.

Why would someone park a horse and buggy on train tracks? Morgan could think of only two reasons. To kill the horse and ruin the buggy, or to stop the train.

Bank robbers would want to stop the train for a ride away from town.

He moved more cautiously. Where were the five men? After a ten minute crawl up to the top of the next small rise, he could see the tracks and the land in between. Fifty yards ahead below the tracks he spotted two people. They sat on something black. They were not eating. They had no fire.

Waiting.

They must be waiting for the train. Morgan wished he'd brought the Spencer. He needed to get closer but there was no cover. He looked at the pair again. Both wore pants but one was smaller, and had long hair. The woman with the boots. So it would be one gun to one with the man.

He put a sixth round in his Peacemaker .45 and stood and ran forward. He wouldn't fire until they saw him. He ran twenty yards and the woman looked up and screamed. The man pulled a pistol and fired.

Morgan's shot came a fraction of a second sooner and jolted into the high chest of the man who spun away and dove behind some rocks that had been pushed out of the way to make the grade level.

The woman rolled with him and vanished.

Morgan crouched to make a smaller target.

No more shots came from the pair.

"Give it up, you two," Morgan called. "We've got you surrounded. Five men are on the tracks behind you. We know you robbed the bank in Laramie. Now you're wounded and bleeding to death."

"Did what?" the man called. "I thought you were a bandit."

Morgan put a .45 round a foot over the rocks. "Of course you did. That's why you shot at me." Morgan fired again into the rock, shattering shards of rock forward.

"You might as well give up. Are you the Reynolds who wrote the note? Clever idea. The sheriff believed you. They went east."

"Why didn't you?"

"I followed your buggy tracks. The horse droppings gave you away."

A hand poked out and fired a hand gun. The round missed Morgan by fifteen feet.

"Reynolds. Yes, I remember you. You're the one from the poker game the other night. You lost. Did you make that a habit?"

"Yes, but it doesn't matter now."

"Who's the woman?"

"Just a whore from town."

"Yeah, but it was my idea to rob the bank. Poor Jared had already stolen three thousand from the bank, and. . . ." There was the sound of a slap and then a scream.

"Don't ever hit me again!" the woman shrilled.

Morgan crawled closer. He took two shotgun rounds from the bandoleer.

"Ever been on the receiving end of a shotgun blast? Keep your heads down and watch this." Morgan fired one barrel then the other from the Meteor, peppering the rock and the surrounding dirt with the double-ought buck.

Quickly he ejected the spent shells and reloaded.

"Now, let's do this the easy way. Reynolds, you throw the handgun out and then both of you stand with your hands on top of your heads."

"Go poke a porcupine!" the woman screamed.

Reynolds fired again around the rock. Morgan blasted the edges of the rock with the last rounds in his six-gun, reloaded and fired all six.

When the noise of the shots died away, he heard the woman screaming.

"Shot me you bastard!" She bellowed.

"Oh, god, I didn't know this was going to happen," Reynolds said. "I can't go back. I'm bleeding so much now I'm getting dizzy. Why didn't you just kill me and be done with this?"

Reynolds stood up, waved the gun at Morgan. When he saw where he was he fired once. The bullet missed by ten feet.

"Go ahead and kill me!" Reynolds screamed.

"I'm not your executioner," Morgan said. "Let a judge decide that."

"I'm not going back," Reynolds insisted.

"It's up to you, Reynolds."

The short, round banker lifted the .32 caliber weapon, put the muzzle in his mouth and pulled the trigger. The lead slug pounded through the roof of his mouth and directly into his brain, chopping and smashing hundreds of vital brain connections. He died almost instantly. Reynolds jolted to the side and lay still.

The woman screamed and kept screaming until Morgan ran up with his gun drawn. She sat behind the rock, not looking at the body near her.

Her right hand covered her cheek and her left hand held the packet of one-hundred dollar bills.

"Look what you done to me!" the woman screeched. She moved her hand and Morgan saw her right cheek was slashed and torn where a bullet or shards of stone had torn through it.

He dropped beside her, holstering his gun. He examined her face. There was no exit wound. Evidently the damage was superficial or the ricochetting slug had gone in her cheek and out her screaming mouth.

"Let me stop the bleeding, miss. It isn't too bad. It'll heal up quick."

She stared at him. He'd never seen her before. Slowly Sunny shook her head.

"Ain't so. Face won't heal up. Saw a girl with a marked up face in Kansas City. She was pretty otherwise and had a good body, but she couldn't work nowhere. No man wants a whore with a scarred up face."

He started to say something but she stopped him.

"No, no, not a word. You don't understand any of this! You ain't been there. I have. A cut up whore is a dead whore, out of the business and begging for pennies and soon dead somewhere in an alley. I seen it too often.

"But . . . but it ain't gonna happen to me. Right now I'm the richest whore in town. Look at this." She held out the banded stack of one-hundred dollar bills. Blood showed on the back and the sides of the packet.

"Got me five thousand dollars worth of good United States greenback bills here. More money than I ever seen before. Yeah, sure, it was my idea to rob the damn bank. That way Jared got away and I got away with ten, twelve, maybe fifteen thousand dollars! So damn much money.

"But now it's no good. I got myself cut up, sliced up, shot up for christ's sakes!" She looked at him and sighed. She put her right hand down from her face. Fresh blood reddened it, some ran down and dripped off her palm. Her hand went under her heavy shirt and she came out with her little derringer.

There was no time for Morgan to draw or even to knock down the deadly little weapon. She put the gun against the side of her head.

"Yeah, it's a .45. Blow my brains half across the county. Remember I got two shots, case you thinking of stopping me. No way you can do that. Why don't you just rest back and let me make my peace and then do it."

"Do what?"

"Kill myself. Jared did, damn well guess I can do the same thing. I ain't had it easy. I'm thirty-one years old and I got my first taste of sex when I was fifteen. I ran away from home the next day and been a whore ever since. Yeah, tough, you're saying everybody has a sad story.

"God knows I've heard most of them, mostly about men and their cold wives who won't spread their legs. Life's tough for us all.

"So, I guess this is the last time. I did Jared last night. He thought he was teaching me a lesson. Hell, I enjoyed it, all three times. So, goodbye."

She closed her eyes and began to tighten her finger on the trigger. Then he could see her finger relax. He almost swatted the gun away when her finger came away from the trigger, but he didn't. Damned little thing might go off when it hit the ground. He waited.

"Oh, hell," Sunny said. She began to cry. The gun dropped between her knees and she wiped tears from her eyes. "Oh, damn, I guess I can't do it." She cried again, sobbing softly. At last she looked up at him.

"You have a name?"

"Lee Morgan. You?"

"Sunny." She watched him a minute. "You've been around, I can tell. You've killed before. Got a job for you. You . . . you do what I couldn't do for me and I'll give you five thousand dollars."

She tossed the bundle of bills to him. Morgan caught it.

"Yeah, I know, isn't mine to spend. So what, I'm doing it anyway. Just don't tell me when it's going to happen." She took the derringer from her legs and handed it to him by the barrel. "Might as well keep this, too."

"Sunny, I've seen women who used to be whores doing all sorts of things. Run stores, have cafes, run boarding houses. A little thing like a few scars doesn't mean the end of the world."

"Does to me. Don't argue, either say you'll do it or you won't. I don't want to do anything else. I'm a whore, and that's all I am."

"Yes, Sunny I understand. Yes, I've killed men before. I've even killed a woman or two. But I did them all with reasons. Just because you want me to kill you isn't a good enough reason for me."

"Damned right it is. It's my life and I get to say what happens to it. If I want to end it here and now, that's what happens. I want it to be over, right here."

They heard a train whistle down the tracks.

"Damn, train's coming. Do it now."

Morgan got up and picked some wild flowers that grew on the side of the slope. Some daisies and some bachelor buttons and two or three others. He gave them to her and she took them, blinked back tears and nodded her thanks.

"If I go back they'll say I helped rob the bank, which I did, and they'll put me in a prison, so this is better."

She looked away from the approaching train. A meadowlark sat on a small shrub. It sang for a moment, and Sunny smiled. "I've always liked birds, such nice little creatures. So soft and kind and gentle."

She was still looking at the meadowlark when Morgan lifted the .45 and put a bullet through her right ear and out the top of her head.

He watched her body slam to the ground.

"Rest in Peace, little lady. Rest In Peace," Morgan said. It was as close to praying as he ever got.

He sat there for five minutes staring at the two bodies. There was no right or wrong here. That didn't bother him for a fraction of a second. He just wished that she could have seen another way out of her problem. But, like she said, it was her life to do with as she wanted.

The train whistled again far down the tracks. He eased to his feet, reloaded the empty chamber in the revolver and made sure the empty rested under the hammer. Then he looked in the suitcases and canvas bags.

Morgan dropped the stack of one-hundred dollar bills in the bag with the bills and went through the others. There was no hidden money. Reynolds had twelve dollars in his wallet.

Morgan walked back and brought up his big gray and tied her to a bush.

He dozed in the sun waiting for the train. It huffed and steamed up to a stop a dozen feet from the skitterish horse. Morgan met two armed men on the wood car right behind the engine. They had rifles and deputy sheriff badges.

They untied the horse from the tracks and led her to a side. The men tipped the ruined buggy down the small bank. Morgan told them he had recovered the bank money and the robbers both had committed suicide. The two special deputies decided they could walk back to town. They helped Morgan tie the two bodies over the skitterish buggy horse and made a lead line from the cut off buggy reins. Then they strapped the canvas bags of money to Morgan's saddle and they began the trip back to town.

The deputies kept up with the slow walk of the horses and they escorted the little procession to the sheriff's office. Coming into town they picked up a parade behind them of more than a hundred curious townsfolk staring at the two bodies.

The sheriff took the two bodies and had them moved to the undertaker. By that time, Henry Fenwick, the president of the bank, came running up. He talked with the sheriff a minute, then claimed his two canvas bags.

Morgan held up his hand. "Mr. Fenwick, I want to go with you and I want the sheriff there while you count the money. It should be all there. If it isn't it isn't my fault and I don't want to be charged. Remember, I'm bringing this back to you when I damn well didn't have to."

Fenwick's grin covered his whole face. "You won't be charged with anything. Fact is, there will be a reward for you. A hundred dollars!"

The sheriff snorted. "Kid saved you more than fifteen thousand you said, Fenwick. You should do better than a damn hundred dollars."

Fenwick frowned. "All right, two hundred. You certainly saved the day here in Laramie."

It took them two hours to count the money. It all was there. Fenwick nearly passed out when he saw the dried blood on the stack of one-hundreds.

When the tally was finished, he gave Morgan the money, in twenty dollar greenbacks. Morgan thanked him and headed for the Emporium. He still had a killer to find.

Inside the saloon all five girls crowded around him. They were patting him on the back and thanking him for bringing back the money.

A half hour later Morgan was working on a cold bottle of beer when Lily at last asked him the question.

"Why the hell did you come back? You could have been half way into Colorado by now with fifteen thousand dollars."

Morgan sipped the beer and shook his head. "Yeah, could have. But a nice lady in a grave out the other side of town would always have haunted me. I've still got one more killer to find. Hell, I can rob a bank anytime I want to."

Lily gave him a crisp new, one hundred dollar bill.

"For you, another reward. You saved me from going broke. Damn, I think I'm going to keep my money in the mattress after this."

She started to leave, then sat back down. "Oh, you had two more rewards. One from the city council. They kicked in a fifty dollar bill, and the Laramie General Store widow lady came up with another fifty. Hell you could get elected sheriff right now if you wanted to run."

"Not today," Morgan said. "But I am looking forward to four o'clock and see what Gwen has for supper."

Lily punched his shoulder. "Men! All you ever think about is your crotch and your belly."

"True," Morgan said. "And soon you'll be making money from both those urges."

Chapter Twelve

That afternoon Morgan walked the town. He stopped in at the General Store to thank Aggie. She held his hand and looked into his eyes and smiled softly.

"You saved the town, Buckskin. If the bank went broke most of the stores would be out of business as well. I had over two thousand dollars in Fenwick's bank. You were just a lifesaver." She hesitated as the front bell rang.

"Tonight?"

He squeezed her hand. "I'm not sure. I have one more piece of business to take care of. I'll come if I can, late."

"Oh, I wanted to ask you about that poor girl. Were—were you there when she. . . ."

"Yes."

"Why? For heaven's sake, why?"

He told her what Sunny had said about being scarred. "She said it was her right to end her life whenever she wanted to."

"That's so sad. She was so young. There were a hundred things she could have done. Oh, I see. She didn't want to do anything—anything but what she as doing. Oh."

He squeezed her hand again as the customer walked up and asked about horse collars.

Outside he saw the Englishman who fell into step beside him.

"Well, I say, you've become quite the local hero. I must say if I had found that much money, I would have been sorely tested not to just keep on riding with the cash."

"Crossed my mind."

"Instead we're walking. Great exercise. You Americans seem to put a lot of stock in walking."

They kept moving down the boardwalk, stepping up whenever a merchant set his front boards at a different level than his neighbors.

"About the doxy out there. Why in the world did she do herself in that way? Nasty."

Morgan told him quickly.

"Yes, yes, I see. That's logical. I'd been with that one a time or two. Loads of fun, but a scarred whore is a lonely one. She was right, you know. Absolutely right."

Suddenly Morgan wanted to be away from the Englishman. He waved and turned toward the shoe repair shop. "Well, I've got some business in here, Harwich. Nice talking to you."

In the shoe shop, Morgan looked at some repair prices, checked a pair of boots that had been given new life with a fancy leather heel and some stain and polish. When the Englishman walked on up the street, Morgan slipped out of the store and walked in the other direction.

Again he began asking store owners and customers about the man, John Larston. The name meant nothing to them.

He came out of the Oak Hill Clothing store and headed across the alley to the next retail establishment. The boardwalk ended at the alley so wagons and buggies could move through. Just as Morgan took the step down from the foot high boardwalk, a revolver shot hammered into the afternoon sounds.

The bullet slapped through the top of Morgan's hat, spinning it off his head. He drew his Peacemaker and darted back to the protection of the clothing store wall, then peered around the wall into the alley from a foot off the boards.

A man scurried around a trash barrel and toward the far end of the alley. Morgan took a quick shot at him even though he was out of range, and ran down the alley. He paused at the corner and looked around into the street. Someone stood waiting behind a buggy 30 feet away.

Morgan jolted into the open, then jerked back. He tricked the bushwhacker into firing. The round splintered into the wooden building and the shooter turned and ran. He was on First Street now moving toward the railroad tracks. Morgan pounded behind him. First Street held a few businesses, several houses and almost no people.

Morgan sent another booming shot at the man, then ran faster. The tall, thin man darted to the tracks, went behind a big box car and then disappeared for a moment. Morgan bent down and looked under the car and saw the man's feet vanishing upward.

Lee grabbed the steel rung of a ladder up the end of the same box car and rushed upward. The other man had just got to the top of the car and heard Morgan. He fired a shot that glanced off the steel of the box car and narrowly missed Morgan.

Then the bushwhacker leaped to the next box car and ran forward. Just then the engine at the head of the train gave a whistle and jolted forward a foot and stopped. The man lost his balance, rolled to the side and dropped off the car. Morgan hurried down the steps and saw the man lift up and run back toward town, disappearing behind a warehouse building.

By the time Morgan got to the corner of the warehouse he saw only the last foot of the killer rushing inside through an open door. Morgan ran ahead, reloading the spent rounds in his six-gun as he ran, making sure he put a sixth round in the chamber. He sprinted down to the door, jerked it open and jumped back against the wall. There were no shots. He ran into the big building and saw it was a storage place. A man sitting on a box looked up from a newspaper.

"Yes?" he asked.

"I'm hunting a bushwhacker. That man who just ran in here, where did he go?"

"Charged straight through and out the back. Said he was lost. He was hunting the hardware store. Only lost man I ever saw who hunted for someplace with his six-gun still smoking."

"What did he look like?"

"Tall and thin, something like a cowboy more than a miner. A bushwhacker? He took a shot at you?"

"Yeah and I'm afraid he got away clean."

"Sorry."

"Did you know who the man was?"

"Stranger to me, tall and thin with a little moustache and one gun for a holster down a little low, but not as tied down low as yours."

Morgan thanked him and went back to the alley off Main and found his hat. It had two holes where the slug had ripped through. Now he could think about buying a new hat.

There was only one man in town who would want to shoot at him, John Larston. So now the killer knew Morgan had his name. Would he run or try again for a kill? He'd try again. This man was a different stripe than the one who ran. This one would wait his chances to make sure he killed Morgan the next time.

Only there wouldn't be another bushwhacking try for Larston. Morgan had to make sure of that. He saw by the shadows across the street that he had missed the four o'clock supper from Gwen's kitchen at the Emporium.

He settled for the next best eatery in town and ordered a rare steak and all the side dishes. As he finished his meal, Harwich, the Englishman, stopped by and chatted a moment. Harwich's bodyguard had eaten at the same table with Harwich and now hung in the background.

"Any more big games coming up?" Harwick asked.

"Not that I've heard of. Now with the banker Reynolds out of the game you'll need another easy mark." The bodyguard moved farther back, then slipped out the door. The man was tall and thin. For a moment Morgan frowned.

"I never did know the name of your bodyguard."

"Oh, he's not much at poker. I haven't trained him yet. He goes by the name of John Larston. Of course out here in the wild West we never know if a man uses his right name or not."

Morgan didn't flicker an eyelash. So, the killer had been under his nose all the time. No wonder his name didn't show up on the hotel register. It would be for Harwich and party.

Morgan pushed back from the table. "Looks like I'm overdue at the Emporium. See you there tonight if you stop by."

Harwich turned and went out the main door. Morgan took the side door and hurried down to the hotel where he knew Harwich had registered. The clerk looked at Morgan slyly.

"I'm not supposed to give out room numbers," he said softly. Morgan slipped him a silver dollar and the man grinned.

"Now I see it. Mr. Harwich is in room 213 and his bodyguard is in 214. But I didn't tell you, I hope you'll remember that."

"I have an excellent memory. Thanks."

Morgan carried only his six-gun. It would have to do. He hurried up the steps to the second floor and went down to number 214. For a moment he pressed his ear against the door and listened. Someone was moving around in the room.

He knocked on the door. The movement stopped.

"Telegram for Mr. Harwich," Morgan said. There was a moment of silence.

"Next door, 213," a voice said sounding muffled through the door.

Morgan stepped back and kicked at the door with his heavy boot. The door latch popped but a bolt high up let the door open only an inch. Morgan heard a window lift. He kicked the door again, higher, putting all of his weight behind the blow. The bolt popped off and the door swung open.

Morgan had his Colt out as he ran for the open window. He saw someone go over the side and drop just before he got off a shot. He crawled through the window, stepped out on the shingles of the roof and ran to the edge. A man scurried down the alley toward the street.

Morgan fired again, but knew the man was out of range. Then Morgan dropped down from the roof, holding by his hands and letting his knees buckle to take the force as he hit the ground in the alley.

The man ran toward Main Street and before Lee got there he heard a shout.

"Hey, thief! Bring back my horse!"

Morgan ran out and saw a man shaking his fist at the rear end of a big sorrel that Larston raced around the corner down toward First Street.

He looked around, soon found a man about to mount his horse. He ran to him.

"Mister, I need to borrow your horse to chase that horse thief. Name's Morgan, I'm good for it."

The man stared at Morgan. "Yeah, you're the guy who saved the bank's money. Help yourself!"

Morgan stepped into the saddle, whirled the mount around and galloped flat out after the sorrel. He got to the corner of Main and looked at Second. No horse was in sight. He rode hard to Second and spotted a sorrel vanishing around an alley that led north.

Why did he always wind up going north. Now Morgan could see the man and horse. The big mount was tiring. Morgan gained on him as they crossed the tracks and raced out the north road along the Laramie River.

He closed the gap until he was 40 feet away and pulled up his Peacemaker. Morgan fired five times and saw the last slug jolt into Larston's right shoulder.

That discouraged the man. He began a circle that led back to town. Morgan saw the move and angled to cut him off. When Larston noticed it he cut back more, avoiding immediate capture.

Morgan reloaded as he rode and it almost cost him his life.

Larston had seen him reloading and he stopped the sorrel and waited for Morgan to close the gap. Suddenly Morgan looked up and saw Larston sighting in on him from 20 feet. Morgan had time only to jerk his mount to the side.

The first slug took Morgan in the left shoulder,

the second hit the horse in the head and both horse and rider went down. The horse screamed a death call and kicked a dozen times as she died.

Morgan rolled when he hit the ground. The jolting pain in his shoulder sent a dark wave over him, cascading into his mind, threatening to push him into unconsciousness. He fought it, he lifted the six-gun to ward off Larston who he was sure was coming back to finish him.

Afterwards, Morgan figured it took him a full minute to batter down the blackness and sit up and see clearly. He saw Larston 30 yards away, slumped over the saddle, blood staining his whole right sleeve and arm red as he angled the mount back toward town.

Morgan sat up and wanted to scream at him. But he didn't. He wouldn't hear, and it wouldn't help. What he had to do was figure out how to get back to town and get some medical help. He shook his head. It pounded like a Fourth of July drum corps.

He looked at his left shoulder. The blood oozed from the wound in front forming a red splotch on his shirt under the buckskin fringed vest. He winced and then screamed as he pushed his right hand over his left shoulder to feel for an exit wound. The twisting of his left shoulder sent flashes of blackness through his vision and he eased his hand back before he fainted.

"Now, stupid, get back to town." He blinked and looked around. Due south. He figured he was a half mile from the edge of town, from the first house. Too far, too bloody far!

"Stand up," he said out loud. "Stand up and walk, or die where you sit!"

He reached down with his right hand and pushed, dragged his legs up so he could kneel, then balancing with conscious effort, he stood up. Morgan stumbled, caught himself. He threw out his left arm and the pain caused him to groan in agony. He'd never had a shot up shoulder hurt like this one was.

Morgan took a step, then another one. Each time he came down on his left foot it sent a knife slicing into his left shoulder.

"Forget it!" Morgan shouted at himself. "Forget it and get back to town."

He walked 20 steps and then stumbled and fell. The black birds hovered over him, their big black wings flapping. But he battered at them, smashing them and hurling them back until he could see plainly again.

Then he gritted his teeth, let a screech of unavoidable sound shrill through his teeth as he stood. This time he watched in front of his feet. Morgan saw where his foot was going to come down before he moved it.

Take longer that way, but he'd get there. He had taken about 20 steps before, because he remembered counting them. Five so far. "Twenty-five," Morgan said. "Twenty-seven." When he got to 40, he stopped and wiped sweat off his forehead. A large black circle clouded the center of his vision. He'd had it before.

A doctor friend said that was lack of oxygen to the . . . no, lack of blood supply to the optic nerve. Whatever the hell that was. He stared at the town. Still too far away.

"Forty-one," he said out loud. "Forty-two."

Now he could see the closest house, an unpainted square with an outhouse nearest him. There was a spiral of smoke from the chimney.

"Maybe," he said.

Morgan thought he saw something moving to his left. Then he shook his head and lost it. He took a dozen more steps and the image showed again, to the left and closer.

A train, he thought. No. Not big enough.

"There he is!" someone shouted.

Morgan stopped, shook his head. He'd heard a voice. The image of the left blurred, then came clear. A man on a horse. No, two men on horses.

The blackbirds swarmed him again and he went to his knees, then toppled over sideways.

"Damn, I think he just died!" the first man to reach him said.

The second man shook his head. "Naw, just lost some blood, and got too much sun. Hoist him up here in front of me, and we'll take him to the barber."

"Mean we ain't got a real doctor yet?"

"Last one left when he couldn't get nobody to pay his bill. Said doctors had to eat, too."

"So the barber it is. He any good at pulling bullets out of people? This one here got one slug going in, but not coming out."

They rode as gently as possible the quarter mile back into town. The second man stripped the saddle and bridle off the dead horse and hauled it in.

"Old Starwell gonna have his hands full with this one. He bled more than he shoulda."

"I'll go on ahead and tell him you're coming." The second horseman rode out faster, the heavy saddle bounding along on the hind quarters of the mount.

Morgan looked up and blinked at the bright light. He couldn't remember anything but those damn blackbirds. Inside. He was in a room. He tried to lift his hand to shield his eyes, but found someone holding it.

"What'n hell?"

"About the size of it, Mr. Morgan. You were

about one or two words this side of hell before
these two men brought you in. You should make
it now. Got the slug pulled out and the bleeding
stopped. Sloshed a cup of good whiskey across
the nasty wound, to kill off the bad blood. Now
you're all bandaged and starting to heal. Least-
wise, I hope you heal."

"How . . . how long has it been?"

"Well, we found you along about six-thirty or
so," one of the cowboys said. "You was plumb
out and laying there in the prairie. By now—" he
looked at his pocket watch, "it's a little after
eight."

Morgan blinked. An hour and a half. He
swallowed. "Got any more of that medicinal
whiskey?"

"Medicinal is all. About two fingers worth."
The barber-preacher poured it in a glass and
handed it to Morgan. He took it in two gulps and
felt it burn right down to his toe nails. Then he
pushed up with his good right arm. He swayed
back and forth a minute, then got his balance.

"You the only medical man in town?" he asked
the barber.

"Yep."

"You treat anybody else tonight? Man who had
a bullet in his right shoulder?"

"Fact is, I did. He also went down on his knees
and confessed that he was a sinner, and he
promised his heart and body to the Lord Jesus
Christ. He's saved tonight and is safe in the body
of Christ."

"Fine, where can I find him?"

"For what purpose would that be, Brother
Morgan?"

"I need to have a talk with him. He in his hotel
room?"

"No, I'm afraid not."

"Here, in this building somewhere?"

"Not at all."

The cowboy who held Morgan on his horse bringing him to town grinned. "Preacher won't never tell you, Mr. Morgan. But I will. I had near a hundred dollars in that bank, and I woulda lost it, weren't for you. Preacher took that guy with the shot shoulder over to the church."

"The church? Why, Preacher?"

"Sanctuary. Not the army or the law or a posse can touch that man now. He's saved for Christ, and I intend to help him regain his peaceful ways. I've already helped the Lord forgive him for all of his sins."

"He tell you about the widow lady and her four year old boy he and his men shotgunned to death a week ago out east of town about thirty miles?"

Preacher Starwell stepped back. "There was nothing to tell. That is a bold faced lie and I challenge you to withdraw it."

Morgan laughed but it hurt his shoulder.

"His name is John Larston. He rode in here near a week ago with two who helped him kill the widow and her son. One of the men died at the ranch. Two of them found their earthly reward here in town. Larston is the last murdering bastard left of the four and I intend to see that justice is done."

"Then I'll get the sheriff and we'll have a trial," the preacher said.

"Won't do. Only my word against his, so the law ain't no way to settle it. We do it the old way, his gun against my gun."

"But his right arm is wounded and tied to his chest," the Preacher said.

"Tough, he'll just have to shoot left handed."

"I can't allow that," the preacher said.

Morgan could feel the whiskey rekindling his

fires. He gritted his teeth and stood up by himself from the bunk. He looked down and saw that his six-gun was still in its holster.

"Good." He looked at the cowboy who had brought him in. "Friend, you like to walk along with me to be sure I go the right direction? I need to stop by the Emporium Saloon on my way to the church."

The man nodded and he and Morgan walked out of the barbershop, across the street and down to the Emporium. Morgan picked up the Meteor ten-inch barreled shotgun from his room and they went up the alley toward the church.

Morgan wasn't sure what to expect when they got there. It shouldn't be all that hard. He had only to find Larston and kill him.

Chapter Thirteen

Morgan had to put his hand on the man's shoulder now and then as they walked. His knees weren't as steady as he wanted them to be.

"Damn little nick in the shoulder and I'm walking like a new born colt," Morgan growled.

"You lost too much blood," the cowboy said. "Another hour out there and you'd be in a pine box."

"I thank you for your help. What's your name?"

"Carlos."

"Thanks, Carlos, and to your friend." Morgan took a deep breath. "Maybe you should stop and rest a minute, Carlos. You don't look none too chipper."

The cowboy chuckled and stopped.

"That little shotgun. How long is the barrel?"

"Ten inches. Built that way. Ten gauge with double-ought buck in the chamber."

"Damn! I'm gonna remember to always be behind you somewhere."

They found the church and looked at it from half a block away.

"I'd guess the preacher came over here to tell him I was coming. My bet now is that Larston is through running. He's shot up, but he knows I am, too. He's holed up in a good defensive position and will wait for me to come dig him out."

"Lots of places to hide in that church," Carlos said.

"Too damn many. The moon is out too bright, and I don't shoot as good as I did a couple of hours ago." They came to the house next to the church and somebody called to them from the shadows.

"Over here!"

"Sounds like the preacher," Carlo said.

They moved that way cautiously.

"Morgan, you might be a hero," the preacher said, coming out of the shadows, "but I still can't allow you go into the church after Larston. He's in a sacred sanctuary."

The preacher stood in the moonlight with a pistol in his hand aimed at Morgan.

"Don't try to beat me. My weapon is drawn, cooked and aimed. No man alive can beat that from gunleather. Now let's have a talk. This man is saved by the blood of Jesus. He is on the high road to heaven now, and I can't let you slow him down. He has promised to give up the gun and the sword, to be a soldier for God. He is on sacred ground and no lawman is permitted to enter therein."

"No disrespect for your calling, Preacher. But all that you just said is so much hogwash. I know it, and Larston knows it. He's used you as much as he can. Does he have a rifle?"

"Hogwash? I don't believe an honorable man would say that, I—"

"Preacher, does Larston have a rifle?"

"Well, yes. He said he needed it for his protection."

Morgan moved quickly into the shadows. He

almost fell, but Carlos caught his good right arm.

"Really, there's no danger. Mr. Larston assured me that he would not discharge any of his weapons."

The crack of the rifle and the sound of the bullet hitting the preacher came almost at the same time. Starwell crumpled to the ground and Carlos caught his hand and dragged him into the shadows and behind the side of the house.

"He's in the belfry," Morgan said. "I saw the muzzle flash." Morgan reached for the preacher. "Where'd he hit you?"

"Leg. He swore on the Bible that he wouldn't shoot. I don't understand."

"That's the problem, most people don't understand how an outlaw thinks. Now do you believe that he's a killer?"

Morgan edged around the house wall and looked at the belfry. It rose 50 feet into the air and commanded the whole area.

"He's damn well got the high ground," Carlos said.

"You were in the war?" Morgan asked.

"Yeah."

"Good. I want you to stay here with the preacher and be cover for me. Just pop a round at the belfry once in a while. Might not even get lead up that high, but he'll think we're still here."

"Where you going, Morgan?"

"Around to the side while he's watching you here. Might work. If he's still up there by daylight he'll be slaughtering half the town just for target practice."

"I'll talk to him," the preacher said. "I know I can reason with him. He's a smart young man." He looked at Morgan who had no objections.

"John," the preacher called loudly. "John Larston. This is Pastor Starwell. Don't shoot, I'm here to help you. I won't hurt you. Please come down so we can talk."

"I'm through talking with you, parson. I got my arm fixed up, that's what I wanted from you."

"But what about the confession you made, the forgiveness, the blood of our savior Jesus Christ!"

"That's all bullshit, parson. Tell it to the little old ladies about to die. Hell, I never did want any of that."

Larston fired a shot that grazed the edge of the house and sent splinters over them.

The preacher moved up and tried again. "Brother Larston. I know you didn't mean what you said. I saw you cry when the Holy Spirit filled you. I heard your confession. I saw your very soul cleansed by the blood of Jesus Christ. There is not a chance in heaven or hell that you could hurt me. I am going to come out into the open so I can talk with you better. I want to talk as pastor to one of his flock.

"I'm coming out and help you overcome this burden of guilt that you still feel. John Larston, I say unto you that you have been forgiven of all your sins. You have been washed in the blood and are free of all sin. You are as white as the new fallen snow. Your soul is pure in the sight of the Lord. Brother Larston, say amen to me. Just once, say amen so I know that you are still in the body of Christ."

Preacher Starwell stepped out into the open, into the bright moonlight and lifted both of his arms toward the belfry.

"In God's house, and close to heaven, Brother Larston, tell me again that you believe in our Lord Jesus Christ."

He paused.

The snarl of the rifle boomed in the night air

and Preacher Starwell jolted backward as the heavy slug tore through his ribs, plunged into his heart and halted his ministry for all of eternity.

Morgan swore softly. He looked at Carlos. "Don't trust this bastard with as much as an elbow around the side of that house. Keep him busy, shoot at him, yell at him. Cover for me."

Morgan lifted the six-gun into his good right hand and walked around the back of the house on this side of the church. When he came to the far corner where he could see the bell tower, he paused and waited for them to talk. Two pistol rounds came from the house.

The man in the tower laughed.

"Out of range, Morgan. Even a silly son of a bitch like you should be able to tell that." The rifle cracked again and Morgan leaned back automatically.

The moon was shielded for a moment by a cloud and Morgan pushed out and walked toward a wagon in the back yard of the house. It was 20 yards away. At any moment he thought a rifle slug might drill through his body.

But the two men at the front were shouting at each other now and evidently that kept Larston looking at the other side of the house.

Morgan slid to a stop behind the wagon. He made it. He knelt down and panted. His arm and shoulder were on fire. He blinked as the pain drilled through him. He had to get moving. The back door of the church was less than 20 feet ahead. Only ten more feet and he would be shielded from the view of the bell tower.

He ran the ten feet and heard the rifle crack, but the slug landed behind him in the hard ground. Then he was inside the church where the back door swung open.

Morgan lifted his Peacemaker and edged into

the darkness of the church itself. He was in an anteroom of some kind. The belfry was on the far end of the building. Morgan had pushed his left hand and forearm into his shirt between buttons to keep it out of the way. It was no good to him at all.

He moved silently to a door and opened it. The hinges squeaked and at once a lead slug bored through it head high and a foot away from Morgan. He dropped down and had seen where the flash came from, but he didn't return fire. He wanted a sure shot.

Morgan put the six-gun into his holster and adjusted the bandoleer of 10 gauge shotgun shells around his chest. He'd refilled it before he left his room at the Emporium. Now he swung up the shotgun letting the strap hold the weight as he used his hand to aim it.

A board squeaked at the other end of the church. It was only about 50 feet to the far wall. There was probably an open stairway there to a small balcony for a choir and then a ladder up to the bell tower. How did Larston climb the ladder and hold the rifle all with only one good hand?

Footsteps sounded along the far end of the structure, but in the inky black interior, Morgan could see nothing. The moon came out again and shone dimly through the stained glass window. Morgan followed the progress of the footsteps until they stopped. The man would have protection.

Morgan realized he had no cover. He dropped down behind the first row of pews and then lifted up. He triggered a round of double-ought into the spot where he had last heard the man. Then he dropped down again.

When the booming echoes of the shotgun round faded the only sound was Morgan reloading with a new round, and a small mirth-less laugh. "Figured you'd have the scattergun. Sawed off, too, from what I saw one day. Hell, no difference. One good .44 slug in your heart will do my work for me. Give it up, sodbuster."

Morgan tried to figure out where the man was from his voice. It seemed to bounce off the ceiling and make the sound come from every corner of the big room.

He waited. Then he lifted up so just his head was over the heavy oak pew. "Hell, Larston, I've got all night. One mistake is all I'm waiting for. Then you'll be shot so full of holes the under-taker will wonder which part to keep to bury."

Morgan jerked down just as a lead slug whispered through the air where he had been and hit the wall behind.

Fire and move.

The bastard wouldn't be in the same spot where the muzzle blast had come from or where the tinge of blue smoke hung in the air. Which side? Most right handed men move to the right. Fire and move right. That was Morgan's left. He scanned that section and saw pews and the aisle down the center of the church and what could be one leg extending from the pews.

Morgan lifted up and fired at the leg.

There was an immediate scream of pain that cascaded through the church with the rest of the thunderous sound of the shotgun. Morgan reloaded quickly so he always had two rounds in the big gun. His left hand had slipped out of his shirt and he realized it had come up to steady the front of the shotgun.

Some magical surge of energy filled him. He couldn't explain it. A wellspring of sudden power and strength and determination. He would beat this man!

The sound of Larston's wailing tailed off to a whimper.

"Bastard! Damn bastard! Damn scattergun. Fair fight, six-gun on six-gun!"

"Like this afternoon when you bushwhacked me out of the alley. Sure, you're always fair."

Morgan moved then. He went to the far end of the pews and crept along until he came to the next to last one. The murdering woman killer had been in the second pew. He couldn't have gone far. Morgan squatted, then knelt and crawled along silently on the floor beside the pew. The moon shadowed again and he could see nothing. He stopped and listened.

A soft keening came from somewhere. The sound bounced so he couldn't tell if Larston was in the same spot. Then he heard a boot scrape. It was directly ahead, across the aisle in the second pew. Morgan went low, aimed down the space between the pews and fired a round from the Meteor.

The booming roar filled the church again. Wood splintered, .32 caliber balls ricochetted from steel floor mounts.

Ahead a man screamed. Then he cried.

Morgan remained quiet. He broke the weapon open, ejected the empty shell and slid a new one in. He let the deadly click of the shotgun going back together sound loud and clear.

Morgan silently pushed under the pew behind to be out of the alley of fire. It would work both ways. By the time Larston figured out the same thing, Morgan was four feet to the rear.

The killer's .44 jolted three shots down the empty space between the pews. Count the shots, Morgan told himself. It was a lot harder to load a six-gun with one hand than a shotgun. He wanted to run into the aisle and blast both rounds into the second pew hoping he could get his shots off before Larston could fire. But the odds on that were poor.

So Morgan didn't move. He was quiet. He would be patient, and live. He'd learned that much from the Indians.

Five minutes later there was a long expulsion of a held in breath and Larston screamed. "What the hell you torturing me for? You know where I am. I can't move with a shattered leg. My arm is almost blown off and now you pepper me with double-ought buck. You like to torture people."

"You're not a person, Larston. You gave that up when you killed Virginia and her little boy."

Two shots blasted in the middle of the words. Lead whizzed within a foot of Morgan but missed.

Five rounds.

He would have put six in the cylinders when he loaded it. One more round. Morgan moved closer against the far side of the back solid oak pew.

"Give you a chance, Larston. You throw out your revolver and your hideout and walk out the back door and I won't kill you."

"Hell yes. You know I can't walk. I never carry a hideout. Don't need one."

"Then die, murdering bastard."

There were several minutes of silence. Then sobbing came, and the man seemed to get control again. "Hell, I'll try to get out there. Gotta drag one leg. I'll crawl. Hear the sound as I toss my weapon over the back pew."

Something hit the floor, but Morgan figured it was a hymnal, several were usually in each pew.

"Go ahead, move out the back door," Morgan said.

"First, a deal. My life, my freedom. Near the back door of the church is a small carpetbag.

Heavy. I've got a ten pound gold bar in there. Picked it up aways back. Ain't had a place to melt it down so I can sell it. You get the gold, I get out of here alive so somebody can patch me up. Deal?"

"Sounds interesting. You shoot the woman?"

"Hell no. I been telling you."

"But you were with them. You tried to back shoot me today."

"Hell, just trying to stay alive. You've been on the run, you know what it's like."

Morgan let him stew a minute. "Yeah. Maybe so. You didn't kill the woman, so I'll think about letting you out free."

"So I'll move for the door?"

"Yeah. No belly gun?"

"Hell no. Told you."

The sounds came then as the man crawled under the pews and paused. Now in the filtered moonlight Morgan could see him again. He was partly silhouetted against the window. The rawhider came under the pew and sat up. He lifted six-gun and aimed at where Morgan had been and fired.

Morgan had crawled silently near the back door after he spoke. He brought the Meteor up and blasted one round into the outlaw, then touched the trigger of the second barrel and finished the job.

Thirty slugs the size of a .32 round chopped and tore John Larston into raw meat. He slammed backward against the pew, then slid down in a mass of pulverized human flesh.

Morgan didn't even go look at him. He bent down and searched around the door for a small carpetbag. It was there. He opened the top and reached inside. A stack of bills, some clothes and at the bottom a smooth sleek and heavy bar. It could be gold.

The dead man had not lied about everything.

Morgan let the shotgun hang by its strap and carried the carpetbag out the church door.

"Carlos?" he called.

"Over here. Is it all over?"

"All but the grave digging. We better go see the sheriff. First we stop by at the Emporium through the alley door."

By the time they got to the Emporium, Morgan had his good arm over the man's shoulder and Carlos carried the small bag.

Morgan left Carlos in the alley, slipped in and left the shotgun in his room and checked inside the carpetbag. Yes, a ten pound bar of gold. It was worth a little over $3,000. That was ten years wages for a cowhand. Larston had owned something to fight for. He should have left town.

Outside, Morgan gave Carlos a twenty dollar gold piece and the cowboy grinned.

"Now if you can help me get down to the sheriff's office we'll get this matter settled once and for all."

The sheriff wasn't there, but his deputy found him making rounds. He looked at Morgan.

"Yep, I heard the shotgunning. Figured when it was over somebody would tell me what happened."

"A real lawman," Morgan said. He told the officer of the court what had taken place since Morgan was bushwhacked that afternoon.

"The man's name is John Larston and I'd expect you may have some wanted posters on him if you'd go through the stack. He won't be missed by many.

"One other thing. Widow lady named Virginia Wilson and her son were shot down by Larston a week and a half ago on her little spread about 30 miles out. Place is hers, homesteaded and proved up. Reckon she might have some kin who would want the place. Figure you might know of any kin she had."

"Don't right off. Wilson, yep, heard of her. Right nice little lady. I'll take care of it."

The sheriff watched him. "Seems like we started having lots of dead bodies around town just after you arrived. Suppose there's any connection?"

"Don't figure so, Sheriff. Now I'm about ready to take a long nap, if it's all right with you."

"It's legal here in Laramie."

By the time Carlos helped Morgan get back to the Emporium he was ready to collapse.

Gwen saw him come in and rushed up to help. They got Morgan onto his bed and Morgan thanked Carlos and he hurried out.

"What *happened* to you?" Gwen wailed. "Oh, I just knew you were going to get hurt." She sat him on his bed and pulled off his boots, then unfastened his pants. He started to protest, but she grinned.

"Hey, I've seen men with their pants off before. And when I take yours off the next time, I'll want you in top physical form so I can give you a good thank you."

Morgan crinkled his brow.

"Lily bought the cafe. This is—was—my last night of work. I just retired! Tomorrow I become a cafe owner/partner and head cook!"

"Great, just great." Morgan blinked. Everything was fuzzy again, sleepy fuzzy. He shook his head and lifted his eyes open with effort.

"Poor baby, you're out on your feet." She lifted his legs under the covers and took the bloody shirt off him and checked his arm.

"It isn't bleeding any more. You'll live. First

you need about twelve hours of sleep and then some good food. In two days you'll be up and around."

"I better be. I still owe Lily a week's work."

"Oh, poooh. Don't worry about that. You've more than earned your money for her. Did I tell you about how big and beautiful the Cafe is?"

Morgan shook his head. He tried to get his eyes open again, but somehow they wouldn't budge.

Gwen saw him trying to stay awake and bent and kissed his forehead.

"I'll tell you about it tomorrow. Right now you have a good night's sleep."

He did.

Chapter Fourteen

Morgan sat up at six the next morning. He started to turn over when gentle hands stopped him.

"No, can't do that," a soft voice said.

He looked up and saw Gwen.

"You see, Lee Morgan, you turn over that way and you'll lay on your arm and you'll yell out bloody murder and wake up the girls. So, I kind of became your nurse. You just lay still and close your eyes and have another four hour nap. Easy now, that's the way."

Gwen's smiling face was what he remembered as he drifted off to sleep again.

Morgan woke up at nine o'clock, slept out and starved. Gwen had dressed, taken the big chair away where she had slept last night and brought him his shaving gear and hot water.

"Figured you'd want to shave before breakfast," she said and vanished.

Ten minutes later she came back with a tray. He smelled the coffee first and reached for it. There were two plates. One with a stack of six hot cakes eight inches in diameter and each half an inch thick. On top lay two sunnyside up eggs. There were two kinds of syrup, three kinds of jam and a plate of hashbrown potatoes and onions, six strips of bacon and three sausage patties.

Morgan looked down at the food. "Something is missing," he said.

Gwen frowned and stared at the food, then back at him.

"What?" she asked.

"No biscuits and pan gravy."

"Oh, you!" she said with mock anger. "You're not as sick as I thought."

He motioned her over beside him. She bent down and he kissed her lips gently.

"Thanks."

Gwen glowed. "Oh, my. You're welcome. Do I get to watch you eat?"

"As long as I get half of the food."

She laughed and sat on the edge of the bed.

Morgan dove into the food, found he could use his left hand a little and began exercising the arm and shoulder so it wouldn't go stiff on him.

He'd have to get one of the girls to do his doctoring now that the town's substitute medical man was dead. If the preacher had just used a little common sense he'd still be preaching and cutting up folks.

Morgan looked at Gwen. "Hey, I thought this was the first day at the new cafe."

"It is. We take the keys at noon after we pay for the place. I was there most of yesterday. Lily will go to the bank soon as it opens and bring back the money. Seven hundred dollars! I can't even imagine that much money."

"You will. How much is rent on the building?"

"Oh, no, the seven hundred includes the building. It isn't all that big. I'm going to build on the back so I can make a little two room apartment. I'll live over there.

"I get the building, all the furniture, the two big stoves and a stack of wood out back that I don't think I'll ever use up. He has an ice box but I'm going to get another one. A new kind that makes the ice last twice as long and keeps even milk for four or five days!"

Morgan finished the breakfast and pushed the tray back.

Gwen was there in a second taking it away from where he still lay in the bed.

"Your doctor says no bath this morning, but one tomorrow. You are to stay in bed today and get your strength back. Lots of fluids."

"Good, I want a bottle of good whiskey," Morgan said.

"No alcoholic beverages and no sleeping with pretty women."

"Good, send me two real ugly women."

Gwen stuck her tongue out at him. "Now you be good or I won't feed you any more."

Morgan started to sit up but realized he wasn't as strong as he was pretending. He lay back down.

"Maybe just a small nap or two."

"Good. Everyone else but Lily is sleeping, so you be quiet. Snoring is permitted." She grinned and headed for the door. "Oh, I'll be back. You have that nap."

About six that evening, Morgan got up and dressed and walked over to Gwen's new restaurant. He was a little shaky, but decided he had to keep moving or he'd go sour. He saw the same sign over the cafe and pushed inside. It was the same as it had been when he stopped by last week.

He figured there would soon be changes. Six people sat in the cafe eating. He moved up to the counter that had six stools in front of it.

Gwen bustled out of the kitchen carrying to plates filled with dinner. She saw Morgan and almost stopped, then kept on going. When she came back she frowned at him.

"What are you doing out of bed?" she asked him.

Morgan grinned. "Walking around, seeing the sights, stopping by for a cup of coffee." He put a nickel on the counter. "How is it going?"

She lifted her brows and blew a strand of hair off her forehead.

"Hectic. The waitress he had quit and went with the former owner. So I need some help. I'm here by myself now, but I'll do it for a day or so. I have a sign in the window for help. I figure a waitress at first, then maybe a cook in a month or so."

She poured him a cup of coffee, refused the nickel and he pushed it at her.

"First rule, no freeloaders. Pay or you don't eat. If some bums come in, check to see if they have money to pay before you serve them."

"Yes, sir!" Gwen said. She rushed back to the kitchen and tended to something on the stove. Two men came in and sat at the counter.

Gwen came out with a pad of paper in her hand and a pencil.

"Yes, gentlemen, what can I get for you tonight?"

"I'll be damned," the man closest to Morgan said. He was in his twenties, thick neck and strong arms. He reached for Gwen but she stepped back. "Damn it's little Gwen, cute little whore from the Emporium Saloon. Sweetheart, I'd like a tit sandwich in the back room."

Morgan cleared his throat and stood. The man

whirled toward him and saw Morgan's right hand inches from the butt of his Peacemaker.

"You, small of brainpower and twice as ugly. You owe this lady an apology or you're gonna be eating a lead sandwich for your supper."

The young man frowned, looked at Gwen then back at Morgan.

"Hell, Gwen, I'm sorry. Didn't mean nothing by it. I was surprised seeing you here. I was just having a little fun."

"It wasn't fun," Gwen said. "Look, I'm gonna be busting my buns off to make a go of this place. You want to come in here for some damn good food, fine. You want to come in here and talk like you just did and cause trouble, expect to get thrown out on your ass."

The man wilted. "Hey, Gwen. Look, I'm sorry. I hear you're a good cook, that's what I want to try. I just shot off my mouth. Forgiven?"

Gwen still frowned at him. "Yeah, I guess. But you spread the word. No grab-ass in here and no dirty talk. This is a respectable cafe, and I intend to make it the best place to eat in town. Now, what will your supper be?"

"You got steak?"

"Sure. T-bone, best in town and it's a dollar and a quarter for the full dinner."

"Done, do us up two of them, I'm buying."

Gwen grinned and hurried out to the kitchen.

Morgan sat down and worked on his coffee. The kid with the fast mouth turned toward Morgan.

"You the one they call Buckskin?" the kid asked.

"Some do," Morgan said.

"Heard you got shot up. Looks serious."

"I'll live."

The man chuckled. "Yeah, I know you will. Hey, no hard feelings about this?"

"Not by me. You like this little lady?"

"Yeah, I like her."

"Do me a favor?"

"What kind?"

"I'm gonna be moving on. Gwen is a special friend. Wonder if you would kind of ride herd on the guys in here. Somebody gets out of line when you're here, you straighten them out. You've had practice on the other end."

The kid grinned. "Yeah, might just do that."

Morgan stood. "Good. The food is worth the trouble. So's the little lady who does the cooking."

By the time Morgan got back to the Emporium Saloon he was ready for a whiskey. Ten minutes later he struggled back to his room and settled down on the bed.

Lily came in behind him.

She watched him a minute. "Need some help?"

"Doing what?" he snapped.

Lily grinned. "You don't need any help with your temper. I was thinking about getting your boots off, but since you mention it, you need help with anything: a job, a place to live, a wife—hell, I'll help you any way that I can."

"Why such a soft touch?"

"Always have been, hadn't you noticed? Us old whores are all like that."

"I'm not doing my job for you out front."

"So forget it. You more than earned your way."

"Can't argue too much right now. In a week, I'll be on my way."

"Where?"

"Wherever I decide. Maybe Denver. It's been a

couple of years."

Lily reached down and grabbed one of his boots and pulled it off with a tug and a quick little turn. She did the same thing with his other boot. He looked at her with surprise.

"Don't ask, it's a secret that will go to the grave with me."

She watched him a minute. "You going to bed with your pants on or should I take them off you, too?"

Morgan grinned. "I like you better when you're a soft touch."

Lily nodded as she walked to the door. "Yeah, you would. So hang around and take your chances."

He waved at her and unbuttoned his fly. Lily left and Morgan eased out of his pants and stretched out on the bed. He wasn't nearly as recovered as he thought he was. Morgan went to sleep and didn't wake until six the next morning.

He sat up and this morning had only a momentary dizziness, then it vanished and he felt nearly normal. He pulled on his pants and his boots and a clean shirt over the bandages. He slipped out the alley door and walked over to Gwen's restaurant. She had just opened.

"A small stack of pancakes and bacon," Morgan ordered as she hurried up to him. She had a girl who was tying on a red and white apron.

"Help," Gwen said. Then she was busy in the kitchen. Twelve men were eating breakfast in the small cafe when Morgan left an hour later. He got to the front door of the Laramie General Store and saw Aggie just lifting the blind on the door. She smiled at him through the glass and motioned him inside.

She pushed him gently away from the door and out of sight of the street and kissed his lips.

"I hear you got shot pretty bad." Her eyes grew tears and she blinked back the moisture.

"Bad enough. Couple of cowboys saw me go down, I guess. My arm and shoulder. I'll heal up."

"Good. I also understand that you settled up your debt with Mr. Larston." She shivered and closed her eyes. "I'm—I'm glad that is all over. Can you stay? I want you here today so we can talk."

"I'm here, I'm glad to stay."

"Good. I'll fix up a chair for you in back and get some cold bottles of beer. . . ."

"No rush, Aggie. I'm going to be in town for three or four more days. Oh, how are you on doctoring? It's time that somebody takes a look at my shoulder."

"I can do it. I used to work with old Doctor Brillhart before he died. I'm not afraid of blood."

"Good, before you get your early morning business."

She took his shirt off and unwrapped the bandages that the preacher had used. She looked at the gouged and cut apart flesh.

"He got the bullet out?"

"Said he did."

"Good. It's going to heal slowly. Cut into some muscles. Try not to do much with your left arm for a while. But still don't let it go stiff and have the tendons shorten up."

"Tendons?" he asked.

"The big strong cords that tie the bones to the muscles. Just keep using it a little."

Aggie put some salve on the wound, then put a compress over it and wrapped it up with strips of a sheet that she tore up. The bandage was smaller then the one before.

She stared at him and shook her head. "I think . . . I think if I ever got shot, that I would never, *never* pick up a firearm again. How can you stand it?"

"Not all that bad. Hey, a customer."

He watched her walk away. Her hips worked their magic little wiggle under the long dress. He remembered how smooth and sleek she was without the dress.

Aggie came back after the customer left. She smiled at him, then kissed him and took his hand and put it on her breast.

"Whenever you feel strong enough." She laughed. "Or even if you don't feel strong enough. I'll do all the work, and you weren't shot down—down below."

He stroked her breasts, then kissed her lips. "Tonight," he said. "Tonight in your soft bed at your house."

He talked with her, drank the beer that a boy brought from the Emporium, and watched Aggie put in her full day at the Laramie General Store. The woman knew a lot about almost everything from a come-along to a bundt cake pan, from a small flat headed brass screw to a roll of the new barbed wire.

That afternoon he asked her about a caldron, a heavy metal pot that plumbers use to melt lead. She didn't have one.

"Not many pipes and plumbers in Laramie," she said. "But I do have something similar. My husband loved to fish and he made his own sinkers. So he melted lead and poured it into the sinker molds. It's around here somewhere."

She found it an hour later. The thick iron pot

was complete with a steel tripod that held it over a small fire or a stove while the lead melted. He looked at the stove in the storage room and found that the thick iron pot would sit nicely down into the hole made by removing one of the lids from the top of the wood stove.

He built up a fire and heated the pot, then scrubbed it out until it was meticulously clean.

"What in the world are you doing?" she asked.

Morgan took a walk to the Emporium and to his room and found the small carpetbag. The gold bar was still inside. He took the bag with him and went back to the general store.

When no one was in the store, he pulled out the gold bar and showed it to Aggie.

"Is—is that real?"

"As real as it comes. Over three thousand dollars worth of what looks like ninety-nine percent pure gold."

"Oh, my."

"It's a little hard to cash in when it's in this form."

"Meaning someone stole it."

"Probably. The man I got it from didn't go into that. And by now there's no way to get it back anywhere near to its rightful owner. So . . . ."

Aggie frowned for a moment. Then lifted her brows. "Yes, yes I guess you're right. No sense letting it go to waste. You want to melt it down into smaller pieces, globs?"

"About the size of it. Nuggets if we're lucky. Where's the best place I can find some sand?"

Two hours later he was all ready. As soon as the store closed that night he had the fire going and pushed the gold bar into the already hot caldron. Morgan did not remember at what temperature gold melted, but it wasn't extremely high. Before long the iron kettle got hot and the gold began to melt and drain into a puddle in the bottom.

When the gold was an inch deep he lifted the gold bar out with a big pair of pliers and held the handle of the caldron with heavy duty pliers and poured the raw gold into marble sized holes he had dug in a box of river sand. The liquid metal sputtered and hissed and soon cooled and formed into a ball with small tails and drips to it.

Morgan worked over the hot stove for two hours and at last was satisfied. Some of it was in small blobs, some larger, many small balls and "nuggets." It would pass in most counting houses.

Morgan waited for the gold to cool. Aggie had gone to the house to start their supper. Morgan brushed the sand off the gold, put it in a small canvas sack and hefted it. It still weighed ten pounds. He had lost none of the gold in the melt down.

Morgan walked out the back door and the three blocks to Aggie's house. He was tired by the time he got there. He went in the back door and Aggie met him with a kiss.

"Supper is almost ready," she said.

He came in, washed his hands and dried them on a towel and kissed her gently. She leaned back and watched him.

"Are you really going to leave all this? Just pick up and move on not knowing where you're going or who you'll meet? Here you have security. A fine business, three thousand dollars in gold, and a woman who will do exactly anything you want her to do, in or out of bed."

He kissed her again and hugged her with his one good arm. "For a few days we can pretend it's that way. Maybe those few days will turn into months and years, who knows?"

They ate the good supper she had fixed and then when he had rested again, they went into the bedroom and she undressed him. When he was bare she slid out of her own clothes quickly and lay beside him.

"Morgan, damnit, I've played all the cards I have in my hand. How do I cheat and get more from the deck?"

"In this game there isn't any cheating. It's five card showdown and we have to play the cards that fate has dealt us. No way around it, no quarter, no bargaining."

"Let's not turn over the last card just yet. Can't we put the game on hold for these last few days? I'm not sure that I want to turn up that last card and find out that I've lost you to the fiddlefooting trail."

Morgan nodded. "We'll wait. No rush. It could take this arm two weeks to heal. When I get back on the road I have to be able to defend myself."

"It won't be easy."

"Life is never easy. Seldom pretty. Almost never this soft and gentle and good."

She caressed him and moved over so she lay half on top of him. "Then lets make it as easy and fine and wonderful as we can. Right now let's make life marvelous and keep at it for as long as you want to."

"Yes, for as long as we can." But already he was thinking of the next trail.

Denver. It had been a year or two since he'd been to Denver. There was nothing to go home for at the Spade Bit. Yet, when he moved it would be Denver.

That decision made, Lee "Buckskin" Morgan

settled down and enjoyed the good life that was at that minute kissing him with a passion that had to be matched.

DOUBLE ACTION

Chapter One

Two .45 slugs snarled over Lee Morgan's head and another one plowed an inch furrow out of the edge of the building he crouched behind. The man lifted up, sent an answering round past the weathered, inch-thick shiplap, and tried to decide on his next move. He was getting low on rounds.

A light rain fell through the darkness and he wiped the drips out of his eyes. At the far side of the street, he saw two black shadows leave the protection of a farm wagon and dart past the rig's two harnessed horses and into the livery stable.

Damnit! That made six of them. Where did they all come from? How could he fight a whole damn army? Retreat, run away, live to fight another day? He looked behind him and saw the flash of a six-gun at the same time he heard the round go off. He dropped to his stomach in the mud and felt the slug jolt through the air just over his head. His hat went sailing to one side.

He looked to the left and bolted in that direction. He had no other option. Two men stood in the street blocking his path. He saw the long gun in one man's hand, a shotgun probably. Morgan fired two shots and the man with the scattergun swore and slumped to one side.

A round from the other man caught Lee in the right calf and knocked him down. He blasted twice more with his six gun at the dark shadows ahead of him, then the hammer came down on already spent cartridges.

A man laughed in the blackness.

"Well, well, well. Look what happened to the big man. He done run out of rounds."

"Fun time?" a new voice asked from in back of him.

"Why the hell not, for now," the first voice answered.

Morgan grabbed the barrel of the empty gun, felt the comforting warmth from the twenty rounds he had pumped through it, and now held it like a club.

Somebody kicked him in the thigh and it jolted him to the left. Another shadow from that direction thrust a rifle barrel at him, jabbing him in the belly, almost causing him to vomit.

A new voice called to him from ahead in the rainy darkness. Before he could spin away from danger, someone clubbed him with a six-gun from behind. Morgan knew he was going down.

Never go down in a brawl or you're as good as dead. He remembered that advice, had used it more than once himself.

When he hit, he rolled to the side and swung his six-gun at the closest shadow. He caught the man on the shin and sent him limping away howling in pain.

Then they moved in closer. Out of the wet darkness, a kick jolted into his side. He spun around on his knees and caught a boot in his belly slamming him over on his back. Then a knife flashed in the faint light from the livery stable lantern, and he felt the searing red agony as the raw steel cut through living flesh on his arm.

He tried to cover up his head. *Protect your head and balls*, was the other advice freely given for a brawl. His hands clasped the back of his head and his arms curved over his face as he brought up his knees to form a ball.

A boot jolted into his shot right leg and he bellowed in pain.

"Damn, he's still alive!" a voice shrilled.

A heavy shoe drove past his arms and slammed into the side of his head. It blurred his vision, his head felt light. Bile surged in his throat and he swallowed it down.

Then a heavy boot hit the other side of his head lifting him up and rolling him over. This time he saw stars and rainbows and all kinds of colored lights before a black cloud came dropping down, only to lift at once.

He tried to roll away. A dozen boots thudded into him. One glanced off his face down across his eye. He could feel a flap of skin hanging down. Twenty, thirty times they kicked him.

"Enough," the first voice he had heard called softly and the punishment stopped.

"Bastard, you come to the wrong town. You picked the wrong boss. Tough luck. That's the way we work up here in the high country. This is your official welcome to hell, cause that's sure as hell where you're going in about ten seconds!"

The sound of the cocking weapon caught Morgan's attention through his foggy mind. Dully, he heard the sharp report of a shot followed immediately by a tremendous pain in the middle of his back. He had never experienced anything so agonizing. Then the blinding black cloud swept down on him again and there was no more hurt, only the blackness.

The six men stared at the body sprawled in the mud and rain on the side of the street.

"He dead? Maybe we should check," one voice said.

The first voice rejected the idea. "Hell, no. I know where I shot him—the bastard is halfway to hell already. Now, one at a time we show up at the saloon, right? Not a word about this. We just got into town."

The voices faded as the men walked up the street.

The rain intensified and the body that lay in the middle of the street just down from the livery stable soaked up the wetness. The body was stretched out on its stomach and the rain water slowly mixed with blood and ran off his back to the ground forming a light red pool.

Faith Davies huddled in the doorway of the closed hardware store half a block down. She had heard the shootout, seen some of the men, and had heard the voices and then the final shot. She cowered back in the shadows of the recessed doorway as the six men walked up the far side of the street on the boardwalk.

They were talking, laughing. One of them was taller than the others and she saw that he wore a high crowned white hat. She waited until they were a half block by before she moved. She had a small umbrella, and she wasn't afraid to get wet. Even though, she shivered. She was sure they had just killed that man up there.

When all six had passed, she hurried down the street to where the man lay. She bent over in the rain and her small hand reached toward the victim's throat and pressed at the side to find the artery that pumped blood to the head.

She could see the wound in his back through a light jacket. Anyone shot in the back there certainly should be dead.

A soft groan came from the body, and she felt a firm steady pulse. He was alive! Faith squatted there a moment huddled under the umbrella. She couldn't help him, he must weigh twice what she did.

Faith stood and aimed the umbrella forward and ran through the rain. She hurried with unladylike speed, but she didn't care. Her father's house was a block and a half away. Not many people out in the rain this time of night.

It was nearly ten minutes later that Faith Davies and her father, Dunc, hurried through the now heavy rain toward the wounded man. Dunc pushed a wheelbarrow. As soon as they got there, Dunc touched the man's throat, grunted, and had Faith hold the barrow steady. He draped the big body in the wheel rig. When the man was on board, Dunc rested a minute. He saw something glinting in the mud. When he reached down he found a six-gun.

"Damn, must have been under his body," Dunc said. "Must be his shooting piece. We'll take it along."

Then Dunc grabbed the handles and pushed his burden slowly down the muddy street.

The rain came down harder, soaking all three of them.

"Six men, Pa. Don't know who they was, but one was taller than the others. Had a kind of high voice and wore a tall white hat that I seen in the light at the saloon."

"Damnation, but he's heavy," Dunc growled through the strain of pushing the barrow through the mud. "At least this infernal rain will wash out our tracks in an hour. Just hope them jaspers don't come back and show the deputy where they seen this body.''

"They said he was dead.''

"Not hardly.''

They continued down a block, then another half block to the alley and up to the back door of the second house. Dunc pushed the barrow right up to the two steps, then both of them dragged the man by his shoulders through the kitchen door and into the big room.

"Build up the fire, Pa, and put on some water to heat. I'll look at his hurt.''

They lit a coal lamp and turned up the wick. Faith found some old washed and opened flour sacks, and gently lifted his jacket and shirt. She used a towel to dry him and gingerly looked at his wounded back. There was little blood there. She pushed a folded compress on the bullet wound and stared at the strange purple line around his back toward his chest.

She showed it to her father. "Whatever could have made that mark?''

"Damnation, look at that. Seen that onct in the big war. Bullet went in this guy's back, hit a rib and slanted along the rib trying to bust through the skin. Skin gets tough, so the slug kept going around just under the skin. Lead tore up the meat in there like a bad bruise and made the purple trail. Could be what happened here. Best turn him over.''

Faith wiped up the blood on his back.

"Let's ease him over on his back,'' her father said.

When they pulled back his muddy shirt they found a small exit wound where the nearly spent round punctured the skin on his chest and came out. There was only a little blood to mark the spot.

"Be dadburned!'' the man said. "Now that is a pistol. By rights this gent should be dead and gone.''

The man looked up. "Faith, we better get him un-dressed and washed and into bed. Hard telling what damage them boots did kicking him that way. Could be busted up inside and his head hurt real bad. Look at that flap of skin off his forehead."

Her father watched her a minute. "I better stay here and help you. Boys down at the saloon have to do without me on our regular Wednesday night poker game."

Faith smiled. "You go on, Pa. You'd rather miss supper than that poker game. Least we know now that he ain't gonna be dying on us. First, though, you help me carry him into my bed. I'll sleep on the couch."

"Yep, I'll help do that. But I better stay here. He's big and has that gun. No telling what he could do."

It took both of them heaving and struggling to get the big man down the hall to the first bedroom. Faith spread an old blanket over her bed, then they lifted him onto it.

"Thanks, Pa. You run along now. Down there you might hear some men bragging about a killing. See what you can find out. I'd sure like to know who those six men were. Anyway, it's been a long time since I got to play nursemaid."

"You sure?"

"Yes, Pa. He's in no condition to be any threat. I'll wipe off his six-gun and hold it if he gets mean. But he won't. Anyway, he needs some care."

Faith peeled the man's shirt half off him, lifted up one shoulder and snaked the dirty, wet cloth out, then took it off his other arm. His broad chest showed thick with brownish blond hair.

"He might not even be conscious for three or four hours yet," Dunc said. "From what you said he took some nasty licks from those guys' boots. Maybe I will go down to the saloon, keep my ears open, maybe hear something."

Dunc Davies put on his hat and an old slicker and opened the back door. "Stopped raining," he said. "I'll put the wheelbarrow away on my way."

Faith waved and then checked the water on the stove. Not hot yet. She wiped the bloody spot on his chest with a cold cloth. He reacted to the cold with a gentle stirring.

A few minutes later she had the hot water and soap and a wash cloth on a chair beside her bed. First she washed off the wound, then his arms and chest and his neck and face. He didn't react at all to the warm water. He was dirty and mud splattered even through his shirt. She dried him off as she went.

Faith hesitated as she looked at his muddy pants and his boots. It had to be done. She wasn't going to have all that mud and dirty mess in her clean bed.

She checked his boots, cowboy type, no laces. Gingerly, she wrapped an old towel around his boot and tried to take it off. It was a task. At last with a lot of pulling and tugging, she got both off. She set them aside to clean later.

Faith paused as her hand reached for his belt, then she shrugged, undid the belt and opened the buttons down the fly. She pulled and tugged again and at last his pants and his summer underwear came off at the same time. She put them with his shirt in a pile for washing.

She looked at his crotch, staring a moment, then she turned, blushing, feeling the heat on her neck and chest. She shook her head, rinsed out the wash cloth and busily began washing him from waist to toes. She finished scrubbing the mud and dirt off him, then rolled him over and washed his back. At last she pulled away the old blanket.

More pushing and rolling and she had him tucked

between her very own sheets. Faith found a roll of white tape and fixed a bandage tightly over both the wounds on his back and chest, then did the same thing to the one on his right calf. The wound in his leg was in two places where the bullet went in and out. She taped up the flap of skin over his eye. It wasn't as bad as it first seemed.

There wasn't anything else she could do for him. She took some of the flour sack strips and bound up his leg so it wouldn't bleed any more.

Then she kept the fire going in the kitchen and closed off her pa's bedroom and the living room so most of the heat would come into the bedroom.

Last she pushed the covers up over him to his chin and made sure his breathing was deep and regular.

Faith spent the rest of the evening watching the man in her bed and keeping the fire going. Usually, this time of night she'd let it go out. Somehow it seemed right to be sure he stayed warm. Once she lifted the covers and felt his chest with her hand. It was warm.

Back in the kitchen she saw by the clock that it was almost eleven o'clock. She'd bank the fire and let it burn out. Her Pa would be home soon.

Faith took the old magazine she was reading and went back into the bedroom. She moved the lamp over to the dresser and went back to leafing through the pages. From time to time she checked him but there was no change. He must be recuperating, his body working hard to repair the damage.

It was almost midnight when Dunc came in. He knocked the way he always did to let her know it was him, then he was inside and holding his hands over the fire.

"Raining again. How's your patient?"

"Still sleeping."

He nodded. "Good. From what I hear that tall man in the white hat you saw was probably Tim Pickering. He and five other gents were in at the Hard Rock Saloon celebrating. Seems they earned some extra money tonight."

"By killing a man?"

"Could be."

"You never play cards at the Hard Rock Saloon."

"Did tonight. Had a feeling one of the shooters might be Pickering. He's been pushing folks around in this town for more than a year now. He just about lives in that saloon."

"Good Lord! I hope he didn't know that you had anything . . . I mean, we certainly don't want him to be angry at us."

"Too late for that, now, girl. We'll just keep our mouths shut and see what happens. If we need to stand up to Pickering, by damn, we will!"

Faith smiled at her father's bravado and touched his arm. "At least we won't have to do that tonight. Our friend is resting well. I think I'll sit up in the rocking chair for a while and see if he needs anything."

Dunc Davies smiled. He was a little smaller than average at five-five. He had a pot belly from too much good food and too little exercise, since he was the only watchmaker and repair man in the small town. His black hair had some streaks of gray and he wore small round eyeglasses with golden rims. Now his usual smile slipped over his concern.

"Yes, you sit a while, Faith. But remember, we don't know a thing about him. He might be just as bad as Tim Pickering."

Dunc went out, and she heard him in his room for a while, then all was quiet.

She sat there in her room listening to the man's even breathing. She figured he must be at least six-feet and two-inches. His hair was blondish brown and he was clean shaven except for a day's growth of stubble.

He had several scars on his body where it was obvious that he had been wounded before by bullet and knife. But his face was gentle, with a strong mouth, square chin. He had a look of a man who knew exactly who he was, what he wanted from life, and had the power to get it.

Could he be a killer and outlaw like Tim Pickering? Not a chance. She watched him a minute more, then turned down the lamp and let the magazine fall in her lap as she dozed off.

Faith woke twice that night, and at last went to the couch in the living room where she spread out two blankets and slid between them, still dressed except for her shoes.

His head hurt like a hundred wild horses were stampeding across it. His chest and back sent urgent pain filled messages to his brain. His leg seemed to be on fire. At least he was warm and dry and in a bed. He decided all this before he opened his eyes. He had made no movement after he awoke. He had done that from long experience, but not because of any present problem or danger that he knew about.

He opened his eyes and saw that he was in a house, that it was daylight, and that an extremely pretty girl stared down at him. Before he wondered where he was, he watched the girl. She was short, slender, with an unruly and mostly uncombed mop of brown hair spilling below her shoulders and covering up half her face.

With a natural move, she brushed her hair out of her face and he saw light green eyes, a snub of a nose, high cheekbones with gentle hollows below and a small, soft mouth with pink lips that had just parted in surprise.

"Looks like you're awake," the girl said. "I'm Faith Davies and I live here."she grinned. "In fact, that's my bed. You were hurt. I found you and my father and I brought you here and helped you."

He looked at her and his grin slowly faded. He was about to introduce himself to this pretty lady, when with a shock that was like being shot, he realized that he didn't have the slightest idea what his name was, where he was, or why he might be in this community.

Chapter Two

The man with two bullet holes in him and a slashed arm watched the woman carefully. "Miss Davies, I thank you for all you've done. Somebody did a good job trying to kill me. You probably saved my life. I can't tell you who I am or why I'm here, not yet. I hope that will be all right?"

She smiled a little tentatively. "Of course. Any time six men gang up on one and then shoot him when he's flat in the mud after he's been kicked twenty or thirty times, I sympathize." The strange look on her face vanished when a little girl smile shoved it aside.

"Now, are you hungry? How about breakfast? I can bring you eggs and quick-fry potatoes and onions, bacon, coffee, toast and jam. Hotcakes if you want them, too."

"Yes, I'm starved." He felt under the covers. "I . . . I don't seem to be wearing much. You have my clothes?"

"Just starting to wash them. Still raining out so I'll dry them in the house. Pa has a nightshirt if you want it." She laughed. "Why not relax and play the invalid for a while and get your breakfast served in bed?"

"Done," he said.

His mind whirled. What in hell was going on? Who was he? What was his name? He must be in this town, whatever and wherever it was, for some reason. That he had to find out first.

Somebody evidently tried to kill him. He felt the bandage on his chest and the pain. It was like one rib had been shattered into a dozen chunks.

Faith watched him, then told him about the wound in his back and chest.

"Pa said he saw something like that in the big war once. A real lucky shot. A quarter-of-an-inch either direction and it would have killed you."

He saw the bandage on his arm, and felt one on his forehead. "You must be a real nurse."

"Not really. I'm a school teacher and out of work. There aren't enough children here in Silverville to start a school. Maybe next year. I stay with my father. He's the watchmaker here in town."

She left then and he heard pots and pans in the kitchen. She was humming a little song he didn't recognize.

Fifteen minutes later she came back in with a tray and his breakfast. The plate held three eggs, a pile of grated and quick fried potatoes, six slices of bacon and three slices of toast, jam, coffee and an apple.

She watched him as he ate with a frankly appraising stare.

"Faith, I've just arrived in Silverville and I don't know much about the town. Can you give me some information about this place? What's going on, who runs things, what kind of law is in town?"

"Sure." She sat in the rocking chair and smiled. "This is Silverville, California. As you know, we're at about four-thousand feet altitude in the edge of the Sierra Nevada Mountains and this is gold and silver mining country. Silverville is a hanger-on after the major strikes. Most of it is worked out around here but we have two big silver mines that just keep going and going."

She got up and poured him another cup of coffee.

"So that's about it. Maybe 500 people in town. Most everybody works at one of the big mines, the Silver Queen or the Big Strike Number One. We have a few stores, not many, and no school, one church, one hotel and seven saloons."

He went on eating. So why did he come to this little mountain town? Surely not to work in the mines. To work for one of the big miner bosses? He'd done that before. That thought stopped him. A bit of memory coming back. He'd worked for a mine owner before. Doing what?

". . . so Pa came here about four years ago and I came last year when they said they would open a school, but they didn't, and couldn't, so I just stayed on." She looked up with those pale green eyes. "More coffee? Another couple of eggs?"

"No, this is fine. More than I deserve. I was very hungry."

He wanted to ask about his horse. There might be something in the saddlebag or bedroll that would help him remember who he was. But she'd want to know what color horse he rode, what kind of saddle. He didn't know. Damn!

He pushed the tray away with the empty plate. "Thanks for the breakfast. One of the best meals I've ever eaten. I wasn't just hungry, I was starved."

She took the tray and came back.

"I'm not even sure who shot me last night. Did you see any of it?"

"Yes. I was frightened half to death. You came

around a corner and the other men were on both sides of you. There was quite a bit of shooting and then a man with a high voice laughed and said you were out of rounds. The six of them closed in and hit you and kicked you and stopped only when the tall man told them to. Then he shot you in the back and they went to the Hard Rock Saloon to celebrate. My Pa said he heard the six of them say something about they had earned some extra money."

"By killing me," the man said. "Great little town you have here."

"We're not all like that."

"I know, and I apologize. You saved my life last night." He watched her a moment. "Who do I thank for the bath?"

She laughed and blushed. "You were all muddy and dirty and bleeding and I wasn't going to put you in my bed like that. It was just part of the job of fixing your wounds."

"I appreciate it, especially the bath. I only wish I had been awake to savor it. Thanks for both the bath and the nursing. Now, what about my clothes?"

She jumped up. "Oh, I forgot, I have to wash them and get them dried. She looked down at him, the blush gone. "You just rest now, you need it. Let me see if you have a temperature." She stepped to the bed and put the back of her small hand against his forehead and let it stay there for a few moments.

"Goodness no, you don't have a fever. Good. I wouldn't know what to do for that. I do need to go over to Doc Johnson and get some ointment for those wounds."

"Clothes first?"

"Sure." She hurried out of the room. He grinned. She was as cute as a ladybug on a pink tulip.

He heard her singing softly in the kitchen. Good,

he thought, she was happy for the moment and he was probably safe from his assassins, whoever they were.

He was in a mining town in California. Why? Two big mines here. From time to time mines hired enforcers, gunmen. How did he know that? Had he hired out as a gunhand?

He saw his gunbelt and weapon hanging on a chair near the bed. With a long, painful stretch he reached the leather and brought it to the bed. It had been wiped clean and rubbed with neatsfoot oil. The watchmaker might have done it.

He took out the weapon. It had been dried off, cleaned and oiled. It was a Colt double action .45. Probably a model 1878 and had a six-inch barrel and checkered ivory grips. The metal was nickle finished. A six-gun. He furrowed his brows. How did he know the model number? He must know a lot about guns.

His hands seemed to know the weapon. He hefted it by the handle, lifted it, pretended to draw and aim. Yes, natural. It was his gun. Now just what the hell was he doing here?

She came in, saw the weapon and shivered.

"Guns still scare me. Always have. Is that loaded?" she motioned with her hand. "No, no it can't be, it wasn't last night. And there were six fired rounds in the cylinder."

"Six? That's a desperation move. I usually carry this piece with only five rounds because a jolt or bounce could make it go off if the hammer was over a live round."

"It was a desperate situation last night."

"Faith, did you clean and oil this weapon?"

"No, Pa must have done that. He appreciates a good watch, clock or well made gun."

"I'll talk to him. Now, is there a local newspaper?

That would be good background for me on the town."

"Sure, only four pages, but it comes out each week. I think I have a stack of them."

A moment later she left the room and came back with some papers all neatly folded.

"Last four weeks worth, will that help?"

"It will."

"Clothes all washed, now I'm drying them. Are you warm enough?"

"Yes, thanks."

He dug into the papers, reading every headline and each story that might give him some idea why he was there. He found a stabbing, two shootings, and the start of a murder trial, but nothing that might help him. There were stories about the mines in each issue, but again, not anything he could get a clue from. He put them aside.

"Any help?" she asked. There was a trace of moisture on her forehead. She wiped it away and still managed to look beautiful.

"Not much. Do you have any .45 rounds in the house? I feel undressed without a loaded firearm."

"You are undressed," she said with a grin. "I think Pa has some around."

She came back soon with a box of .45 rounds and he pushed out the six spent casings and filled the cylinder with five loaded rounds. He put the revolver under the pillow.

"Now that you feel safe from me, I'm going to leave you on your own for about half-an-hour while I walk over to Doc Johnson and get some salve for that cut."

He looked in his weather beaten wallet that lay on a small stand where she evidently had emptied his pants pockets. It held six dollar bills but no letters, cards or addresses. It had been a chance.

He took out two greenbacks and gave them to Faith.

"Buy two dollars worth if you can."

"He won't have a bottle that big." She took one of the bills and waved. "Don't go jumping around too much on that leg. It's going to hurt for a week."

Once she was outside, he sat up and began testing body parts. His left arm hurt like fire when he flexed it or lifted it. Easy with that one. He swung his legs out from under the blankets and looked at his right leg. Slug must have gone right through. That was good.

He frowned. How did he *know* what was good? Maybe he'd been a doctor. No. He put both feet on the floor and tried to stand. He screeched from the pain in his leg. He sat down on the bed and winced. A slow twist with his torso brought a dozen more pain reports from his back, his chest and all over his trunk. He looked down and saw the boot marks on his body that were slowly turning black and blue.

Again he tried to stand and this time made it with only a small groan. He saw a mirror on the dresser and moved toward it. He took two painful steps and held on to the dresser, then looked up to stare at a stranger's face.

No, not entirely a stranger. Somehow he knew there would be no beard, just two days' growth of whiskers. The blondish hair was a surprise. A face that could be hard, strong mouth, square chin, no sideburns. He pulled free the white tape over a small bandage and checked the skin over his eye. A boot must have scrubbed off some skin. A half-inch piece hung down on his eyebrow. Already his eye was turning black. There were some twitches and twinges in his brain. Something was coming back, but not fast enough, maybe not quick enough to keep him alive.

When Faith's Pa came home, he'd level with them and hope they could help him discover why he came to town. Then maybe there would be someone who hired him and he could dig out his name.

"Hired him," he said it out loud. He had used the term automatically. Was he a gun for hire? As soon as he could, he'd go out in the woods and shoot. He'd find out if he was good with a six-gun or not.

Someone knocked on a door somewhere. He listened again. Front door. He waited. The knock came again, then once more. At last whoever it was, left. Must be a friend. He doubted if the door was locked.

He looked at his naked body for a moment, then moved back to the bed. He was sure his clothes weren't dry yet.

Laying there in the bed, he tried to jam the pieces together into something that would make sense, but he simply didn't have enough parts yet. The rest of the day to rest, then in the morning he'd start solving this damned puzzle.

Faith woke him a half hour later when she touched his shoulder. "Hey there, you sleeping in my bed. You feeling better?"

"Almost human," he said, blinking awake in an instant. His hand had stabbed for the revolver under his pillow. That told him something.

"Don't shoot, I'm friendly," she said as his hand touched the weapon. "Told Doc that Pa got some scrapes and scratches and a cut on his arm, and he gave me a jar of ointment and salve. He said it was good for cuts and tears and even gunshots. Let me fix up your hurts, then we'll think about some lunch. If you're hungry at all."

She treated his six different wounds, lifting the covers up from his feet to treat his leg. When she was through she bandaged the leg again and his eye.

Faith replaced the slightly bloody bandages on his chest and back.

She put the doctoring things on the dresser and walked out of the room. When she came back in a few minutes later, Faith carried a round, galvanized washtub.

Faith didn't say a word. She set it down and went out of the room and came back with a bucket of water. She poured three buckets of hot water into the tub, then brought in one of cold water and turned to look at him.

Her face was tinged with traces of doubt and uncertainty, then they faded away and she smiled. "Pa won't be home until about six tonight."

"So you're giving me another bath?"

"Oh, no," she said and grinned. "It's time for my bath. I figure that fair is fair. I mean, I gave you a bath. I undressed you and all. It's only fair that . . . that . . . that you get to help give me a bath. Any objections?"

He laughed and grinned. "Hell, no! I might have got kicked in the head a couple of times, but I'm not dead and I'm not crazy!"

Faith sighed and laughed nervously. "Oh, good, that makes it ever so much easier."

She walked over to him. "I'd like you to help me undress."

He frowned slightly. "Are you teasing me?"

"I never tease. I'm not a complicated person. I see something that I like, I make every effort to get it. Now please, help me undress."

He unbuttoned the fasteners down the front of her dress to the waist. She lifted it off over her head and stood there in her chemise and white cotton drawers that came to her knees.

Faith smiled. "Does your arm hurt too much to help me get my chemise off?"

"What arm?" he said as he sat up and lifted the chemise over her head. Her breasts were modest sized, pointed with softly pink areolas and small pink nipples that even now were starting to grow.

She was slender and well formed and she watched him.

"You're not disappointed?"

"To see a beautiful lady half naked? Who could be disappointed. I'm delighted."

She stepped away from the bed, turned her back, opened buttons and squirmed out of the tight drawers that went down each leg to her knee. Then, naked, she turned slowly. "This is me, here I am."

She looked around, then grinned and looked at his crotch and up to his eyes. "I . . . I . . . I'm not used to doing this. But I want to."

She moved to the tub, tested the water and then stepped in and sat down facing him. She took a small cloth and soap and began to wash herself.

"If you want to come over here, you can wash me. It's only fair because I washed you."

Another small note of memory flashed through his brain. Yes, he had washed a girl in a tub before. He kicked out of the covers and stood naked beside the bed. A flash of pain daggered into his brain but he beat it down. He paused for a moment so she could see his body, then he walked toward her.

Chapter Three

By the time Morgan reached the small bathtub and knelt beside it, his penis was erect and urging him on. Faith looked down at it and grinned.

"How nice, I see now that we're both excited."

She handed him the wash cloth, but he put it down, soaped his hands on the bar and then began to wash her chest and her breasts. She glanced up at him, her smile edging with desire.

"If I were a kitten I would be purring by now," she said softly.

He bent and kissed her lips. They were stiff at first, then warmed and pressed hard against his. His tongue flicked at her lips and they parted and he let her come into him first. Her tongue darted in, a flaming sword that seared him and made him forget all of his aches and bruises. Slowly their lips parted and he kissed her nose, then both her eyes.

"A woman is so marvelous, do you know that? All bristle and bluff one minute, then all heat and passion the next. You never know which woman is in her body at any time. I like them both, but I love the passionate one best."

His hands concentrated on her breasts and then she caught one hand and pushed it down below the water. She sat crosslegged in the tub and his hand caught at the swatch of floating brown fur. She shivered, then reached out and touched his erection.

"Yes," he said as he nibbled at her ear. "Play with him."

She sighed and washed off the soap from her breasts. She held his shoulder and got up on her knees.

"You forgot to wash one piece," she told him. Then her lips found his again and he reached down and soaped her crotch, now out of the water. He washed her thoroughly until one finger penetrated her soapy vagina and she gasped in surprise and pleasure. He washed off the soap and bent to kiss her wet breasts

Slowly he licked them off, then bit her nipples gently until she growled at him and began to stroke his penis.

"I . . . I . . . I think I've had enough of a bath," she said, her eyes shining as he'd not seen them do before. He caught up a soft, fluffy towel she had laid out and dried her hands and arms, then her chest and gently dried her breasts.

She grabbed the towel and dried her legs and back and then caught his hand and urged him to her bed. She lay on her side and watched him. He eased in beside her and kissed her available breast.

"Seduce me," she said so softly he barely heard her. He glanced up and she nodded.

"Have you made love with a man before?" he asked.

Her reply was faint and he had to strain to hear. "Once, when I was sixteen and he was fifteen. He barely penetrated me but he said it counted. I think he was keeping a running total. Please, seduce me slowly."

He did. When he got down to her breasts, he kissed them and petted them. She panted and smiled and urged him on, holding tightly to his penis all the time.

When he touched her clitoris twice she broke into a climax that he thought would never stop. For almost two minutes she raced from one pounding, shattering climax into the next, until she was so exhausted she lay beside him panting, her eyes closed as she gulped in air.

"Oh, lordy," she said. "Oh, lordy!"

When she had recovered she looked at him a long time, then slowly bent and kissed the purple tip of his penis.

"Oh, yes!" he said.

She looked up. "You like that?"

He nodded. She kissed it again, and again, then opened her mouth and pulled the purple head inside. Her tongue teased him and stroked him. Slowly he drew partway out, then eased back in. She picked it up and bounced up and down on him for a moment, then he pulled her head up and kissed her lips.

"A guy can stand only so much of that pleasuring," he said.

She grinned and he moved his hand back down to her thighs. At once they parted and her knees lifted.

For the past twenty minutes he hadn't felt a single hurt. What good medicine a little sex was!

He rolled toward her now and his lance touched her soft little belly. She looked at him, eyes wide. Slowly she began to nod.

"Yes, yes, please. Right now. I'm ready."

He moved between her legs and lowered and found she was wet and more than ready. He was surprised how easily he slipped into her, then her legs lifted from some primal urge and locked around his back. The two bodies rocked and plunged and crashed into each other like a pair of over-anxious cow ponies trying to pull as a team in harness.

Faith whooped and shrieked and then she climaxed again, and again. She was shuddering and vibrating and spasming so fast and repeatedly that he gave up counting. Slowly he built up his own feelings and he realized he had learned something else about himself. He was used to making love. He was not a quick shot artist. It took some time and that took some performances.

When he at last powered over the final obstacle and raced down the other side into his climax, it was so good he didn't see how it could ever be that good again. He shattered into a million pieces.

At last he rolled on his side to take his weight off her small frame. She began to cry at once. He quieted her and kissed away her tears.

"I always cry when I'm happy," she said at last. "Right now I'm so happy I can't think of ever being so happy again. It was pure heaven and I know that now every time I'll compare making love to this time, and it'll come up short."

He kissed her. "Don't compare, just enjoy it every time, get the most feeling and pleasure that you can. It's a part of living and one of the best parts."

They lay there in each other's arms for ten minutes more, then she stirred.

"Maybe I should get up and get dressed," she said.

"Why?" he asked.

She laughed, kissed his nose and snuggled in his arms again.

A half an hour later they at last sat up on the bed.

"I'll get your clothes," she said. "They should be dry by now." She stood and ran to the door.

"Hey," he called. She stopped and turned, naked and glowing from making love. "I just wanted to see you that way. What a beautiful sight."

She grinned and hurried out, her round little bottom twitching until he couldn't see her any more.

By the time she had a fire going and was getting dinner ready, he had learned more about the town.

"We figure another two or three years at the most," Faith said. "Then the silver will be gone, and so will Silverville. There's nothing else here for a town to live on. This will all be just another ghost town in ten years. The cold winter winds will whine through this house, flapping the shutters, and it'll become a house for coyotes and a bear, or maybe just squirrels and rabbits, with some blue jays and hawks in the attic.

"The miners are used to it," she said. "Most of them are used to moving every year or two at the most. The exception is the Mother Lode over in Virginia City. But there's only one spot like that around."

Faith had stitched up the bullet hole and cut in his shirt. He felt downright comfortable in front of the cookstove, warming his hands over the hot metal sides. The rain had stopped again.

She looked at him. "Put on your gunbelt," she said. "I want to see how you do it."

He shrugged, got the gunbelt from the back of his chair and strapped it on, then he tied the rawhide thong low on his thigh to keep the holster from riding up when he drew.

"There!" she said. "The way you tie down your holster. A man once told me I could tell a fast gunman when I saw a holster tied low that way. He said it was so all of the movement of a fast draw went into the weapon coming out of the holster, not of the leather moving up even a hundredth of an inch. Are you a gunman?"

He looked at her. It was time. He shook his head. "Faith, I just don't know. I guess I've lost my memory. You said I got kicked in the head a few times. My brain must have gotten rattled around and I can't for the life of me remember what my name is, or why I came to this town. I didn't even know the name of the town or the state, until you told me."

She was at his side in a minute, her arms around him, her head against his chest. "Poor darling!" She leaned back. "No wonder you wouldn't give me your name. You didn't know it!"

"I also don't know why those six men tried to kill me. Not knowing that could get me killed for sure the next time and you right along with me."

"Don't worry about us. Pa said he heard some men talking last night in a saloon. We think the man who wore the tall white hat and had a kind of high voice, is Tim Pickering. He's a no-good who most people think is a hired gun for one of the mine owners.

"We can find out for sure," Faith said. "But what about you? You're well spoken, so you have some book learning. You know firearms, so you could be an outlaw, a fast gun or maybe a detective or a lawman, a federal marshall, maybe!"

He grinned and chuckled. "That lawman label makes me laugh. I don't know why, but my guess is I'm not a lawman."

"Lots of other reasons them six could have been after you," she said.

"Like what? I'm open to guesses," he said.

"A detective, a Pinkerton detective tracking down some no-good who came through here."

"This isn't exactly on the main line to anywhere, is it? I'd guess the road goes only in one direction out of town, downhill."

"Yeah, but still. . . ."

A knock sounded on the kitchen door. It was three knocks followed by a pause and then one more.

"That's Pa, he'll have some ideas." She ran to the door and unbolted it, then opened it.

The man who came in was short, with a pot belly, black hair and a big grin around gold frame spectacles.

"Well, you look a bit better now than when I saw you last," Dunc said as he took a quick inventory of his guest. He held out his hand. "Dunc Davies," he said. "I live here and this is a whelp of mine."

"Pa, don't ask him his name. Those kicks to the head made him lose his memory," Faith said.

Dunc tossed his hat toward a chair. "Memory gone? All of it?"

"Afraid so, Mr. Davies," Morgan said.

"Dunc, everybody calls me that." He squinted and twisted his mouth into a scowl. "Then you don't know *why* them varmints were trying to ventilate your hide last night in the rain?"

"Not the slightest idea, Dunc. I didn't know where I was when I woke up. I didn't even know what state I was in."

"Glory, glory, glory. We are in some kind of big trouble right here." Dunc looked at him. "Not a glimmer?"

"Straws. I knew I was using a double action Colt, little bits and pieces like that come to me now and then. Nothing to build on," Morgan said.

"We know one thing," Dunc said. "Tim Pickering is mad as a wet rattlesnake today. He expected somebody to find your body and get the deputy to haul it off last night. Kept waiting. Now he can't prove he killed you. I heard he took a quick trip up to the Silver Queen mine to report in to his boss, Sylvester Bibb. From what folks say, Pickering doesn't even go to the bathroom unless Bibb tells him to. When he gunned you down there was a reason, and an order from Mr. Bibb himself."

"Good," the taller man said. "All I have to do is ride out to the mine and ask Bibb what this is all about."

"You'd find out on the hot lead end of a couple of high powered rifles and be underground within ten minutes," Dunc said. "Not a good plan."

"I've got to do something. Maybe I should catch this Tim Pickering alone and have a heart to steel-bladed talk with him."

"Might work, but damn risky," Dunc said. "Let's ponder this. First, we do nothing tonight. Instead we think and plan and try to work out a good strategy."

"First, you have to stay out of sight," Faith said. "That means staying right here inside the house. Outside, one of them six could see you and I'd have to patch up more bullet holes. You've had about enough of those for a while."

"I can't stay here," Morgan said.

"Why not?" Dunc said. "Ain't the chow good enough?"

"It's fine, only . . . I'd be imposing on you and Faith."

"So I'll charge you rent," Faith said. "I've been wondering when you'd remember this." She went to a broom closet and lifted out a heavy cloth money belt. She carried it by one end and dropped it in the tall man's lap.

"What's this?" he asked.

"What's it look like?" Dunc asked. "A money belt that's been dried out some."

"It's yours," Faith said. "I took it off your wet body last night when I took off your shirt."

"What's in it?" the man with no name asked.

"I don't know. It wasn't mine so I haven't looked." She grinned. "I'm curious as a cat, though."

He opened the flap and reached inside. His hand came out with a sheaf of bills. Then another handful. He spread them on the table. They were twenties and fifties.

Dunc counted it. "Be damned. Over two thousand dollars here. That's more than I make in my shop in four years. You might not know who you are, but whoever you are, you're rich."

"Or maybe an outlaw," he said. "Any banks been robbed lately around this area?"

"Stop that, you're not a bank robber," Faith said. Her father looked at her.

"Yep, daughter, I'm thinking the same thing. A tied down gun and lots of money don't necessarily mean a bank robber."

"But it could," he persisted.

"Could just as well mean you're a rich man from St. Louis looking over your mining interests," Dunc said. "Now let's settle down here and figure out what's going on."

The tall man took a twenty dollar bill and gave it to Dunc. "This is for board and room. No arguments. And remember, I like lots of bacon and steak."

They all laughed.

He got up and began walking around the kitchen and living room. "Just exercising," he said. "I got to keep that leg working or I'll never walk again. I've been shot in the leg before.''

"Ha! You remembered something else," Faith said. "I don't much like the sound of it, but it's something.'' She ran into her bedroom and came back with a tablet and a pencil. "I'm writing down everything we know about you. You tell me what else you remember and maybe we can get your memory back without somebody else kicking you in the head.''

"Maybe," he said. "Maybe. But just in case, I'm going to sit in at the Hard Rock Saloon tonight for a beer or two, and see what I can hear or remember.''

"Not a good idea," Dunc said.

"You got a duster?" the tall man asked Dunc.

"Yep, be a mite short, but some folks like them short.''

"And an old slouch hat of some sort?''

"Yeah, I guess.''

"Good, I'll be going to the saloon tonight. If you're there, you don't know me, hear?''

"Damn poor idea," Dunc said and paused. "But if I was in your place, I'd do the same thing. We got to call you something. How about Harry?''

"Why not? I used to have an Uncle Harry." He stopped. "Write that down. We may get there yet.''

The meal that night was mashed potatoes and chicken gravy, fried chicken and green beans and corn on the cob. He ate until he nearly blew apart.

"Good supper," he said.

"Thanks, Harry. You going to help me with the dishes?''

He winced when she said the name, then remembered that was supposed to be him.

"Might as well, got time before the serious drinking starts down at the Hard Rock Saloon.''

Chapter Four

After the dishes were done, Morgan, now called Harry, settled down to talk to Dunc. The older man knew this town inside out, and he might know something about a gunman being hired.

"Can I look at your side piece?" Dunc asked.

Morgan handed it to the older man who looked it over critically. "Nice piece. I used to deal in some firearms as a favor to a few good customers. No more. Now we've got a guy in town who's a real gunsmith, part time, but he's good at it." Dunc looked at Harry and tossed the weapon back to him. Morgan caught it, reversed it and slid it into the holster without a flicker or a wasted motion.

"Well now, neatly done." Dunc looked at Faith. "Write that down, too, the man is handy with a six-gun." He rubbed his chin, then blew his nose that had been dripping all day since his impromptu walk in the rain the night before.

"Just for fun, Harry, let's see you draw that weapon as if it was for real. Take on the kitchen stove over there, but don't shoot the poor thing."

Morgan had been itching to try a few draws

himself just to find out. He walked to the wall away from the stove and stood facing the iron heater.

"Now!" Dunc barked.

Morgan's hand had been hanging below his right thigh. Now it darted upward, caught the butt of the big .45, and started its upward trip out of leather. At the same time the handle came into his hand, his bottom three fingers closed around the grip and his first finger found the trigger guard and slipped into place.

As this went on, his right thumb caught the hammer and pulled it back cocking the weapon. The millisecond the muzzle cleared leather, his hand rammed the weapon forward bringing it up slightly in a perfect point-to-aim movement.

"Bang!" Dunc said. He looked at Morgan for a minute with his mouth open. Then shook his head. "Holy Christ! I've seen some gunmen in my years in mining camps. Never have I seen anything like that. No chance you learned to draw like that in some church pew, or even some lawman's office.

"You can draw, but can you shoot?" He walked around the table. "Hell, I got to know," Dunc said. "Come on out to the wood shed."

"You aiming to paddle him, Pa?" Faith asked.

"Yeah, and twice on Sunday. Final test for Harry. I'm gonna hold a stick of kindling, and call out, and Harry is gonna try to draw and hit the stick fast as he can. Want to try it, Harry?"

"Like you say, Dunc, we both got to know."

The woodshed was about twenty feet long from the edge of the inside kitchen door to the back wall. It was only half full of wood, it being July. They set up three lamps and a lantern down in the far end of the shed, and Dunc stood on the chopping block. He picked up a piece of one-by-four about a foot long and held it in his right hand.

"Better put on a glove," Morgan said. "Be easier on your hand just in case I do hit the wood."

They found a work glove and Dunc put it on.

"I'll hold the stick out arm's length. Don't shoot my hand off or I'll kill you myself. A watchmaker is damn useless with just one hand."

They both chuckled. Faith looked worried.

"Aim for an inch from the far end of the stick. I'll call out, 'now,' like I did before and you draw and fire."

Morgan took his stance, made sure that there was a round in the chamber next to the one under the hammer and nodded. "Ready."

Dunc looked at him and lifted the piece of wood. He held it steady at arm's length. "Now," he barked.

Again Morgan's right hand whipped up in a perfect draw, thumbed the hammer back, point-aimed and fired so quickly it was hard to see his hand.

The piece of wood jolted out of Dunc's hand and slammed against the wall behind him.

"Keeeeeerist in a bucket!" Dunc screeched. "I was trying to count how many seconds it would take you. I never even got off my one thousand, let alone 'and one.' Less than a second. I just never . . . never have seen nobody draw and shoot and hit anything that fast. Keeeeerist in a teacup!"

"That was one of your .45 rounds," Morgan said. "Maybe it wanted to do a good job for you." He rubbed his hand over his face. "All right, I guess that about finishes that part of the argument. I'm a gunman. Now all we have to figure out is if I'm on the side of the good guys or the bad ones."

Faith looked up quickly. "You could be somewhere in between."

Back in the kitchen, Morgan reloaded the spent casing and turned the cylinder so the hammer rested on the empty chamber.

They sat at the kitchen table. "I've got to go to the saloon and see what I can learn," Morgan said. "All I'm going to do is sit and have a beer and listen a little. I'm tired of not knowing who I am and what I'm supposed to be doing. Damn tired of it. I'll be needing that duster and old hat now."

Faith brought them.

"Stopped raining again," she said.

Dunc put on a jacket and his still wet hat. "I'll be having a beer or two as well. Different table. Hard Rock Saloon. Got to serve yourself from the barkeep. His name is Lewis."

They headed for the back door when Faith called.

"Hey, you two. I don't want either of you getting into any trouble down there." She held up the money belt with its $2,000 inside. "What do I do with this?"

"Hide it in the flour bin," Morgan said and she stuck her tongue out at him.

When Morgan entered the Hard Rock Saloon, he saw that it was one step up from a sawdust floor establishment. It was rough and temporary, but it had lasted six years. He took a mug of draft beer and paid his nickel. There was a table at the far end of the dimly lighted saloon and he sat there with his back to the wall. The place was only half filled.

A dozen miners were drinking, a few played poker, a couple gambled at the monte table. Nowhere did he see a tall man in a white hat.

Five minutes later Dunc came in, talked with the barkeep for a minute, rented a deck of cards for a dollar and set up a small poker game with two men he evidently knew. They used a table halfway between Morgan and the barkeep.

All Morgan could do was listen to voices. He

didn't hear any that he recognized from the night before. He went and bought another beer and thought of joining Dunc in the poker game, changed his mind and went back to the table.

He sat there another hour nursing the drink, then gave up and walked past Dunc's table.

"Any room for a new player?" he asked.

Dunc shook his head. "Not a chance, this is our last hand. Been playing together too long to let a stranger in." The other two nodded so Morgan walked out the front door and back toward the Davies' house. He took a detour down Main Street. Nothing looked familiar. The sheriff's office was on a side street and he could read the sign. The windows were dark but there might be someone there.

He gave up and headed back to the Davies' house. He could almost walk without pain now. There was the hint of a limp when he forgot himself, but with some willpower he could force himself to walk straight and even.

He knocked on the back door, three knocks, then two more.

"Harry?" the voice came through the door.

"Right," he said.

Faith unbolted the door and let him inside. She looked at him a minute, then walked up to him and held out her hands for his hat and the heavy duster. She put them in the coat closet then came back.

"Learn anything?"

"Not a thing."

"You don't like the name 'Harry,' do you?"

"Nope, hated that uncle, fact be known."

"I won't use it much."

She came close to him and reached up and kissed him. He kissed her back and put his arms around her, pulling her willing body close to him.

"I'm not a demanding woman, but anytime that you need some relaxation and Pa isn't around, I'll be more than pleased to help you release your tensions."

He put his hand on her breasts and caressed them gently.

"I appreciate that." He kissed her again, then let go of her. "I'm about stove in. I do need some more sleep. Tonight I'll be on that couch or the floor. You're back in that soft and warm bed of your own again."

"Yes, sir. First, let me check your dressings. I'll change them and put on new ointment and salve. Doc Johnson says it's the best healing combination he's ever seen."

A half hour later she had rebandaged him, and spread some blankets on the couch in the living room. He was asleep five minutes after he lay down.

She watched him for a few minutes, then found her magazine and read a little. Faith would wait up for her father.

When Morgan left the saloon, the trio did make it the last game, and then Dunc went out the front door with one of the players, Deputy Sheriff Telford Sanders.

"Look, Dunc. I open the office door and show you the papers, six or eight people might come in for some help. I just want to get home and to bed."

"Damnit, Telly, you promised me, that's why you got in the game with only two dollars. Now come on, a promise is a bond."

"Hell, all right. Don't see why you're so interested anyway. I'm the law here, not you."

"Keep telling you, the Sheriff over at the county

seat told me to watch out for jewel thieves selling stones. If I know who to watch for it's easier, that's all. Damn, Telly, what's another half hour?''

They went down to the Deputy Sheriff's small office with one cell in back and he lit a lamp and moved it to the inside office and closed the door. He opened a top drawer with a stack of wanted posters in it.

"Hell, Dunc, here they are. You look these over and lock the door when you leave and push the key back under the door. I got one myself. I'll see you tomorrow."

He left.

For the next hour, Dunc looked through the drawer full of wanted posters. He was almost at the bottom of the stack when he pulled one out that had a picture that was a remarkable likeness. Most of the pictures were fuzzy and hard to make out. This one was plain and true to life.

"Wanted for Murder. DEAD OR ALIVE. Lee Buckskin Morgan. Reward $2,000. Tombstone, Arizona Territory. For the shooting death of Wilfred Potts. Contact Tombstone Sheriff, Tombstone, Arizona Territory."

The picture was perfect right down to the slight squint of his eyes, the square jaw and tumbled blondish hair that covered the tops of his ears.

It was the same man. Lee Morgan was the name of the man in his house. The man with the quick gun and the poor memory. The man at home alone with Faith. He folded the wanted poster and put it inside his shirt, then slammed the drawer and hurried to the door. He fumbled with the lock, then he took a deep breath. He had to calm down.

There was no rush. Morgan was not the kind of man to take advantage of a woman . . . unless she wanted to be pleasured. Faith was a grown woman now, and what she did was up to her. Anyway, he'd learned a lot more about Morgan in talking with him tonight and watching him that the damn piece of paper said.

He'd heard of wanted posters being put out that really shouldn't go out. Too late to call them back then. They might sit around in drawers in sheriff offices for twenty years. Most of them were not dated. Lots of wanted posters were sour grapes over legal self defense shootings.

He wouldn't tell anyone about the poster, he decided. He'd see what developed. If somebody did hire Morgan to come into town as a paid gun, it probably would be Bibb. But if that was so, why would the mine owner tell his hatchet man, Tim Pickering, to gun down Morgan?

No, it had to be the other way. Maybe the other mine owner, Janish Lang, had sent for Morgan to try to even up the fire power from Pickering. Now there was an idea.

Dunc walked slower as he neared the house. He couldn't slip up and use Morgan's real name. Why not change the name they called him? He and Faith knew a relative named Buck. Buck Wilhouse, a cousin of hers in Michigan. He was a tall guy, too. Yeah, he'd give it a try in the morning.

Dunc had looked at Morgan's hands as he ate. He had no callouses, no rope burns. He was not a miner or a cowboy. If he were, his hands would show it. What did that leave? A gambler or a gunman.

When Dunc came in the door, Faith held up her hand to quiet him. Dunc saw Morgan sleeping on the couch. He had a drink of water, and found his nightshirt and crawled into bed. He had a mystery to solve. There was nothing Dunc Davies enjoyed more than a good mystery.

When morning came, Faith found Morgan was up before she was. He had a fire going and coffee boiling. She stared at him sleepy-eyed and realized she must look a fright. She hurried back into her room to wash her face and comb out her long brown hair so it billowed around her shoulders.

When she came back out, Harry and Dunc were talking over cups of coffee at the table.

Dunc looked up. "We just decided that Harry doesn't fit this young man. We're gonna call him Buck instead. He's tall like your cousin Buck, and should be easier for us to remember. He's agreed. So, goodby Harry, and hello Buck."

"What kind of orders do I have for breakfast?" Faith asked.

"Usual for me," Dunc said. "Stack of cakes and some hot syrup and a gallon of coffee."

"Nothing for me," Morgan said. "I'm off on a walk so I can make sure this leg works when I want it to. My left arm is a little tight too, but it should be healing. I'll be back in an hour or so."

Morgan finished his coffee, waved and put on the slouch hat that pulled down over his face and headed for the alley. The first stop he was going to make was the livery.

The six men had attacked him outside the livery. That should mean that he had already left his horse there. That was the only way to come into Silverville, by horse or stage. He doubted he came on a stage.

The morning was bright and cool for July. The sky was washed and bright, the green from the rains lush. He walked down two blocks, saw the livery at the end of the next block and got there just as the stable hand was cleaning out stalls. The kid was sixteen, and had red hair.

"Were you on when I brought my horse in two days ago?" he asked the young man.

"Dunno, which was your nag?"

"I rented her and I'm not sure. There was some shooting just after I left outside the livery here. You probably remember it. Shooting in the rain," Morgan said.

"Oh, yeah. Heard some guy got blasted, but nobody ever found a body. Couple of guys came around the next day thinking he might have crawled in here and died. But I told them he didn't. I'm the only one dying here. Yeah, I remember the roan. You rode her hard and gave me a dollar to walk her out and rub her down. Did it, too."

"Good. Where is she?"

"Down this way." The stable hand led him along a shed to the next one and a stall where a big roan stood. She had on a feed bag.

"Oats?" Buck asked.

"You said oats every morning, hay every night and gave me five dollars in advance. I'm using up your money." The horse was unsaddled.

"Where's the tack?"

The young man pointed to a shelf behind the horse. "Right there, saddle, saddlebags and blanket. Now I got work to do." The kid took off with the five tined pitchfork growling about all the shit he had to throw around in this job.

Buck grinned and went to the saddlebags. The first side was empty. The other side had a pair of socks, a small notebook stapled on the top, the kind just big enough to slip into a pocket. He put it in his pocket and felt around again. A slip of paper. He took it out but couldn't read the faint writing in the poor lighting. He put it with the notebook.

That was all the bags had. The saddle was standard western, no marks, no number, no hand made artisan's signature. Just another ten dollar saddle.

He went out and found the stable hand. He took a five dollar bill from his pocket and held it out.

"Two things. Take good care of that horse. Remember who it is if anyone asks if the owner has been in. Right now I want you to forget that you ever saw me or know who in hell owns that horseflesh. Agreed?"

"Yeah, no trouble on my part. Oats and hay just a quarter a day. You're paid up for eighteen more days on that first five dollar bill."

"Keep that five yourself. Remember, you never saw me."

Buck headed out of the livery by the back door, circled around along a little stream hard against the slope of the mountain and found a log in the sun. He sat down, watched the creek a minute, then dug out the notebook and the piece of paper. Maybe now he could make some sense out of this whole affair.

Chapter Five

There was no hesitation on Morgan's part. He wanted to know who he was. He unfolded the piece of paper from his pocket and read it quickly.

It was a bill of sale for a horse, a roan mare, the one he must have ridden into town. The receipt was made out to "bearer" and was dated a week ago. No help. He couldn't remember ever seeing it before.

He turned the small notebook over in his hand. He couldn't remember it either. The mare certainly didn't start any memories flowing for him.

On the first page of the notebook there was one word. 'Silverville.' So evidently he had intended to come to this small mining town. He flipped the pages. Three blank pages later he found some more words that made little sense.

One phrase was, 'missing three weeks.' On the same page was the word, 'miner.' A third entry was 'Chinese.'

The rest of the notebook was blank. Dandy! Why wasn't he the kind of man who wrote down everything in detail? That would have been a big help. His name and address on the inside flap would have helped, too. It also would have been too easy. His luck hadn't been running that way lately.

He almost threw the little book away, then stuffed it in his pocket and went back toward the main part of town. Buck, they were calling him. Fine, a damn lot better than Harry. He wasn't sure why he didn't like the name. Now he wasn't certain that he even had an uncle named Harry.

As soon as he went in the back door of the Davies' home, he smelled the fresh bread. That reminded him of home when his mother had baked bread. He frowned. Yes, his mother, the little ranch out west in Idaho. He had been very young, three or four, then they told him his mother went away and wouldn't be coming back. Another small fragment. Idaho. Yeah, that did feel right, familiar.

Faith looked up. Brown hair framed her face and covered one eye. She blew it away with a gust of breath.

"Just in time. You like fresh baked bread before it gets cool?" she asked.

"Does a range bull like to get to the young heifers?"

She laughed. "I don't know, but I'd guess they do. I'll write that down." She sobered. "Right now I feel like one of those young heifers." He went to her and kissed her lips lightly, felt her push her breasts hard against his chest. Then he stepped away.

"Faith, you don't know anything about me. I'm a gunman, right? That's all we know so far. I might even be wanted somewhere. Let's just slow down a little."

She shook her head, light green eyes giving her away before she spoke. "I don't care! You can have killed the governor and I'd still love you. There, I said it." She hugged him tightly and pushed against him all the way down to her knees. He could feel the heat coming from her slender body.

Gently he unstrapped her arms from his back. "You said something about hot bread? My all time favorite. My mother used to bake when we lived in Idaho. You can write that down. I wasn't more than four when they told me she had gone away. Now I know that she must have died or left us."

"We're making progress!" She kissed his cheek. "One of these days it's all going to come back."

"God, I hope so." She cut a slice off a just baked loaf, and tried to keep it from crushing together. She did well. He spread just churned and salted butter over the steaming bread and watched it melt into the whiteness. Then he added fresh apple butter on the bread and leaned back savoring each bite.

"A man could go soft and easy around here, around you. I bet you know that."

"Counting on it so hard it hurts."

"No matter what happens, I never want to harm you. Remember that. You're a beautiful, special, marvelous little lady, and you always will be. No matter what happens to me, you remember that, live long with that thought."

"Don't. That kind of talk scares me." She caught his hand and held it so she would have some contact.

"Don't worry yet. I still don't know why I'm here. As soon as the Hard Rock Saloon opens, I'm going to be watching it. Bet there are a few chairs sitting outside stores along Main Street, right?"

Faith nodded.

"I'll use one and watch for our tall man, Tim

Pickering. One way or another I'll find out what's going on."

Tears brimmed Faith's eyes. "You be careful. You go and get yourself killed, I'll come and spit on your grave!"

"Nicest thing anybody's ever said to me that I can remember," Morgan said. This time he kissed her cheek. "Now, I hate to bother an important, busy person like you are, Faith. But could I have another slice of that fresh baked bread?"

Two hours later, Morgan settled into a tilted back chair against the Silverville Hardware store's front wall and pulled the slouch hat down over his forehead so he could see a slot from under the brim. He aimed the opening at the front door of the Hard Rock Saloon and waited.

Once he almost went to sleep in the lazy morning sun, but he roused as men began going into the drinking establishment. After sitting there for an hour, he hadn't seen the tall gent with the white hat.

Morgan got up, stretched and knew his leg was stiff. He walked halfway down the block and back to loosen it up. He didn't hurt quite so much this morning. Faith had changed his bandages and said his back was coming along nicely. The swelling along the purple mark tracing his rib was starting to go down. He could see some of the black and blue of the tissue was fading.

His left arm still hurt like fire when he moved it wrong. He was most concerned with his leg. Without two good legs a gunman was about as much use as tits on a boar. Thinking about the use of such a phrase stopped him. Now where did he come up with that? It was a farm term. Would he know farmers in Idaho? What part of Idaho? He had no idea. One more bit of information for his catalog of himself.

Back at the Hard Rock Saloon, Morgan turned in, scanned the place quickly but didn't find anyone tall and no one with a white hat. He got a nickel beer and slid into a chair at a small table with his back to the wall.

A sharp-eyed dandy with a bright vest and a deck of cards in his hand walked up and nodded. "Got time for a little game?"

"Not hardly. Ride on down the trail."

The gambler shrugged and walked to a table where two miners had just sat down. He got a game there.

Buck took out the small notebook and stared at the page with the three entries on it. The word miner was obvious enough. Or was it? Did he come here to pretend to be a miner? To go to work underground and unearth some kind of conspiracy of highgraders, or maybe a killer? Maybe.

But if you put all the words together you had "Chinese miner missing three weeks."

Who was worried about Chinese, especially Chinese miners? The railroad had brought in thousands of Chinese late in the Sixties to help push the Central Pacific through the Rocky Mountains.

After the railroad was built and completed in 1869 the Chinese stayed in the country, some of them moving back to San Francisco where they established a real Chinatown. Others drifted into different kinds of work. He had heard that some mines in the west used a lot of Chinese. But in the short time he had walked around Silverville, he hadn't seen a single Chinaman.

The old problem came back. He was a gunman. So who brought him to town? Who had hired him?

Sure, he could ride up to each mine and ask the

owner if he was waiting for him. But if he picked the wrong one first, he was dead and buried and Faith was spitting on his grave.

Six men came in the door. They seemed to be together, but none of them was anywhere near six feet tall and none had on a white hat.

Morgan had another beer, got a deck of cards and played some solitaire. Two hours later he decided he never would win even one game of solitaire.

He was about to ditch the whole plan when he looked up at two men coming through the door. One wore a high crowned white hat, the kind that he'd seen some Mexican *vaqueros* wear south of the border.

He made a note to remember that. He'd been in Mexico and knew about Mexican cowboys.

The man with the white hat got a beer from the apron which he didn't pay for, swung his leg over a chair back and sat down at a table. He started to look around. Morgan concentrated on his beer and shrugged a little lower in the chair.

The white hat gave up his visual search and talked sternly to the other man he had come in with. It was clear even from thirty feet away that the shorter man was getting a lecture. Five minutes later the shorter man went to the bar and brought back two more draft beers. He pointed to the white hat and didn't pay for them. The barkeep shrugged.

Morgan moved to see the man better and groaned softly, his back was hurting more now. He had an almost overwhelming urge to jump up, rush up to Pickering and smash him in the mouth, knock him over backwards, and then shoot the bastard dead when he went for his gun.

Instead, Morgan finished off the mug of beer, stood and went to watch a poker game at the table next to the white hat. He heard the man's voice as he called to someone at the next table. Pickering's voice was high, a real tenor. He had to be the same man.

Morgan walked outside and sat in a different chair across the street by the barbershop. He could stand a haircut, but no time right now.

After about twenty minutes in the chair, Morgan spotted Pickering coming out of the Hard Rock Saloon. It was getting on toward noon. The tall man adjusted his white hat and walked across the street, past Buck and down several stores. Morgan followed him. He went into a small neat store front that was well painted and had a sign over the door that read: "SILVER QUEEN MINE, Town Office."

Pickering went into the office and closed the door. Morgan walked on past without looking in the windows. This was not a good time. He went into the General Store next door and bought a paper, then a box of .45 rounds and looked at the shotguns. Too damn obvious. Maybe Dunc had one.

He walked back to the Davies house. After his knock on the back door he went inside.

Faith had just finished baking a green apple pie. She ran to him, then stopped and walked ahead slower before she hugged him.

"I'm just so terribly glad every time I see you come back," she said, tears almost brimming out of her eyes.

"I'm glad to be back, too," he said. "That means I'm still alive and fighting." He led her by the hand to the kitchen table and sat her down. Then he put the small notebook in front of her.

"Any idea what these words might mean?" He told her where he found the notebook and the bill of sale for the horse. She stared at them and then slowly shook her head.

"Evidently, you knew that you were coming to Silverville. Somebody must have told you there were mines here and that we had some Chinese. Actually, there aren't any Chinese in town now. Used to have quite a few. Don't know what happened to them. Probably moved out to a new railroad job somewhere. They liked the railroad work better than going down in a mine any day."

"Missing three weeks?" he asked.

"No idea. Maybe someone you're trying to find has been missing in the mines here in Silverville for three weeks. About all I can say."

She jumped up. "You want a piece of warm apple pie with a wedge of cheese and some soon to be whipped cream?"

"Don't ever ask a starving man if he's hungry, woman!"

She grinned and hurried to the stove. The apple pie sat there all cinnamon and sugar coated on the crust and oozing apple goodness through three slits in the top.

They each had a piece of pie after she whipped the cream. Then they sat back and smiled.

"That was your dinner," Faith said. "Not good nutrition, but we'll make up for it at supper. Can I have half of the new paper?"

They both read it then, but it proved to have no story that would help Morgan in his quest. She took his shirt off and checked his back and chest wound.

When she looked at his back, she frowned. "Put your shirt back on," Faith said. "We're going to see Doc Johnson."

"It's not healing?"

"Looks worse now than when it first happened. You need some of his professional treatment."

"No."

"Why not, Morgan?"

"What if Pickering has someone watching the doctor's office for a man coming in shot in the back? He could be there before the doctor got my shirt off."

"Could be. Could also be that you die of blood poisoning. It happened a lot during the big war. You've got the start of a red streak up your back. Blood poisoning doesn't take long, so get your shirt on. We'll go in the back door from the alley. Anyone tries to hurt you, I'll shoot his damned head off."

She fussed in a kitchen drawer and came up with a .32 caliber Smith and Wesson rimfire tip-up revolver. "I said I hated guns, not that I don't have one and can't use it. Yes, it's loaded with four rounds but I don't figure we'll need it." She put it in her reticule.

"Is this really necessary, Faith?"

"Yes. The gun is a safeguard, and as your nurse I'm scared to death the way your back looks. I've never lost a patient, and I don't want you to be my first."

She caught his hand and they went out the back door.

"I'll go ahead. You follow me. Don't get lost, and don't decide to lose me, or you get no more apple pie or fresh baked bread. Deal?"

"Deal."

They got to the doctor's office with no trouble. No one noticed either of them. Morgan waited outside the back door after Faith went in, but he could see no movement up or down the block long alley. After five minutes, he went inside and locked the door behind him.

Faith almost tackled him. "Where have you

been?"

She led him into a small room and a moment later the doctor came in. He was a short man with wild gray hair and a full beard that he kept trimmed close. His forehead bulged slightly accented by a receding hairline. He wore spectacles, the half kind you can look over the top of. Now his sharp blue eyes stared over the top at Faith.

"I see. So this is the father of yours with the cut on his arm. More like a shot in the back. Let's see, let's see."

Buck took off his shirt and the middleaged doctor whistled.

"Be damned. Only saw something like this once before. It was an underpowered .44 with almost no bang left."

He looked from back to front following the path of the slug.

"Should make one Tim Pickering damned mad, fate turning this kind of a trick on him," the doctor said.

"You know about Pickering?" Faith asked.

"Story has been all over town for two days. He told me it was my duty to report any gunshot wounds to the sheriff. Made it plain that if I didn't, he'd have me arrested."

The doctor worked as he talked. He completed taking the dressing off, examined the back wound again.

"You're right, Nurse Davies, it could be the start of blood poisoning, but it isn't, not yet. This is going to hurt, young man."

Almost as he said it, Dr. Johnson swabbed Morgan's back wound with alcohol. Morgan let out a grunt and bit his lips together.

"Everybody is talking about this new problem

called germs," Dr. Johnson said. "Seems these germs we can't see get into a cut or wound and cause all sorts of problems. The alcohol is one way to kill them off. Sorry I had to surprise you. No way to make it hurt less unless I get you drunk first, and we don't have time for that."

As he spoke he swabbed Morgan's chest wound which was not as large and Morgan merely winced.

"Got some good juice here for you to use on him. Twice a day, and make him drink lots of fluids. Probably won't have to come back. Now, young man, what's the matter with your leg?" Doctor Johnson aimed the last question at Buck.

"Mosquito bite."

"Let's look at it."

He pushed up Morgan's pants leg and saw the bandage. When he had it off he shook his head.

"Mosquitoes are growing. This one must be a .45 caliber size. This one looks cleaner." He put some salve on both the wounds and bandaged it again.

"You've got a good nurse there, young man," the doctor said. "I want you to take care of her. Don't let Pickering know where you are. Can you use that Colt on your hip?"

"I shoot some."

"Good. Last man I heard say that was Bat Masterson. I won't be reporting any gunshot wounds, but you stay out of sight. Pickering is mad as hell from what I hear. His job is on the line. Either you're dead or he's hunting work."

"We'll go out the back," Faith said. "Thanks, Dr. Johnson."

Morgan pushed his hand into his pocket and came out with a wad of bills. He dug out a five and handed it to the medical man. The doctor looked surprised.

"Real money? I'm not used to this luxury. Usually I barter my services for eggs, bacon and milk. I'll get change."

"No change, we're even," Morgan said. "Thanks, Dr. Johnson."

They went out singly, Morgan first this time, walking normally, then fading behind a bushy shrub and watching the alley both ways. He could see no hint of danger.

He headed for Faith's house and waited for her at the back door.

"Now," Morgan said. "Tonight we see what kind of action we can stir up in this town. I'm ready to take on Tim Pickering."

Chapter Six

Tim Pickering stood in front of the heavy oak desk trembling. He was a tall man, about thirty years old, and without a lot of weight or substance. His pants hung on his hips from wide suspenders. He wore a jacket to help fill out his shoulders. He was six-feet two-inches tall but weighed only 165 pounds.

Pickering's face was pale now, his hawk nose looking less severe than usual. Dark eyes wary, his clean shaven jaw quivered slightly. His bony hands turned his white high crowned Stetson around and around but he wasn't aware he was doing it.

"Pickering! Stop turning that damn hat. Drop it on the floor." The one who thundered the order was a huge man, perhaps five-eight and weighing almost 400 pounds. Rolls of fat nearly hid his small brown eyes. His cheeks puffed as he breathed with difficulty. He slumped rather than sat on a huge benchlike chair that had four pillows on it and a large, reinforced back rest also layered with pillows. He was totally bald, his head perfectly smooth and round with no humps or lumps. It was pristine white since no one could ever remember Sylvester Bibb being in the sun, or indeed, leaving his combination office and living quarters.

A huge black man stood impassively behind and to the right of Bibb. The man helped Bibb move from place to place, was his servant and companion, and it was rumored he had once broken a man's back simply by picking him up and slamming his back across his knees. Not a flicker of emotion showed on the ebony face. He was six-four, heavily muscled and weighed about 240 pounds. There was no fat anywhere on his body.

Pickering's white hat dropped to the floor on command. He looked up at his employer.

"Still no word?" the fat man boomed. "Your spies haven't learned anything yet? It's been more than forty hours since you failed miserably to do the job assigned to you."

"I been looking. I've got six people out scouring the whole town. We took the livery apart, warn't no body or no wounded man there nowhere."

"You going to smash down every house in town until you find him?"

"Uh . . . no sir. I guess, maybe not."

"On the other hand, that way you would find the bastard, wouldn't you?"

"Yes sir, Mr. Bibb."

"You're supposed to be my outside man, Pickering. I've been putting my trust in you. I'm not getting my money's worth."

"I did just as you said. We busted him up some, then he ran out of rounds and I shot him right in the middle of the back. No way he can't be dead."

"Corpus delecti, Mr. Pickering. Where the hell is the body? I won't believe Lee Morgan is dead until I can touch his corpse. Are you significantly clear on that point?"

Pickering quelled some of his shivering and nodded. "Yes, sir. Yes sir, Mr. Bibb!"

"Pickering, I'm afraid you need a gentle reminder that we are dealing with a tremendously important matter. I've known this man before. The whole future of our endeavor here could be hanging in the balance. You must find him and if he isn't dead, *kill him at once!*"

Bibb caught a bit of drool from his lips as he roared the last of the demand. He turned toward the black man. "Mr. White, one for Mr. Pickering."

The tall, heavy, black man surged toward Pickering with seemingly no effort, swung one massive arm that looked like a big man's thigh. His balled fist hit Pickering in the shoulder and slammed him to the side four-feet before he tumbled to the floor and jolted against the near wall.

"A gentle reminder, Mr. Pickering," Bibb crooned. "Those who fail me simply never have the chance to fail again. If I don't hear that Morgan is dead within the next 18 hours, you'll have to tell Mr. White here why. As you know, he can't speak, except with his hands and feet. I'm sure you know what the outcome of Mr. White's questioning always is."

Pickering got to his knees, then slowly to his feet.

"Yes, Mr. Bibb, I know. I'll . . . I'll go right now and find him, I promise!"

"Do that. I want to know the moment you find him, day or night. But don't wake me up to tell me bad news."

Pickering shook his head and hurried to the door. It opened into an outer office where two heavy faced men sat. Each had a loaded revolver in his holster and a sawed off twin-barreled shotgun primed with double-ought buck on a small shelf near the desk. The shotguns could not be seen over the counter that stretched across the room. It was there more for protection than any other reason.

The men both looked at Pickering, then they relaxed and nodded to him as he went through a locked door in the center of the counter. It could only be unlocked from the inside. Pickering closed it and one of the big men went to lock it.

Pickering took one look behind him at the closed door that shielded him from Mr. Bibb, then he hurried outside.

Behind the closed door, Sylvester Bibb sighed and shook his head. "It is impossible to hire responsible men anymore. Twenty years ago a man could command absolute loyalty from all of his employees, such as I receive from you, Mr. White."

There was no acknowledgement, no flicker in the black eyes. The figure seemed, just then, more like an ebony statue than a man.

Bibb chuckled. "Good, it's after three o'clock, time for my mid afternoon snack. The kitchen, Mr. White."

The black man moved to the back of the chair and pulled it down a foot. Sylvester Bibb lay back with it which freed the front wheels. Then Mr. White rolled it like a wheelbarrow on the large back wheels through a wide pair of double doors and down a five-foot wide hallway to a large kitchen on the right. It had been built with everything at a low level so Bibb could work from his chair.

The big black man seemed to know exactly where the fat man wanted to move. He went from one cupboard to another, then to a chopping block, to the stove which was glowing hot and had a variety of frying pans and pots hanging within reach of the man in the wheeling chair.

In twenty minutes the snack was ready. It included a sear-fried two-pound steak raw in the center, a heap of country fried, previous boiled potatoes, three kinds of vegetables, a half loaf of bread and a jar of jam, plus a quart sized cup of milk.

As Bibb ate, Mr. White stood behind his chair awaiting directions. Most of the orders were given with hand signals that the two had worked out producing a maximum of efficiency.

The mass of food was devoured quickly, then the large man motioned and the black man wheeled the chair into a bedroom. There was no bed. Bibb gave another signal and the chair was lowered to the floor on the front wheels. The whole back of the device unlatched and lowered. It soon rested on swing down legs that touched the floor. The chair was now a nearly flat bed.

Mr. White lowered the blinds in the room, left and closed the door. A moment later another door on the other side of the room opened and two small Chinese girls, thirteen years old, ran up to the big bed. Both girls were naked. They laughed and giggled and crawled on his bed-chair and on him and the after-snack snack began.

The girls chattered in Chinese and it was soon apparent neither could speak English.

The huge man chewed on any breast he could grab and hold. The girls tickled him, held his nose, rubbed his bald head. After five minutes of grabbing and poking and playing with the girls, he clapped his hands once and they turned and ran out the same door they had entered through.

A few moments later, the tall black man came in

and handed Bibb a piece of paper. He read it and swore.

"Not now. Tell him I'm resting, that I can't be disturbed."

The black man ignored the protest, lifted the head of the bed so it moved back into a broad chair. Then he tipped it as before and rolled the bed/chair back to the office area.

When Bibb was situated behind his desk and had some papers spread out in front of him, he nodded at Mr. White. The black man went to the door and opened it.

A man came in wearing a brown suit and holding a brown hat. Under his arm he carried a leather case. He was average height but his body was misshapen as if the pattern was cut slightly askew. His right shoulder tilted down four inches and his left slanted upward four inches. His slightly larger than normal head was tilted perpetually toward the high shoulder.

When he spoke it was with a clipped, superior sounding British accent. "Mr. Bibb, good to see you looking so well today. I'm here with the weekly report. Things are going quite well, actually. Our production rate is up well over what it was last week, and the richness of the ore is actually improving. A wider vein, I believe the tunnel foreman indicated."

He spread out four sheets of figures on the wide desk and pointed to the first one.

"Do you have time for a brandy, Mr. Hyde?" Bibb asked. "I find a brandy particularly refreshing at this time of the day."

"Oh, goodness, no brandy for me. But you go right ahead, sir. I know nothing of spirits. Only mining. But I do know mines. I've been called one of the best mining engineers and general managers that you'll find in the colonies, don't you know."

He waited as Mr. White brought a bottle and poured a brandy glass with a half-inch of the drink. Bibb sniffed the aroma, then swirled the brandy again and took a swallow.

"Ahhhhhhh, yes. Delightful. Now, you've told me what I want to know, production is up. Any kind of trouble, disturbances?"

"None to mention. We did lose one of the workers, but it should be an object lesson to the others. This one had highgrading down to a science. He placed his treasure just beyond the fence each night. Had bribed a guard. Both have been severely disciplined."

"Do you need any more workers?" Bibb asked.

"No, not at the moment. We have two tunnels working and that's the only veins we have to follow now. If one of them branches, we could use another twenty-five. But not yet."

"I still have the contacts in Sacramento."

"Good, good, Mr. Bibb. We shall have some need from simple attrition before long, for say, four a week."

"Anything else?"

"No, sir. I think that tells the story. I'll be back next week about this time." The Englishman stared down at Bibb with a smug, almost superior expression.

"I don't have to remind you, Mr. Bibb, that we are full partners in this endeavor. You'll see my share of the weekly profits plainly spelled out in the report."

"Yes, yes, Mr. Hyde, it always is. But you remember it was my genius that set this up. All you did was the leg work."

"But that is work that you are not able or willing to do yourself, Mr. Bibb. Together we make a good operating team."

"Out, Hyde! Out of my sight, you misshapen, ugly devil of a man!"

Mr. Hyde smiled. "Coming from a mountain of lard, a tub of fat, a monster of the supper table and eight meals a day, I consider that to be a compliment. Good day, sir."

When Mr. Hyde closed the door, the fat man roared with laughter. He had been fat all his life but not this big. That was because he never could afford to eat this much before. He loved being huge. If he could eat enough he might weigh 600 pounds! That was a goal to strive for.

His cook would be here at four and they would go over the menu for the two evening meals, one at six and another at nine. He was looking forward to some really fine gourmet suppers tonight.

Bibb flicked his hand and the ebony tower was beside him. Bibb relaxed as Mr. White rolled him into his parlor where he could look out across an empty lot at the surging mountains to the north. He never tired of watching the mountains and the changing seasons. Now at the height of summer, the mountain held their greenest splendor. The recent rain seemed to brighten everything.

Outside the neatly painted front door of the town office of the Silver Queen Mine, Mr. Hyde turned toward the hotel. He smiled as he anticipated the rest of the afternoon and evening.

The clerk at the hotel put the two dollar bills in his pocket and smiled.

"Yes, sir, Mr. Hyde. Right away. Your usual, but somebody different, I understand. Should take only about 15 minutes. You're in room 22 on the second floor."

The misshapen middleaged man walked to the driveway and up to room 22. Every week he got this same room if it was available. Inside he sat on the bed, then opened the window to let some fresh air into the room.

It wasn't a hot day, not often did it get hot up here. The altitude and the breeze kept things cooled off even in summertime. He took off his hat and put it on the dresser, then his necktie and his jacket and vest, hanging each carefully on a wire coat hanger.

Hyde sat beside the window looking down on Main Street. Mining towns were all alike, but this one was slightly better simply because it had been here longer.

The knock on the door came before he thought it would. When he opened the door he saw two women outside. One was tall and slender, had henna red hair and freckles. The other one was younger, maybe 25, with large breasts and soft blonde hair around her shoulders.

"Ladies, I do believe that you've come to the right place. Won't you please step inside."

"Ya really wanted two of us?" the older, taller one asked, her voice like sliding gravel.

"Oh, absolutely. I haven't seen either of you before. Is that correct?"

They nodded.

"We don't do nothing outlandish or that will hurt us," the younger one said.

"Ladies, I'm sure you don't. My name is Horace. Yes, one of my shoulders is tipped up and the other one down. It doesn't affect my mind at all. I'm a mining engineer and you are each earning ten dollars for yourselves and ten dollars for the saloon. Does that sound interesting?"

"Sure," the older one said with some enthusiasm. "Christ, I'll do anything for ten bucks."

"Good, the blind is down, let's start with names."

"I'm Cathy Lee," the older one said.

"Ruth," the other one.

"Fine, now Ruth, I want you to lie down on the bed." He waited for her to do it. "Take off your shoes. Now Cathy Lee, sit on the side of the bed. It takes me awhile to get excited, ladies. To help me, I want the two of you to make love. Undress each other and then have sex with each other."

Ruth sat up. "Ain't that unnatural?"

"Not at all, Ruth, what can it hurt? You do want that ten dollars, don't you? All I'll do right now is watch."

"Hell, why not? You done it before, Ruth. Told me once. I think it might be fun for a change," Cathy Lee said. She bent forward and kissed Ruth on the lips and reached for her big breasts. Slowly, Ruth let Cathy Lee push her backwards to the bed and quickly the older woman had pulled open Ruth's blouse and was fondling her full breasts with nipples as round as a thumb.

Horace moved his chair closer to the bed and sat there watching. After awhile his hands went down to his crotch and he rubbed slowly. It would take awhile. It always did for him. But he had plenty of time, all night.

He watched at Cathy Lee slowly seduced Ruth. Their dresses came off and the two women looked at each other for a moment. Then Ruth closed her eyes, caught Cathy Lee's head and brought her mouth down to her big breasts. Cathy Lee sucked one in her mouth and made small noises in her throat.

Already Ruth was grinning, and reached for

Cathy Lee's smaller breasts, tweaking the nipples, petting them, watching as they grew in size.

As he watched them, Horace began to take off his shirt. He worked at it slowly. Before he had it off, Ruth had pulled Cathy Lee off her breast and pushed her head down to her crotch. Cathy Lee moaned with delight as Ruth spread her legs, showing a blonde fur patch and pink nether lips.

Cathy Lee gave a small cry and pressed her mouth over the pinkness. Ruth thrilled in pleasure and fell backwards on the bed.

At last, Horace felt a lump rising in his crotch. He grinned. Oh, yes, this was going to be a fine night. He thought of the whip and the ropes and chains he had in his suitcase and he smiled a devilish mask. This was going to be a wonderful night!

Chapter Seven

Tim Pickering was not a brave man. He hated being called on the carpet that way by Mr. Bibb. But the man was right, he did owe his employer an honest day's work. He rubbed his shoulder where the black giant had hit him. Pickering had been smart enough to know it was coming and he jolted sideways just as the blow came.

He had done it before. The effect was a hard push rather than the battering blow it looked like. Mr. White didn't care if they fooled Bibb. Pickering sometimes felt he saw a glint of satisfaction when they put something over on the fat man.

Now Pickering set his jaw and marched down the street to the Hard Rock Saloon. Few in town knew it, but Mr. Bibb owned the saloon and seven or eight other business firms in the community.

He pushed past the bar and into the back room where two men sat at a table playing cards and a woman lounged on a couch with heavy cushions.

"Trouble," Pickering said. "We find Morgan in eighteen hours or we're all out of work." He grabbed the woman by one arm and pulled her to her feet. "That means you, too, Big Tits. We all get on the street and find the bastard!"

The woman had been combing her hair. She was in her twenties, plump, and wore a skirt and a blouse that barely covered her surging breasts.

"What can I do?" she mewed.

"Go to all the whore houses in town and show them that picture on the wanted poster and see if any of the girls have seen him. He's bound to need a woman sooner or later."

He stared at the other two. One was Shorty, he was nearly six-feet tall and slender as a hoe handle. Twin revolvers hung on slender hips. His face was thin and strained as if he didn't eat enough. He didn't, because he drank his meals out of a whiskey bottle. His eyes were just a bit bleary.

"Damn! Told you I should have checked him the other night after you shot him," Shorty said.

Pickering put all of his weight into his blow as he powered a fist into Shorty's shoulder. The man didn't see it coming and it slammed him across a chair and into the table which fell over as Shorty crashed to the floor.

"You remind me once more, and you're the one we'll be digging a grave for. Christ, how many times you going to tell me that? Shorty, work the saloons again, no more than ten minutes in any of them, and keep going to one after another until they close tonight. And no booze until we nail the bastard. I find you with a drink in your hand and you're a dead man! Get out of here."

Shorty got up, brushed off his clothes and walked out the door with a scowl.

"You're next, Tits. Get moving or the free ride is over and you're back to working with your ass. Get out there now."

The woman scowled, put on a light sweater to cover herself a little better and left.

Pickering stared at the other man who still toyed with the deck of playing cards. He was a wide-shouldered square-cut man who looked like a brawler. He was.

"So why are you still here, Nate?"

"Cause I know where Bilbray will be at four o'clock today. He's got to go see the banker."

Pickering grinned for the first time in a half hour. "Yeah, got the bastard. You and Shorty know where to be, the alley. Yeah! Now, this other matter. Bilbray won't matter much if we don't find Morgan. Where else is there to look?"

"Hotels, restaurants, he know anybody in town?" Nate asked.

"Not that we know of. He's a loner. Come to do a job and now we lost the bastard."

"I'll check the streets, the stage, the stores, but most of all, the eating places," Nate said. "He's got to eat somewhere."

"That's what worries me. He is eating somewhere. You suppose some citizen found him and took him in and is taking care of him? I'll talk with Doc Johnson again. I can tell if that old sawbones is lying. Let's get it done. We've got to find that bastard Morgan."

At the doctor's office, Pickering pushed aside the doctor's wife and barged into a room where the medic was bandaging a man's arm.

"Pickering, might have guessed," Doctor Johnson said. "What do you want?"

"You know. You treated any gunshot wounds yesterday or today?"

"Why would I tell you?"

"Because if you don't, I just might mess up your face with my fists. Can you set your own broken nose?"

"Easily. Can you repair your own heart after it takes a .45 slug through it?"

Pickering looked down and saw the six-gun in the doctor's hand.

"Move out the door and right on out of my office or I'll put a round through your leg and I won't treat it. Take your choice, move or get shot. I'm through letting you push me around."

"You couldn't do it, Doc. Not a chance."

The .45 went off in the small room and it sounded like a cannon. The hot led snarled through Pickering's pants leg narrowly missing flesh.

"Still think I'm bluffing, Pickering? I'm damn good with one of these things. The next one will go through your thigh and I'll be aiming at the bone. You want a broken leg, too?"

Pickering began to back out the door. "All right, just relax. I didn't touch you."

"And I won't touch you, Pickering, but some hot lead damn well will. Out!" The doctor kept the weapon trained on the man until he pushed out the back door and into the alley. Then the furious doctor fired three times beside and behind Pickering as the tall, thin man ran at full speed down the alley.

Two blocks down the street, Nate had folded over the wanted poster of Buckskin Morgan so it showed only the picture. He let the waitresses in the hotel restaurant look at it, but both of them shook their heads. They hadn't seen him.

"Handsome man like that I would have remembered," the younger one of the two said. "He sure ain't been eating here."

Nate tried the three cafes in town with the same results. They would know. Morgan had not been eating at any of them. That meant he'd been staying with a family somewhere in town.

Nate gave up and went into the General Store, but still drew a blank. He checked in at the three other saloons, and ran into Shorty, but he was having no luck either.

The woman, whose real name was Fanny, was still in the first saloon that had girls. She was having a drink with a miner who couldn't keep his hands out of her blouse.

"Told you I'm retired, not in the business any-more," Fanny said with a grin.

"Yeah, yeah, you'll never retire. You like getting poked too much."

"Not by you." She finished the beer, rubbed his crotch and went upstairs to talk to the girls. All four came out of their rooms within the next half hour. They looked at the picture on the poster and shook their heads.

"Wasting your time, Fanny," a faded soiled dove called Princess told her. "A gent like him won't be paying for his loving, you can count on that. He's got some little sweetie all bundled in the haymow somewhere. We'll never see him."

"Yeah, my luck. Without him my man is about done in for good. You got room for another girl here?"

"Think you can still stand the grabbing and pawing and stink of these miners?"

"Used to, guess I can again. Where's my crib?"

"Anyone that's not got the door locked, just as it always been. You sure, Fanny?"

Fanny grinned, shrugged. "Yes, I'm sure. I better get to work."

Outside on the street, Tim Pickering walked the short three blocks of the town's shopping area, watching faces. He had the features of Buckskin Morgan burned into his brain. He almost drew on one man, but when he turned fully around the face wasn't right.

Twice he almost got into fights when he lifted hats on men who had them pulled down on their faces. Neither man was Morgan.

As he walked, he watched the time. He needed to end up in the middle of the street outside the dentist's office right at four o'clock.

Bilbray wouldn't be able to back down. Not with the big mouth he'd had around town lately. It was a matter of honor, of living up to what you claimed you were going to do. For a week now, Bilbray had been trying to get the people stirred up to run Tim Pickering out of town.

He even tried to get a court order, but the judge wouldn't be through here for two more months. The deputy sheriff laughed at him, then quickly told Pickering about the legal try. Now was when the braggart had to answer directly for his big mouth, had to put his six-gun in back of his accusations.

Four o'clock in front of the dentist's office.

Pickering moved down the street and went into the Watchmaker and Jewerly Shop. The bell on the door tinkled and a face came up from the workbench behind a small counter.

"Dunc, is my watch ready yet?" Pickering asked.

Dunc Davies looked up, startled at first to find the man they had been so concerned about right there in the shop. He let the eyepiece fall out of his right eye and blinked as he always did.

"Yes, let's see, Pickering, right? That was a nicely made silver pocket watch for cleaning and setting.

Looks like it's all ready. That'll be a dollar."

"A dollar? Damn, last time cost only fifty cents."

"Let that be a lesson. Keep it away from moisture. Looked like it could have been dunked in water even. Had to scrape off some rust and work over some of the mechanism. But she'll run like a railroad now."

"Yeah, all right." Pickering gave him a dollar and looked at the time. "This set right?"

"Down to the tenth of a second. Right now it's three, forty-two and about eighteen seconds."

Pickering looked at the timepiece, put the leather thong around his belt loop and let the watch sink into his pocket.

"Yeah, close enough." He turned and walked out of the shop without a goodbye.

Dunc watched him go. He seemed to be in a hurry now. One of these days Buck was going to catch him without his friends and settle their small shoot-in-the back problem.

Outside, Pickering paced down the boardwalk faster now. He didn't see the step up at the General Store walk and tripped, nearly sprawling on the boards. Someday all of the levels of these damn walks had to be the same, he told himself.

He made it to the dentist's office five minutes before four o'clock. He peered inside but saw no one in the small waiting room just inside the door. The dentist was new in town, and Pickering had no idea what his name was. The sign simply said "General Dentistry." It had been there through the last three dentists Pickering could remember.

Pickering leaned against the front of the blacksmith shop next door and waited. He unsnapped the leather strap that held his six-gun in the holster and trailed the leather down behind his leg. Then he eased the weapon in and out of the holster twice to be sure it moved easily with no hangups.

Two minutes later he saw the slightly bow legged man with the little pot belly come rolling down the boardwalk. He had on a pair of cotton trousers and a checkered shirt. On his right hip hung a holster filled with iron. Pickering grinned.

When Bilbray was six feet away, Pickering moved onto the boardwalk directly in front of him.

"Mr. Bilbray, I'd say we have an argument to settle. Don't you think this would be a good day to take care of it?"

"No. I mean yes, we have an argument, but I won't draw against you."

"In that case it'll be easy for me, won't it? I'm going to shoot you down, Bilbray. You might as well have the satisfaction of trying to outdraw and outshoot me."

"You're too fast."

"Should have thought of that when you kept spreading those lies about me. Out into the street, Bilbray. No reason to shoot up any store windows."

Bilbray hesitated. His lower lip trembled. Sweat beaded just under his old felt hat. His right hand twitched as he looked down at the gunman's low tied holster.

"It's no better than murder, Pickering." His voice raised to a shout. "This man Pickering is trying to kill me!" he shouted.

One or two people turned, but most of the towns folks within hearing went on their way.

"You could be next!" Bilbray screamed. "You, Halsteen the butcher, he could get mad at you next and call you out." The man called Halsteen never turned around.

"Where's the Deputy Sheriff?" Bilbray screeched.

"I demand to have the Deputy here."

"He's busy right now," Pickering said. "You moving into the street, or you want to die right there on the boardwalk?"

Bilbray kept looking around. No one came to his aid. At last he groaned and stepped into the street.

'It's murder, plain and simple. Murder!"

The dentist's office was right beside where the alley cut back through from Main Street. The narrow slot between buildings was murky with afternoon shadows.

The two men stood in the street now, twenty feet apart.

"I'll make it easy for you, Bilbray," Pickering said. "I'm gonna count to three, then draw. You go ahead and draw just anytime you want to, Mr. Bilbray. One." He waited a moment. "Two . . . Three."

Pickering was moderately fast.

Morgan had come out of a saloon across the street and stared at the scene. He'd seen it many times before. This was familiar. He saw Pickering's right hand dart down for his weapon, grab it and pull it free and lift it.

The shot that rang out seemed a little fast and almost in the same moment he heard what he swore were two other shots. The second man in the street facing Pickering never got his weapon out of the holster. He jolted to the side, then slammed to the rear where he sprawled on the dust filled street and never moved again.

A curious crowd gathered when the gunplay was over. Somebody went up to the man on the ground and looked at the body, then rolled him over.

"Right through the heart!" the man said. "Damn, that was good shooting."

A man with a star on his chest came through the crowd. He looked around.

"What happened here?" he asked.

"A shootout, Deputy," the man who had checked the body said. "Looked like self defense. Both of them drew at the same time."

The deputy looked at Pickering who had walked forward. "That right?" he asked Pickering.

"Yeah, Deputy. He called me out and we talked and he started to draw and damned if I didn't beat him."

"Come down to the office. You'll have to sign a statement." The Deputy was a stout man with a fat little belly. He pointed to two men. "You and you, get that body down to the undertakers."

Morgan scratched his jaw. Why would a body jolt to the side when it was shot from the front? Answer, it wouldn't. He wandered down a dozen feet to the alley and stepped into the shadows. He sniffed and at once knew why the body had been rocked to the left.

He smelled the unmistakable odor of gunpowder smoke. Somebody had shot from the alley just before Pickering had fired. The shots came close enough together to make it hard to tell them from one round.

Morgan eased along behind the men who carried the dead man. He saw where they were going and waited ten minutes after they came out of the office before he went in.

The undertaker was a small round man with a red face, fringes of red hair, spectacles and a perpetual smile.

He looked up as Morgan slipped through the office door into the room where the corpse laid on a table.

"Sorry, nobody allowed back here," the man said still smiling.

"Sorry yourself, but I just have a quick question for you. How many slugs you find in that body?"

"Hell, one, right in the heart. Why?"

"Check his left side," Buck said.

"Check . . . who are you, anyway? Why should I check?"

"Take a look, you have to take his clothes off anyway. Take a look."

"Hell, if only to get rid of you." The undertaker unbuttoned the man's shirt and pulled it out of his pants and lifted up a light undershirt.

"Be damned!" the body carver said. "Look at that! Two more bullet holes in his side." The undertaker looked up quickly. "You some kind of lawman or something?"

"Not so you could notice. Just thought it strange when I hear three shots at a shootout and the winner fires only one and the loser none at all. You don't need to mention this to anyone. Be better for your health if you don't."

Lee pulled his six-gun and laid it next to the red face of the little man pressing the muzzle ever so lightly against his head.

"You mention to anybody that I was in here asking about this, you'll be your own next customer. Understand?"

The small man with the fringes of red hair nodded. When Morgan eased out the door into the office, the Silverville undertaker was still nodding his sweating head.

Chapter Eight

Morgan left the undertaker's establishment and meandered around on the street where the shooting had taken place, but did not see Pickering. The two of them had to have a serious "nigh unto death talk" and the sooner the better. But maybe not today.

Morgan turned back toward the Davies house. He still wished that he could remember. Damnit! He was walking around like a blind man. Maybe Dunc had some information for him. He felt like he was just half a man not knowing his background, where he had been or what he had done. All just one big damn blank page.

An hour later they sat around the supper table in the Davies' house. Here he felt at home, safe, secure. Faith had put on a pretty blouse and combed out her long brown hair until it shone in a tawny wave around her shoulders. Whenever she glanced up at him now she had an expression he recognized at once. He knew the look and wasn't sure that he objected. One afternoon making love with him and she wanted him to stay and be with her for the rest of her life. He had seen the expression on women's faces before and before he had been terrified by it. Now it didn't seem to be so bad.

Dunc had started talking as soon as he got in the door that evening.

"The other mine in this area is the Big Strike Number One. You know that. The man who runs it is Janish Lang, about my age. Far as I know, he's honest, realiable, a good man. His mine is closer to town, about a quarter-a-mile, and the men walk out or ride every day to go to work. Seems he runs a good operation, is making money and we just never hear much bad about him. He lives right here in town."

"He comes to church, is married, has a family and seems like a nice man," Faith said.

"You've probably been thinking the same thing I have," Dunc said. "Somebody in town must have hired you to come here. If Bibb and his gunmen tried to stop you, it must mean that it was Lang who hired you."

"So I should go see this Mr. Lang and come right out and ask him if he hired a fast gun?" Morgan asked.

Dunc nodded. "Don't rightly see any other way to figure out exactly why you're here." Dunc remembered the wanted poster and squirmed. He probably should tell Buck he was wanted, but he didn't think this was the right time. Anyway, those posters could be put out by anybody.

Morgan worked on the thick steak, mashed potatoes and gravy and three kinds of vegetables. "I know I'm getting fat eating this well, Faith. Tomorrow, let's have burned biscuits, hard fried eggs and maybe some greasy strips of bacon. I'd feel more at home."

She smiled at him and he could see a cottage with curtains in the windows and three kids waving at him from the door. He shook his head to get rid of the image.

Lang lives right here in town," Dunc said. "Fact is, he's down the street just a couple of blocks. Nice house but not a palace."

"Does he have guards and fences and dogs protecting him?" Morgan asked.

"Not at all." Dunc said. "No guards at all, I know of. Just a regular man like the rest of us."

Morgan sipped at his second cup of coffee.

"All right, it's decided. Right after supper, I'll go over there and see this Mr. Janish Lang. Might be able to clear up a lot of things that way."

He waited until almost seven-thirty, then headed for the address Dunc gave him. It was a modest house for a mine owner, wooden construction, three stories and painted white. No fence, no door bell. He knocked sharply three times and waited. Lights were just starting to come on around town.

A moment later someone came to the door. When it opened a man looked out. He was shorter than Morgan, had thinning hair and a broad smile.

"Yes sir, can I help you?" Lang asked.

"Mr. Janish Lang?"

"Yes, that's right."

"Could I talk to you for a minute?"

A frown flickered across the man's face, then he nodded and stepped back and Buck moved inside the house and the door closed.

"Mr. Lang, I don't know quite how to start. Did you send out of the area to hire a man to come and work for you, a man who had some experience with guns?"

Lang looked up quickly. "I sure as hell did. But I hear that Pickering and his gang of thugs shot down the man. Too damn bad, I needed him."

"Mr. Lang, what was the man's name you hired?"

Lang looked at him closely. "Not sure that should be any of your business. Why don't you tell me who you are and why you're interested in this man I tried to hire."

"Mr. Lang, that's part of my problem. I'd like to tell you who I am, but I rightly don't know. My new friends here in town tell me that I was in a fight with six men and then Tim Pickering shot me. But somewhere along the action, I lost my memory."

"Pickering shot you? You could be the man I hired. Does Idaho mean anything to you? A place called Grove, Idaho?"

Lee furrowed his brow, then shook his head. "Sorry, doesn't seem familiar at all."

"Damn! Well, come into my den, I'll show you a copy of the letter I wrote and see if that stirs any memories. If Pickering and his goons beat you up and shot you, I'd say it's more than likely that you're the man I sent for."

Down the hall way they came to a den with heavy furniture, a desk, a globe on a stand, and one wall covered with bookcases that were well-filled. Lang lit a lamp on the desk and looked through a drawer a moment.

Then he brought out a piece of paper. "Not too good with my handwriting. I'll read it to you. It's addressed to Lee Buckskin Morgan, Grove, Idaho." He looked up sharply. "That name mean anything to you, young man?"

Buck shook his head. "Friends here in town call me Buck, but that's just a coincidence."

Lang gave him a long look. "Maybe. Date on this

copy of the letter is two months ago. I asked Buckskin Morgan to come here to Silverville to help me with a problem I have. Another mine operator in the area has a fast gun who is hurting me and my miners. Also, this other miner is turning out twice the ore that I am and I want to know how he's doing it." He looked up from the paper. "That's about all there was. I also offered you a thousand dollars for a month's work if you can help me with these two problems."

"I don't hire out for straight killing jobs," Buckskin said. "You can find plenty who will do that." He stopped and looked up at Lang. "Now where did those words come from? Must be the real me talking there. I didn't think that through, it just blurted out."

"Good, good," Lang said. "I think part of your memory is coming back. Your name is Lee Buckskin Morgan. You come from Idaho where you have a ranch."

"Yeah, the Spade Bit, where me and my dad raise horses, only my dad is gone now, killed in a shoot-out."

Lang watched him. "Had you known that before, about the Spade Bit?"

Morgan began to grin. "Not a particle of it. Another sentence just busted out of my lips. I think my old brain is trying to help me get my memory back."

Lang pulled a bottle from his desk. "Could you use a spot of sipping whiskey?"

"Rightly so, Mr. Lang. I'm feeling better than I have since I woke up two days ago after Pickering shot me in the back."

Lang looked up suddenly. "Shot you in the back two days ago and you're up and moving?"

"You won't believe this either. I better show you."

Five minutes later Morgan had stripped off his shirt and showed Lang the entry point and how the bullet traveled around his rib and came out.

"Be damned! I never would have believed it if I hadn't seen it."

"Pickering can't believe it either. So you see, I've got a personal score to settle with him. I'm not too fond of back shooters, especially when it's me who gets shot and I'm half unconscious laying in the mud and rain on my belly."

Lang tossed down the rest of his glass of whiskey and paced the den. "Buck, I'm sure you're my man. Can you use that iron you have tied down?"

"I shoot some."

Lang chuckled. "Only good men with a gun say that. So, Pickering is covered. How can we find out what's going on up at the Silver Queen mine Bibb owns? They have fences and rifle toting guards around the place day and night."

"Talk to the men who work there."

"That's part of the problem. The workers up there live up there. It's near ten miles into the hills from here. Only other mine in this stretch that isn't worked out. Nobody seems to know where he gets his diggers, or anything about them."

"What about the law in this area?" Morgan asked. "How does Pickering get away with his gun talk?"

"Almost no law here. Don't know if you've met our deputy sheriff. He's about as close to no law as you can get. I'm sure that he's on Bibb's payroll at three or four times what the county pays him. We're in El Dorado County, but the county seat is over twenty miles away. The Sheriff has been to town only once."

Now it was Morgan's turn to walk the room.

"How did you hear about me? What did you hear?"

"If you're the same man, and I'm about convinced that you are, I heard about you in Sacramento. The word was that if there was an especially tough job to be done, you were the best man in the West to do it. I heard you spent some of your time at the Mile High Hotel in Denver," Lang said.

"Denver? I can't ever remember being there," Morgan said.

"That's where I mailed your letter. The hotel evidently knew you and forwarded it to you wherever you were."

"That's possible."

"People I talked to said you were good with a six-gun, but that you weren't over the edge. They said you used a little style and conscience in your work," Lang said.

Morgan laughed. "Nice to learn all these things about myself. What if I'm not this guy after all? I could have gunned down this Morgan, taken the letter and come here for the job. How would you know the difference?"

Lang rubbed his hand over his face, then stared at Morgan for a moment. "Possible, yes, but I don't think so. I think I'm a good judge of character, and I don't see anything to make me believe you aren't the man I sent for." He sat down in the big chair behind the desk.

"At any rate, the job is yours, if you want it. The thousand dollar offer still stands. I need to get a little breathing room here. Pickering is either chasing out of town or shooting down two of my workers a week. I can't stand for that."

Morgan turned and held out his hand. "Deal," he said. "I like the way you lay your cards on the table. I'll see what I can find out about the Bibb mine, and

I'll damn well put Pickering out of business. I'm not sure which one first but I'll dig into both the problems for you.''

The men shook hands and Lang smiled. "I'm pleased. I think you can do both jobs. How you fixed for cash? You need any advance on your wages?''

"No. I'll do the job first. If Pickering is faster than I think he is, or if he gets me in the back again, you won't be out any money.''

They had one more shot of the sipping whiskey, then Morgan asked if he could go out the back door just in case anyone was watching the front. No sense in taking any chances. He slipped into the blackness and waited. Nothing moved. No sound came. He waited for five minutes, then headed down the alley toward the Davies house.

He was starting to remember. The Spade Bit in Idaho. He didn't do straight killing jobs. Yes, a little was coming back, slowly. His brain must have been really scrambled. Pickering was going to pay for this, not just a straight shootout. There had to be something special for Mr. Pickering. Something damn special.

It was still early. Maybe he could find the sonofabitch tonight.

Morgan checked one saloon but saw that Pickering wasn't there. He left and went to the Hard Rock Saloon, bought a beer and sat with his back to the wall working on the mug of suds. He waited fifteen minutes, then he got restless. He didn't know why, but he figured he shouldn't stay there any longer. He went out the back door leaving his beer half finished on the table. He didn't care who noticed.

When he got to the alley he hurried his pace and then he was running. Why? He wasn't sure. It was a damn bad feeling he had in his bones. Something was wrong. Something was wrong at the Davies' house.

He picked up his pace, felt his leg screaming at him with pain but he battered down the knifing sensations and ran faster toward the Davies' house. He just knew that he had to get back there as fast as he could.

Chapter Nine

If Morgan hadn't surprised them, he and Faith and Dunc would all be dead.

He ran up to the front of the house. It was closest. It was the fastest way to get inside from downtown. That was what saved them all.

Morgan was panting when he stopped just short of the front porch. He bent over to get his breath and to try to slow down the daggers from searing through his right leg and even his arm now.

He already had the six-gun in his hand. With the double action Colt .45, he didn't have to cock it between each round. The trigger pull cocked the hammer and then let it fall. He could fire five times as fast as he could pull the trigger.

Morgan stood straight and eased up the steps to the front door. It was never locked. He turned the knob silently and pushed the door inward a half inch. No chair, no bolt, no chain. He edged the panel inward a full inch and listened through the crack.

He heard a woman sobbing. Faith.

Two voices mumbled low and in the background.

Where were they? Inside somewhere, not watching the front door. So they would be in the kitchen or the bedroom. He eased the door inward again six inches so he could see past it down the short hallway.

Nothing there.

He stepped in. The floorboards creaked. Sweat popped out on his forehead in a nervous reflexive action.

He hoped the voices in back blocked out the floorboards noise. Morgan lifted the six-gun and stepped forward. Nobody in the small living room. Beyond that the kitchen. He could see no one. There was a lamp burning in the kitchen.

They had to be in the bedrooms. One of the two. Closest one was Faith's. He remembered it well.

Before he could move a man stepped out of Faith's bedroom and saw him. The stranger swung up a sawed off shotgun and his finger touched the trigger just as Morgan fired. His round ripped through Shorty's chest, plowing a wide hole through his heart and out his back.

A hundredth of a second after Morgan fired, Shorty's dead trigger finger spasmed forward on the trigger, dropping the hammer. The double-ought buck round exploded, most of the .32 caliber size pellets thundered into the wooden floor. Two of them bounced off and one hit Morgan's boot heel nearly knocking his foot out from under him.

For a moment after the shotgun blast the echoes dribbled off to total silence. Morgan stepped around the hall partition into the living room just as a shotgun poked out of Faith's room and blasted a round of double-ought buck down the hallway. It was followed by the sound of someone smashing a window.

"Getting away!" Morgan growled. He charged down the hallway into Faith's room in time to see the last of a man vanishing over the window sill and into the darkness. He charged to the window and fired four more times at the figure running away into the darkness before Morgan's weapon ran dry.

Only then did he look around the room.

On the bed lay Faith, naked and tied spread eagled to the bedframe. Her eyes were red. His boot knife came out and Morgan slashed the torn up sheets that kept her tied to the bed.

"Look for Pa!" Faith shouted as he cut her bounds. "He must be in the kitchen."

They ran to the kitchen and found Dunc sprawled on the kitchen floor on his face. Faith knelt beside him. Morgan had reloaded his Colt as they ran. Now he turned over Dunc Davies. He was still alive. His breath came in gasps. A bloody bullet hole in his chest must have just missed his heart but cut a torturous hole through his lung.

"I'll go get Doc," Faith said. Then she realized she was still naked.

"Get that shooting iron of yours, get a dress on and watch the front door," Morgan ordered. "I'll run and get Doc Johnson. Don't want to move Dunc right yet until the Doc looks at him. It's bad, you know it's bad."

"Hell yes, bad," Dunc said. "Where you two been?"

Morgan caught Faith's hand and held it. He looked at Dunc. "You're still alive. Figured it'd take more than one slug to kill an old watchmaker like you. Faith, you watch him. Don't move, Dunc. Doctor will be right here. Remember who the bastards were. I got one, the tall bean pole."

Then Morgan hurried out the back door. He went

down two alleys and came out half a block from the doctor. He knocked on the door and a light flared.

Two minutes later Doctor Johnson was walking rapidly beside Morgan toward the Davies' house.

"Hit him high in the chest, left side you said. Must have missed his heart."

Morgan gritted his teeth as he walked. His leg must have broken open. It hurt like hell.

They went through the back door, calling to Faith as they did. She had put a pillow under Dunc's head and a blanket over him. She also had on a dress and shoes.

"He said he was cold," Faith said.

Doc Johnson went to his knees and began checking Dunc. He looked up. "Did you notice if the slug came out Dunc's back?"

"Didn't see any sign of blood, but we really didn't look," Morgan said. They eased him to his side and Doctor Johnson's hand explored his back. At last he nodded.

"Yes, a small exit wound lower down. Good, we won't have to dig in there after it."

"Suits me fine, Doc," Dunc said. "How's your garden this year?"

"Dunc, glad you're still with us. Just so you'll stay around a while I don't want you to talk any more for a spell. Have you spit up any blood?"

Dunc shook his head.

"Hurt to breathe?"

Dunc nodded.

"We're going to get you into bed, then I'll see what the hell I can do to help you. Not an awful lot, I'm afraid. Fifty years from now medicine will know exactly what to do. Guess I was just born too early in the century."

It took them ten minutes to get Dunc into his bedroom. At last they let him stand up slowly, then had him walk.

"Can't put any pressure on your chest," Doc told him.

When they had him bedded down and bandaged, they turned down the lamp and went into the kitchen where Faith had coffee going. Doc turned to Faith, his face serious.

"Now, for you, young lady. Did you get hurt?"

"No, just scared half to death."

"That's easy to treat. Did they rape you?"

Faith looked quickly at Morgan, then lifted her brows. "No, Doc. Buck got here in time to stop them. That's part of the scared to death part."

"Same treatment." He walked up to her and put his arms around her and held her tightly. At last he bent and kissed her cheek and stepped back.

"Now, is that better? What I call H & K care. Works every time. H & K stand for hugs and kisses. As for Dunc, we can only hope. He looks good right now. If that round went through high enough up in his lung it won't do a lot of damage. He'll be sore for a week or so, and if there's no infection from those damn little unseen germ things, he should be fine.

"You keep him home for at least a week and let me know if he spits up blood or has any trouble breathing, wheezing, that sort of thing."

Faith nodded and walked the doctor to the door. Morgan brought out a ten dollar bill and gave it to the medic.

"You're downright spoiling me, Buck. While I'm here let me look at your various cuts and bullet holes."

He checked over Morgan in the living room, changed the dressing and worried a minute over the leg wound.

"Don't look the best, but might come out all right. I'll look again in three days."

They let the medic out the front door and Faith ran into Morgan's arms. She began to cry softly and he took her to the couch where they sat down.

"They were waiting for you to come back," she said. "They told us they would kill you and then us too. When you didn't come right away they started touching me and feeling me. Then they tied me on the bed and they cut off my clothes! I've never been so angry or frightened in my life.

"Pa kept yelling at them and fighting with them. Finally he went at them with a knife, and the tall one shot Pa with his pistol almost point blank.

"Then they took me to the bed and tied me down. I don't know who the tall one was but the heavy set one was called Nate. He's almost as tall as you are with big shoulders and arms."

"Good, I have a name and description." He bent and kissed her cheek and then held her tightly for a minute.

"Now, I have to clean up some trash. You stay right here." He went to the body in the hallway and picked up the sawed off double barreled shotgun. He found half a dozen rounds in the dead man's pockets. Then he boosted the body on his shoulder and carried it out the back door and down the alley. He walked with him two blocks over and dumped him alongside the street.

Back at the house, he found some blood spots on his vest and washed them out the best he could.

Faith still lay on the couch. She had curled up with her head on a pillow. "I think I'll sleep right here tonight," she said.

"We'll talk about that later. I'm going hunting.

Not sure when I'll be back. You lock all the doors and windows and don't let anyone in. Keep that five-shot revolver in your hand and use it if you need to."

He hefted the sawed off shotgun, slid the extra shells in his pocket and reloaded the one fired barrel. Morgan slipped on the ankle length duster and hung the shotgun by a rawhide thong around his neck. The duster covered the scatter gun and its ten-inch barrel completely. He put a sixth round in his Colt and then stepped out the back door and headed for saloon row.

In the first three drinking emporiums he found no one who even looked like he could be Nate. In two of the saloons he asked the apron if he had seen his old buddy Nate. The barkeeps simply shook their heads and looked away. Nate was not well liked in the community.

The Hard Rock Saloon had been most productive finding Pickering so he went back there. These two men must be working with Pickering. He bought a beer and sat under his slouch hat for ten minutes in the Hard Rock before he saw Pickering himself slide into the saloon and vanish past the bar and into a back room.

Interesting, Morgan decided. Pickering moved like he owned the place. Another man came in, large, broad shouldered, with arms the size of oak limbs. He had to be the one. He wore a pistol on his hip but it didn't look much used. The man stepped up to the bar and got a beer but didn't pay for it. Figured.

Morgan took the small notebook from his pocket and wrote on it with a stub pencil.

"Nate: You hunting that guy who got shot in the rain couple days ago? I know where he is. Meet me in the alley in back of this place, right now."

Morgan found a man deep in his cups with an empty beer mug. He showed the note to the man and waved a quarter at him.

"You take this note to the barkeep and I'll give you a quarter. You understand?"

The drunk grabbed at the quarter. Morgan had written "Nate" on the outside of the note and folded it over once. The drunk sobered up a little, stared at the note, then at Buck.

"Take the paper to the apron . . . and I get the quarter."

"Right. I'll be watching you. If you don't do it, I'll throw you out into the street."

"Yeah, yeah."

Morgan made him repeat his orders again, then gave him the quarter and the note. Morgan moved toward the back door but stayed in a spot where he could see the bar. The drunk stumbled once, almost dropped the note, but at last got to the bar. He threw the note on the glistening top and yelled at the apron.

The bar man came over and looked at the name on the note, picked it up and glared at the drunk, then shrugged and carried the paper down the bar where the big shouldered man sipped on his beer. He read the note, looked around and the barkeep pointed at the drunk.

Two minutes later Nate must have figured out he wasn't going to learn from the drunk who gave him the note. He snorted, lifted the six-gun from his holster and angled for the back door. Morgan was right behind him. As soon as Nate pushed open the outside door, Morgan drove into him from behind, hitting him in the back with his shoulder, slamming the stocky man through the door and face down in the dirt of the alley.

The six-gun in his hand skidded away into the darkness. Morgan rolled off the man, cringing at the pain in his left arm, and came up with his own weapon trained on the other man.

"We have a nice little talk right here Nate, or you die slow. How does that sound?"

"You're Buckskin Morgan, right?"

"I ask the questions, Nate. Don't get up, stay right there, face down on the dirt, where you belong."

Morgan put his foot in the middle of the big man's back and pressed down. Nate squirmed but didn't complain.

"Who sent you after me at the Davies' house?"

No answer came. Morgan tromped down hard with his boot heel into Nate's back bringing a howl of pain.

"Who sent you?" Morgan asked.

"Pickering." Nate said.

"How did you know I was at the Davies'?"

"A neighbor saw a man going in and coming out of the back door. She was curious. I . . . I know this lady well."

"Who shot Dunc?"

"Shorty did. He's the man with the two guns."

"And you stripped Faith and tied her on the bed?"

"Yeah, both of us." Nate said.

"You bastard." Morgan pulled his foot off the man. "Roll over on your back." Morgan waited for him to turn over slowly. Then Morgan shot him in the left knee. The heavy .45 slug drilled through his knee cap and exploded the knee joint. Nate curled into a ball, screaming in pain.

"You bastard!" Morgan yelled at him. "It's pay up time. You were with Pickering that night you shot me in the rain, right?"

Nate wailed in his pain. Morgan kicked him in the

side and he uncoiled and lay there sobbing. Morgan repeated the question. Nate wiped his eyes with one hand and looked up through the faint light of the alley.

"Yeah. You should be dead."

Morgan kicked Nate in the crotch, crushing one testicle against his pelvic bones. Nate bellowed in agony for a moment, then passed out. He came to at once, screaming.

Someone started to open the back door of the saloon. Morgan whirled and fired a round into the wall over the top of the door. Whoever it was who was coming out changed his mind.

Nate lay there cringing, trying to hold his knee and his crotch.

"You're scum, Nate. You're the original bastard, do you know that? You probably shot Dunc. You would have raped Faith if you had time. You'll never rape anyone again."

Lee kicked him alongside the head, then again and saw the man's head jolt from side to side. He walked a dozen feet down the alley, then turned and fired two shots into Nate's head.

For a moment a surge of emotion billowed up in Morgan. It was familiar. He had sensed that feeling before. Not pleasant, but not terrible either. It was a combination of power and life and death and doing right and knowing that he had just killed a man and that it was a man who well deserved to die. Then the feeling evaporated.

That's when Morgan knew that he had killed men before, that in the balance he might not be much better than the man he had just killed. At least he had a good reason.

He walked to the end of the alley, almost hoping that Pickering would hear his man had been tricked into the alley. He wanted to be done with Pickering right now and get on with the job so he could learn as soon as possible exactly who he was and all about his regular, normal life.

Once out of the alley, Morgan walked faster. He had to ask Dunc something while he could still answer. Why had Dunc suddenly suggested that they call him Buck until they found out his real name? It wasn't coincidence. Morgan didn't believe in chance. How did he know?

Chapter Ten

Morgan knocked at the Davies back door. Faith asked who it was, then let him in quickly. He had a grimly satisfied expression and Faith noticed it at once.

"You found him," she said.

"Yes, he won't bother you anymore. You can relax. How is Dunc?"

Her slight frown faded and her mouth opened in silence and then she sobered. She shook her head a moment as if trying to realize that two men were dead. She didn't say anything.

"How is Dunc?" Morgan asked again.

"Oh, he's doing fine. Hasn't got to sleep yet."

"Good, I need to talk to him." He held her hand and they went into the second bedroom where Dunc lay on the pillows, his head up, the light up bright. He was looking at a Ned Buntline Wild West dime novel.

"You got the look of a man who just took care of a problem," Dunc said.

"True. I have another problem. I talked to Mister Lang. He wrote a letter to a guy named Lee Buckskin Morgan. Did you suggest that we call me Buck because you knew who I was?"

Dunc nodded. "In the bureau there, top drawer."

Buck opened the drawer and found the wanted poster.

"I'll be damned. Arizona. Says I killed a man. Sure as hell does look like me."

"I went through the deputy sheriff's stack of wanteds and came up with that one. He hasn't seen it. That stir any memories? Thought better not to say anything about it."

"Just as well. I don't remember a thing about Arizona." He dismissed it. "How are you feeling?"

"Hurts like hell."

Morgan grinned. "Yeah, getting shot tends to do that to a guy. You do what your nurse tells you to. I'm heading out toward the Bibb mine. Mister Lang hired me to get Pickering out of his hair and to see what's going on at the Silver Queen mine. Guess I better get started doing my job."

Dunc nodded, frowned as pain stabbed through him and then took a long, slow breath.

"Yeah, you take care of that. I got that one scattergun right here beside me. Nobody gonna push us around again."

"You're feeling better, Dunc." He pointed at him with his finger and went back to the kitchen.

Faith poured him a cup of coffee.

"You planning on leaving tonight for the mine, or in the morning?"

"Thinking about right now."

"I have a friend, Maxine Garrison. Her husband worked up at the mine. They let him visit her one day every two weeks. She hated it and wanted him to quit. But three weeks ago he didn't come home and hasn't been back since. She might be able to tell you something. I'll write you a note and you can talk to her in the morning. You can't do anything up there tonight anyway."

She put down her coffee and walked to where he still stood near the stove. She pushed hard against him, her breasts crushed on his chest as her lips sought his. The kiss was long and she sighed gently.

"Faith, we can't make love tonight. Not with your father in the house . . . especially since he has that sawed off shotgun!"

She smiled. "I know. I can get a little hugging and kissing, though." She kissed him again and put his hand over her breast.

"A little encouragement, a few dreams," she said. "At least you can play with me a little. I need it after what happened earlier. Right then I thought I'd scream if a man ever touched me again. But now . . . now I want you. So just touch me a little, then I can go to bed happy."

He put his hands inside her blouse and caressed her breasts feeling them get warm and her nipples rise. She spread her legs and pulled one hand down and he rubbed the soft wet spot there through her soft cotton drawers until she shivered. Then he touched the hard node and she climaxed gently against him as they both stood there beside the stove.

Her hand kept his pressed there and he rubbed her again. This time her climax was harder and she moaned in total joy and clung to him. At last she pushed away and rubbed his crotch tenderly.

"Next time big fella, it will be your turn." She grinned at him. "I'm going to say good night to Pa and turn down his lamp. I'll hear him if he even wiggles." She shook her head. "You are more man than I'll ever have again, you know that? Now get to bed before I rip off my clothes and embarrass myself wantonly."

He slept that night on the sofa with a blanket draped over him. The sawed off shotgun was beside one hand and his Colt double action by the other.

The next morning Morgan took a note Faith had written and found the home where Maxine Garrison lived. It was near the edge of town, needed paint and was rundown. He knocked and waited.

He heard a baby cry. A moment later a woman opened the door with a child in her arms. Her hair was carefully combed and she looked scrubbed fresh and clean.

"Morning, I'm Buck Morgan. Faith Davies sent me over to talk about your husband and the Bibb mine. Would you have a minute?"

"About the mine? You hear anything?"

Her face was open, her emotions floating on the surface as the hurt and longing showed through.

"No, ma'am. I'm about to go up there and see what I can find out. Faith said your husband had been gone for three weeks?"

"Come in, come in. I'll put this little punkin' down and we can talk." She turned toward the hallway. "I'll be right back. Sit down."

He sat on a straight chair. The furniture was sparse, and inexpensive. The living room had three wooden chairs, a small table and two pictures on the wall.

She came back and held out her hand. "I'm Maxine Garrison, and Faith is right. Only it's been nearly five weeks now and I'm frantic. I don't know what I'll do. Yes, I'll tell you all I know about the mine."

"I'm not promising I can help. But I'll try."

"He went to work there about three months ago, and then he said that the number of men hired from town was going down. Finally, he said the mine had almost shut down and there were only six of them still there, but that the foreman, Arch Sibling, said they were going to be going full steam in a few days.

"Then Wid went back to work that Monday and I've never seen him again."

"That's all you know?"

"Yes."

She looked up, her brown eyes pleading. Her dark hair was short and neat. For a moment her chin quivered, then her mouth opened and showed white, pretty teeth. Her blouse was open down three buttons and a slice of cleavage showed. She had put on a few pounds after the birth of what must be her first baby.

"Mr. Morgan, you can see how it is here. I don't have any more money. My husband is missing. My baby is hungry. I'm not sure what we're going to eat today. Anything you can do to find out what happened to Wid will just be wonderful. I can do nothing from here.

"I . . . I can't pay you any money, but I want to give you something. I don't know a lot about men, Mr. Morgan, but I do have one thing I can give you. If you wouldn't be offended."

Slowly she unbuttoned her blouse, watching him, waiting for him to tell her to stop. Morgan didn't. He wanted to see her breasts. The buttons came open one by one and her breasts swollen by milk surged out.

"If . . . if you want to, Mr. Morgan, I'll be proud to take you into the bedroom."

The blouse came fully open. She shrugged it off her shoulders and her breasts jiggled, large, taking up half of her chest. They was only a little sag from their bulk and they were milky white with small brown freckles.

She held out her hand. "Mr. Morgan. I believe in paying for services. Since I'm asking you for a favor, the least I can do. . . ."

She stood and caught his hand and he stood.

"You don't have to," Morgan said, his voice hoarse with the urgency of his desire as it surged into fire.

"I understand that, but I want you to be encouraged to look for my husband."

She led him into the bedroom. The baby lay in a crib at one side sleeping. Without a touch of embarrassment she slid down her skirt, then the short underthings she wore until she stood there naked.

Her hips were wide, her belly with a slight rise, and a large triangle of black hair covered her treasure. She walked toward him, hips swaying, breasts bouncing, then she kissed him and held him close. Her tongue went into his mouth at once and she sighed and reached down to his crotch where she rubbed gently.

They didn't say a word after that. She pulled him to the bed and sat him down and undressed him. She frowned at the bandages on his chest, back, arm and leg.

Tenderly she kissed each one, then pulled his mouth to her breasts. They were hot already, burning brightly. He kissed them and nibbled at her nipples until she moaned in pleasure. Then he sucked one breast into his mouth and chewed gently on it. Soon she moaned again and eased backward on the bed flat on her back, open, inviting.

She pulled him with her, her legs spread wide as he lay out over her luscious, hot body.

At once she settled him between her thighs and moved his erection to her wet slot. She looked at him and nodded and he edged forward, then slid into her easily. She made small noises and smiled, then he felt her inside muscles gripping him, relaxing and gripping him again.

Now it was his time to moan in delight and begin his thrusting. She worked with him. He had no thought of his hurts, she was a talented lover, matching his speed and movements, opposing them so it created twice the effect. Quickly he was beyond the point where he could delay. She nodded and he roared into a climax that he wasn't sure he would live through or that he even wanted to. At last he exploded in one last surge and fell on top of her in total exhaustion.

"Wonderful," she said.

He had nearly recovered when he realized she had not climaxed. He pushed his hand between them and found the small hard node and began to rub it.

She looked at him quickly. "Why?" she said.

He kissed her and hit the button again and again. Slowly she began to breathe faster, then her hips began to rotate and in another minute she surged over the top, smashing into a long set of spasms that shook her like a rag in a puppy's jaws and then dropped her. She was limp and spent and her eyes were closed.

"My god! That's the first time!" she breathed.

He kissed her lips softly. "It won't be the last time."

Soon they came apart and he saw a new glow in her face. She looked at him with wonder and awe.

"I've never been able to do that before. No reason. Maybe Wid was not a good lover. I've only made love with two men now, so I don't have a lot of comparisons."

She laughed softly and smiled. "So wonderful! I'm not going to let you leave this house! I'll make a love slave out of you, using you five or six times a day until we both die of exhaustion."

She touched his wounds. "Do they hurt when you get so excited that way, pumping so hard?"

"No, I forget all about them."

"Good. I want you to forget again." She went up on her knees and pushed one of her big breasts into his mouth. "I just love it when you chew on me that way. Can I chew on you? I never have. Wid doesn't want me to."

Her hands went down to find his softness. She played with him and worked and slowly he came hard again. When he did she gave a little cry and pushed him away and eased him down on his back, then knelt at his crotch.

"So beautiful! So big and thick and long and just pulsating. Wid only does it at night with the lights out. I like this way better. You said I could chew on you?"

He nodded. She bent and kissed the purple tip, then down the shaft.

"He's so good, so yummy!" Then she looked at Lee and slowly slipped him into her mouth. He nodded. Her eyes thanked him and she sucked as much of his shaft into her mouth as she could. She made contented noises deep in her throat and then without any urging, she began to ease back and forth on him.

"Oh, god, you don't know what that does to a man," he said softly. He reached down low and found her breasts and rubbed them.

Her lips devoured him, triggered nerve endings he had forgotten about. Slowly he pumped his hips and gradually she held her head still. Then it was time to get serious. He was close to shooting it all.

"Do you want to continue, to let me come?"

She nodded and he felt the first urges, the first closing of valves and opening of channels and the short quick trip of the juice up the tubes.

He wailed and punched harder with his hips, but carefully. She had her hands up now to keep him from spearing all the way through her. His hips bucked again and again and he knew the world had come to an end.

His brain exploded and melted into jelly and his body vaporized and flowed into a crack in the floorboards. Then it all gushed into one huge ball of flames.

She pulled at him after his hips quieted. Then she came away reluctantly and stared up at him.

"I'll never forget you Buck Morgan, not if I live to be 200 years old. Two marvelous experiences. Tremendous."

"The pleasure was mine, Maxine. I'll do everything I can to find your man. I better get ready to go."

They both sat up. He dressed and she watched him. Maxine lounged on the mussed bed, staring. Her breasts hung down and he reached over and petted them.

"The most wonderful, marvelously beautiful part of a woman," he said. Then he kissed both hanging marvels and stood. He put on his gunbelt and cinched it up. He'd left the shotgun and rifle on his saddle.

Maxine got up on her knees on the bed and hugged his chest, pushing her big, soft breasts against his shirt and staring up at him with huge brown eyes.

"I want you to go, but I don't want you to go."

"I have to. I'll look for your husband, I'll demand to know where he is or what happened to him."

He undid her hand and bent and kissed her again, then petted her breasts and she flashed him a big smile that made him want to stay all day and all night.

"Time for one more? It's been a long time for me."

He smiled and shook his head. "I have to find the mine and get ready to go in there tonight. You say there are fences and guards and dogs and everything?"

"Yes, that's what Wid told me." She smiled as she let go of him. "Be careful, Buck. Come tell me what you find when you get back. I'll . . . I'll be waiting for you."

He left quickly then, hurried to his horse and stepped into the saddle. He took the quickest way out of town, then swung around to the north trail that led deeper into the mountains. He'd have the wagon road to follow. Up this valley, across a ridge and into another valley.

Easy. Earlier he had saddled his horse in the livery and paid for another week's stay, then went out the back gate so nobody would see his horse leaving. Now was not the time to take a chance for Pickering to spot him. He'd deal with Pickering later.

Right now, he had a mine to find, he had to earn a thousand dollars, and he had to discover some secret that Mister Bibb plainly did not want found out.

Chapter Eleven

The first five miles went quickly as he cantered the horse and then walked her. They made good time. He wanted to get to the mine area so he could slip up on it and observe it, recon the place before it got dark.

Recon? That was military. Had he been in the Civil War? With a start he realized he didn't even know how old he was. That would come in time, he decided. It plagued him that he had lost his memory. So he probably was this Buckskin Morgan. Who the hell was that?

Was he really wanted in Arizona for murder? If he was an outlaw there, he might also be a wanted man in maybe half a dozen other states, including California. Damnit to hell! He wished he knew all about himself!

He rode harder then, and eased off when he figured he had covered about nine miles. He was into the second valley. Far ahead he could see smoke, smell it now too. Smell it? He must be something of an outdoorsman. A hick from Chicago would not be able to smell smoke out here from ten feet.

He moved up to corners in the wagon road cautiously now. He had met no one, nor seen a soul since he left Silverville. What was going on up here anyway?

At the next corner he could see the mill ahead. A collection of unpainted buildings. He could make out the hoist house, the two mine entrance tunnels, a larger place where the ore must be broken down and refined somehow, and a big stamping mill. He scowled. So he knew what they were, he couldn't remember how or why he knew. Maybe he was a hard rock miner.

He backed around the corner and rode into the woods. Silverville was about five-thousand feet in elevation. He had been steadily on an upgrade since he left the small town and figured he was around the seven-thousand foot level here. Lots of trees, pines and firs and lots of brush from the winter rains and snow pack. He would have no trouble riding almost up to the mine through the cover.

When he spotted it, he had been about half-a-mile away from the mine. He rode another quarter-of-a-mile north, located a patch of dense brush and worked into it. Soon he found a small clearing where he could picket the horse. Nobody would find it unless they charged right into that spot. It would make a good hidden camping spot if he had to stay over the night. He had matches for starting a camp fire if he needed them. Always come prepared was his policy.

Morgan left the shotgun hidden behind a tree, took his borrowed Remmington single shot rifle and began working his way uphill through the brush toward the mine.

It took him half-an-hour. He moved like an Indian, slowly, not making a leaf rustle or a branch creak. He faded from one tree to the next, and soon could look out on the Silver Queen mine from fifty yards. A well made eight-foot-high barbed wire fence was less than twenty feet in front of him.

The fence was carefully built with the barbed wire strands no more than four inches apart on posts set every ten feet. The fence was hung with tin cans that would rattle and clatter if anyone tried to climb it and probably if anyone even touched or bumped it.

On top of the fence a two foot extension came down at a 45 degree angle to the inside. This, too, was layered with barbed wire. The fence looked like one he had seen at a prison once. Bibb didn't want anyone to get out of his mine location. Now just why was that?

Morgan lay there concealed by brush and tall grass and watched the mine. The layout was about what he expected. A small building with windows that was obviously the mine office. He figured it had living quarters in the back. The stamping mill clattered as iron struck iron mashing the ore into small pieces so the chemicals could go to work extracting the silver and any traces of gold that was in the silver bearing quartz.

The smelting operation building was just down from the stampers. He saw men moving around. Set back from the other buildings, up the little creek that ran down through the mine enclosure, were two buildings that looked like dormitories. If the miners stayed up here, the management would have to furnish them a place to eat and sleep.

The mine entrance tunnels were both busy, with

men pushing out cars loaded with ore. Once it hit daylight, the car was hitched to a pair of mules and it was pulled toward the stamping mills, working up a slight incline so the ore could be dropped into the stamping chambers.

Nothing out of the ordinary so far. How did he know that? Had he been a miner? From that distance, he couldn't see the men who pushed out the ore cars plainly, but they looked small. Why? Were small men an advantage in mining so the tunnels could be smaller?

It was past midday. He wondered if the men had been fed a meal? Probably they got two meals a day so they could stay underground at midday. Were there shafts in there that dropped deep into the mountain, or were the tunnels directly to the rich vein on this same level? He could see no ventilation shafts up the side of the mountain. But if there were no shafts, why would they need a hoisting shack and mechanism?

He was working up too many questions.

Five men pushed an ore car out of the tunnel, helped get the mules hitched and an outside man drove the mules up the incline. One of the men from the mine slipped away to the side behind a pile of tailings and stretched out. The other four men from the car went back into the mine, evidently to push out another car of ore.

Now Morgan saw the guards. There were three men walking the fence. All had rifles. The closer one came toward him on this section of the fence, the clearer it became. He carried a Spencer repeating carbine. It could fire eight shots of .52 caliber without reloading.

That was a mighty good and expensive weapon for a guard to be carrying. He checked the man hiding in the slag heap. Twice he had rolled over to keep out of sight of the patrolling guards. When the two guards on the part of the fence nearest to the slag pile were at the farthest point from the man hiding, he began crawling toward the fence.

Morgan lifted his rifle to help the man, but at once he knew he could not fire a single shot. If he did there would be guards out through the gate hunting him. He could lose them in this brush and get away. But that would not be helping out anyone like this man who evidently was being held here against his will. Why else the guards, and fences?

The escapee had made it halfway to the fence. The guards turned now and started the boring job of retracing their steps.

Suddenly the man trying to get away must have realized he was running out of time. He lifted and ran for the fence twenty yards away. He got there without being seen, then used a pair of wire cutters and broke one of the wires about waist high. The snapping wire and the clanging of the tin cans set up a reaction around the whole fence.

The guards checked their sectors quickly and a cry went up from the man just to Morgan's right.

"I see the bastard!" the man called. His rifle came up and he fired twice, missing both times. The man trying to escape cut two more wires and lunged through the fence. He got only halfway through, then the barbed wire caught on his ragged pants. He tried to pull them free.

Three rifles snarled almost at once and two of the rounds hit the runner, jolting him against the fence. He struggled again and surged against the wire, falling half on the outside. Two more shots slammed into his body, then it hung on the fence, motionless and lifeless.

Morgan turned away. He could have helped the man! Sure, and he could have been shot himself. He wanted to earn his $1,000 and report back, not get himself killed.

The guards blew whistles and three more men ran out of a guard shack with rifles ready. They talked with the head guard and then the three new men hurried away and came back with wire splicing and tightening equipment. They pushed the body of the dead man out through the hole and left him there. Then they quickly repaired the spot and put on one extra strand of barbed wire just to make sure.

The men worked about thirty yards from where Morgan lay concealed in the brush. The three looked like anyone else, 20 to 30 years old, white, wearing suntan pants and shirt, evidently a kind of guard's uniform.

At the far side of the complex, he saw smoke come out of a smaller building he guessed was a cook shack. He checked his watch. Nearly three in the afternoon. He wondered how the food was, but decided he couldn't break in and then get in line for chow call.

Powder shack? Where would they keep the dynamite? Any good mine had lots of the new dynamite and caps and fuses around for rough tunnel faces. He looked over the entire place again and found a wooden door over a dugout to the far right next to the fence. Looked like a safe place. They must have dug a hole and put logs over the top and a slant door. If the goods blew up they wouldn't blast down every building at the mine.

Morgan watched. He saw a few more guards as they changed places. The mules were behind now as a dozen small ore cars had been pushed out to be dumped into the stamping mill crushers. They might build up a surplus so the stampers could work all night.

Morgan dozed. He snapped his eyes open and looked around. No one was near him. He had no idea how long he had been sleeping. His watch showed that it was after five o'clock. Then he saw what had awakened him.

A line of men came out of one of the mine tunnels. They were chained together with ankle irons on their right ankles. They marched in a long row. None of these men wore shirts, only grimy pants and shoes. He tried to count them. Over forty of them.

They walked with their heads down. A rifleman guard led the way and marched them to the barracks at the far end of the camp.

Slave labor! No wonder no one had returned from this place. He was too far away to get a good look at the men, but somehow they all seemed to be small. All were smaller than the guards. But the guards might all be six-feet four.

There was no doubt now. He had to go into this place. He had to free those prisoners. So it wasn't his job. This kind of inhuman shit he wouldn't stand for.

Morgan pulled back from the fence and worked his way through the brush uphill toward where he had seen the powder magazine. He found it again and edged up as close as he could get to the fence. The trees were all cut down inside the fence, but they hadn't bothered with those outside. He found a pair of young pine trees growing close together.

He could use them to get inside. Once inside getting out would be no problem. But first he needed the shotgun. He took the rifle and ran downhill through the brush. He was confident now that they had no outside sentries or scouts. They figured they were safe inside their barbed wire!

He found his horse and moved her closer to the bottom of the fencing, then took the shotgun and his supply of shells. Good thing he had remembered to pick up a box of the double-ought buck rounds. Now he moved them into his pants pockets front and back and his shirt pockets. When he needed them he would want them fast. He left the rifle on the horse. It was a daylight sharpshooter's weapon. Tonight he needed the scattergun and all the rounds he could pump out.

He jogged back up the hill and got there just before the sun slid behind the far mountain top. He saw the cooks in the cook shack take food to the building he figured was the headquarters. Then they used a wheelbarrow and took large pots up the hill to the barracks. These men were not going to have a gourmet supper.

Morgan memorized the layout of exactly where the buildings were. Everything depended on there being a good supply of dynamite in the powder bunker. If it turned out the place was a potato cellar, he was in lots of trouble.

But at this place he figured the management would be more likely to have more dynamite than potatoes.

An hour later it was totally dark. He checked on the twin pine trees he had seen. They grew six feet from the fence and were about 30 feet tall. Buck tied the shotgun around his back with a stout rawhide thong, then began climbing the pine trees.

Within seconds his hands were covered with sticky pitch from the pines, but that would help him hang on. He got above the fence and kept climbing.

When he was ten feet over the fence he tested one of the young pines by swinging out to the side toward the fence. It bent gracefully to the side, then held.

Morgan climbed another ten feet until the trunk of the pine was less than an inch in diameter and stretching only six feet over his head. He would need only one of the pines. This time when he leaned to the side, the tree bent to the left toward the fence. He grabbed the trunk with both hands and swung outward, pushing away from the bending trunk with his feet.

The added weight on the top of the tree bent it smoothly to the side. He cleared the fence by six feet and just before the bending branches of the pine touched the top strand of the eight foot high barbed wire fence, he let go. His feet were only four feet from the ground. He landed easily and kept his feet.

The pine made a swishing sound as it straightened into its previous position.

Morgan grinned. He was inside and he had left no evidence of his entry for a fence walking guard to spot.

Chapter Twelve

Morgan ran to the wooden door leading underground and checked it in the soft moonlight. He could see no warning wires or safety devices. There was a padlock on the hasp over the door but one smash from the butt of his Colt and the lock popped open. He swung one of the doors up and saw steps going down. He went in until he was shielded from the outside, then he struck a match.

Yes. The powder magazine. There were at least twenty cases of dynamite there. He lit another match and found boxes of dynamite caps and rolls and rolls of fuse.

Morgan figured he could set a lot of charges in ten minutes, so he cut off 20 ten-foot lengths of fuse, making them all the same length, doing it by feel. When he had those ready he set them on the ground outside of the bunker and then lifted out three 50-stick boxes of dynamite. They were packed in sawdust so they wouldn't jostle against each other and explode.

Morgan struck another match in the bunker and

picked out ten dynamite caps and put them in his one pocket without any shotgun shells. He just hoped that they didn't bang together too hard, or he would be the next explosive item to be heard from.

Outside, he closed the bunker door and pushed the padlock back in place, pressing it together so it looked to be locked.

Then he moved cautiously toward the buildings and settled down to wait. He had to spot where the night guards were. They wouldn't need fence guards since the workers were all locked in ankle chains.

Ten minutes later he saw one guard leaning against the hoisting house. He was smoking a cigarette and gave himself away by the glowing ember on the end.

The second guard coughed. He was just outside the mine office building. After another half hour, Morgan could find no more guards. These two should go off duty about midnight, he figured. He could wait. He had work to do.

First he lifted the wooden tops of the boxes and took out dynamite. He carried an armload of 18 sticks and took six lengths of fuse and went to the fence across the bottom of the compound farthest from the office building. He wedged three sticks of powder under the wires on the first post just at the ground level.

Then he made a hole in the soft dynamite with a stick, and pushed in the dynamite cap. Next, he pushed the end of the ten-foot long fuse in the hollow end of the cap and it was ready. Then he went to the next post. He mined six posts in a row and hurried back to his dynamite.

He would light the fuses later.

Just to be safe, he carried all the dynamite, fuses and detonators a hundred feet from the powder magazine to a little spot of brush. Then he began to plant bombs everywhere that the guards would not spot him. He put ten sticks at the entrance to the mine, another on the back of the cook shack. One more fused bomb went under the back side of the mine office.

The mine office deserved the most, a half case of dynamite—25 sticks. He set a fuse into the whole batch. What a bang that was going to be! It would be the first blast to go.

He moved cautiously up to the back side of the hoisting building and set a ten-stick package under it. All the bombs so far had ten minute fuses. He hoped this fuse was normal and burned at the rate of a foot a minute.

Next, he circled the barracks. He watched them for ten minutes, but could find no guards. Without a sound, he slipped into the back porch and tested the door. It was locked. From his pocket he took a piece of stiff wire he had brought with him, bent it, and a moment later had the simple skeleton key lock open.

He stepped inside and listened. Men sleeping. A few muttered in their sleep. He risked a match and checked. Single bunks and the men were chained to the bunks. The locks on the leg irons were good ones. He couldn't open them. He'd need a key. One of the guards would have one in case of fire. He checked one sleeping man again with a match near his face.

He was Chinese. Morgan used another match and checked two more faces. Chinese. No wonder the men had looked small.

He slipped out the door and faded into the night

to a spot where he could watch the two exterior guards.

He looked up at the moon, then at the north star. The pointer stars on the big dipper were angled up at the north star as if they were coming from the '8' on a watch. That made it almost midnight. He had no idea how he knew that.

Five minutes later, a shaft of yellow light streamed from the mine office building and a door slammed. Two figures walked into the night, and a few minutes later the two guards were relieved and went back into the office building with the fresh ones taking over.

Now he would eliminate one of the two guards, then get the prisoners released.

Morgan worked up through the darkness to where he could see the two guards. He found the first one at the same place next to the mine office. It took him some time to locate the second one near the hoist shed. This one positioned himself around the corner, just out of sight of the mine office building guard. So much the better.

Morgan circled, came up behind the hoist shed and then began to edge around the wall. He moved like an Apache, no noise, no sudden changes in shadow patterns. He pulled out his boot knife and crept forward.

Now he was at the corner and could see the guard leaning back against the wall, his automatic rifle hanging over his shoulder by a sling. His hands came up to his face to light a cigarette.

With the flare of the match, Morgan drove forward. He ran only eight feet away. The match blinded the guard for a moment. In that half a second, Morgan slammed into the man, drove his six-inch knife deeply into the guard's side and ripped it out to the front.

He felt the blade reach the ribs and grate off them, then ease outward and the guard dropped limply from his grasp. Morgan caught the rifle before it clattered to the ground. The guard slumped face down into the mountain dust.

Morgan took a deep breath, bent and worked through the guard's pockets. He would have to keep a key in case of some disaster so the slaves could be freed during the night. Morgan found the key in the dead man's second pocket. He slipped it out. It was a long thin rodlike affair, more like a wrench.

He pushed it into his pocket, took the rifle and hurried away toward the barracks with the hoist shack shielding him from the other guard.

In the barracks with the door already open, he slapped the first Chinese man gently. He awoke with a start.

"English?" he asked softly. "Do you speak English?"

The man blinked, shook his head, but pointed across the aisle at the second bunk.

Morgan shook that Chinese awake and asked the same question.

"A little," he answered.

"I have the key to release all of you. You're going free tonight. I want you to wake each of the men and tell them all to be quiet. Not a sound. Understand?"

"Yes."

"Are there men in the other barracks?"

"Yes, Mexicans, about thirty. Also a few white men."

"I'll unlock these men, you come along and tell them to be quiet."

Morgan hurried down one aisle and up the other

unlocking the hated leg irons. He warned the man again to keep everyone quiet until the explosions, then they should run to the fence and when the shooting stopped, they could go through the fence and away.

Morgan ran to the second barracks. He unlocked the same simple door lock and was inside.

At once he found the white men. He told them what was happening and they told the Mexicans. Five minutes later he had the thirty men free. Then he asked if Wid Garrison was there.

"That's me," one man said.

"Come with me," he said. "You ever use a rifle?"

"Yes, sir."

They ran to the fence and Morgan found a place for him where he would have a field of fire covering the office building.

"How many guards and bosses?"

"Twelve guards and four others."

"Wid, you ever killed a man before?"

"No, but I damn well can kill any of those sixteen right now!"

"Good. I'm going to start lighting the fuses. First I'll get the mine office, then the other buildings. Last, I'll come down and light the fuses for the fence. I should be able to get them all before the first one goes off.

"Remember, if the Chinese or the other prisoners forget and come charging through here, don't shoot at them."

Morgan ran into the night. He got in back of the big mine office building and lit the fuse, then ran to the hoist shack and the cook shack lighting both there. He continued to the entrance to the mine and lit the fuse there, then on down to the fence.

"Hey, Willy," the guard at the front of the mine

office building called softly to the second guard.

Willy couldn't answer.

The guard tried it again. "Damn, Willy. You sleeping again on duty gonna get your ass whipped."

Still no response.

"Hell with you. Ain't my ass."

Morgan continued on to the fence and lit the fuse. Each of the six fuses here was low enough in some weeds so it wouldn't be seen by the guard. He lit the last one, then sprinted for the spot where Wid Garrison crouched.

"Damn soon now this place is going to blow up," Morgan said. "I talked to your wife in town. Faith Davies told me to ask her about this place. I'm working for the other guys. When I saw those damn leg irons and chains, I got a little mad."

Garrison blinked tears out of his eyes. "I was about ready to give up and die. We lose one man a day up here. I don't know where he gets the Chinese and the Mexicans."

Just then there was a brilliant flash and the rear twenty feet of the forty foot long mine office lifted off the ground and disintegrated, showering half the mine camp with bits of lumber and roofing.

The guard standing in front of the building was knocked flat. He struggled to his feet. Wid aimed at him and fired twice. The guard screamed and jolted to the ground.

Two men ran bellowing in fear from the front of the bulding. Morgan stood and slammed a round from the shotgun at them, then realized he was too far away with the scatter effect of the cut off barrels.

He ran forward, came within twenty yards and fired again, blowing both of them four feet backwards into hell.

Glass broke on the far side of the building and someone jumped out. Two shadowy figures rushed away into the darkness.

Just then the cook shack exploded and a moment later the hoisting building.

When that explosion died down, the ten sticks of dynamite blew up at the mine entrance.

Morgan ran around the shattered office building looking for any survivors. He found one, a guard evidently who had his arm blown off. He lifted his hand for help, then slumped to the ground, dead of shock and loss of blood.

Morgan fired twice into the broken windows, then heard the string of explosions obliterating a fifty foot length of fence.

That sound died away and Morgan looked at the barracks.

"Now, Chinaman friend," he bellowed. "Get your people out of here."

He heard chattering along the far fence, then saw shadows slipping down the side of the enclosure to where the smoking remains of the fence lay flat on the ground.

The Mexicans and six white men came down along the fence a moment later. Morgan saw no new targets. He ran back to where he had left Wid Garrison. He and another man were crying on each other's shoulders.

"My friend," Garrison said to Morgan. "We kept each other alive these three weeks."

"You might as well go with the rest of them, Garrison. I've got a little clean up to do when it gets light. Nothing else much is going to happen here tonight.

"Try to make as little noise as possible. I'm watching for a pair that got away. Who lived up front in the building nearest the front door?"

"That would be the mine general manager," Garrison said. "He's a real geek named Mr. Hyde. An Englishman who is a sadistic bastard."

"The foreman lived up there, too," Garrison's friend said. "I still think that Englishman likes little boys. Damned if I don't."

"Might have been the pair who survived the blast and got out a window," Morgan said. "I'll be watching for them right here until daylight."

Garrison shook Morgan's hand, as did his friend. Then they stepped gleefully over the blasted down fence and hurried out to the road.

Morgan moved to the midpoint between the gap in the fence and the gate. If one of the survivors was Mr. Hyde, he would have a key to the gate. Now was no time to be sloppy.

Buck waited the rest of the night. Near daylight he heard someone moving toward him. Just as it grew light enough to see more than twenty yards, two men with partly burned clothing came away from the fence on the far side and headed toward the gate.

One of the men seemed misshapen with one shoulder higher than the other. He walked with a limp. The man behind him held a pistol and kept searching the area around him.

Morgan took the Spencer and made sure there was a round in the chamber, then lifted the rifle and put one round through the pistol waver's heart.

At the sound of the shot and the sudden death of his friend, Mr. Hyde held up his hands.

"Don't shoot, old boy. I surrender. I don't know where you all are, but there must be half an army of you. I give up. I capitulate, for god's sake."

"Walk over this way," Morgan said. Hyde knew where he was by then from the small cloud of blue smoke from the .52 caliber Spencer round. "Easy does it, or you're as dead as the rest of your slave mongers."

"Slaves? Certainly not. These men all worked for wages."

"Sure, Hyde, sure. And you're the Prince of Wales." Morgan had tied the shotgun over his back, and held the Spencer loosely. He had not used his six-gun.

"Let's take a tour of the office and see what's left, Mr. Hyde. You first."

"You did a jolly good job of bashing it in. Found our dynamite, did you?" He looked around. "Where are the rest of them?"

"Aiming their rifles at you at this moment from just beyond the fence. A security force. We weren't sure how many guards you had up here."

"I daresay not enough."

He led the way to the office and stepped inside through the door knocked off one hinge.

Morgan slung the Spencer carbine and drew his Colt.

"Don't grab a weapon, or any tricks, Mister Hyde. If that happens I start shooting you in the elbow, then the knees and work up toward your black heart."

Hyde nodded and opened a door marked "private." Inside, the window had shattered inward from the twisting of the frame building. A large desk had not moved. Pictures on the wall had fallen.

"The cash box," Morgan said. "And open the safe. I'm taking over as official administrator of this mine as of today. So dig out all of the valuables, now."

"I hardly think that's fair," Hyde said.

Buck brough the Colt down across Hyde's forehead, slamming him to the floor, tearing two gashes across his head that dripped blood down his face.

"Do it, now!" Morgan said, his voice steady and edged with a deadly steel that Hyde reacted to automatically.

He opened a locked drawer to his desk and took out a metal box. He lifted the lid to reveal stacks of greenbacks. He went to a picture hung low on the wall and pushed it aside. Behind it was a wall safe that extended into a closet.

Inside was a heavy bank cash bag, nearly full. Hyde pulled it out and nearly dropped it. It took both hands to lift it to the desk top.

"Gold double eagles," he said. "Then there are the pure silver bars ready to be shipped to the mint in San Francisco. There are ten of them, each weighing ten pounds."

"Where?"

"In the safe."

"How many men have died at this mine since you've worked it, Hyde?"

"What? I really don't know. I didn't keep records."

"One a day?"

"No, not that many. One a week perhaps in the past two months."

"I heard it's one a day, that's sixty. How many died on the wire trying to escape?"

"What? Oh, three or four, we warned them."

"So you and your men here killed sixty-five men, and worked the rest half to death as slaves. That's highly illegal, even for a fine talking Englishman like you."

"I'm ready to face the court," Hyde said.

Morgan had what he wanted.

He turned to one side and let his gun drop down a ways. Hyde reacted better and quicker than Morgan expected. He kicked the gun out of Morgan's hand, pushed him over the desk and darted out the door. Morgan picked up his gun and walked to the broken window. Hyde came racing out the door heading for the blown down fence.

Morgan fired twice. Both rounds hit the man in the back, the first smashing his spinal cord, the second jolting through one shoulder. He died before he crumpled into the dirt.

"Yes, Mr. Lang, I'll be able to give you a complete report on what is going on at the Silver Queen mine," Morgan said.

Chapter Thirteen

Morgan stared through the window at the man lying on the ground. Was he dead? Hyde was the sneaky kind who just might play possum. He went out through the broken door and turned Hyde over with his foot. There was no breath, no pulse at his wrist.

Good. As Morgan stood, a sudden wave of dizziness hit him. It sometimes did when he stood up too quickly. Only this time it was worse. He put out one hand to steady himself, then knew he was falling. His hands went out but then he passed out and slammed into the ground hard, his forehead bouncing off the packed dirt.

Morgan came to slowly, shook his head to clear it and tried not to move. If he didn't move they might think he was dead. Then he realized that it wasn't raining. In fact, he wasn't even wet.

"What the hell?" Morgan said and sat up. His head spun again but then settled down and he looked around where he sat. This wasn't a street. He'd been in a shootout with five or six guys and ran out of rounds, then he got kicked about a thousand times.

He looked around at the mine.

"Oh, damn. I came to this town to work for Janish Lang."

He looked down at the body in front of him and memories of the past few days came flooding back.

He remembered it all; Faith and Dunc, him getting shot, the shootout in the alley and the guys with the shotguns. Then he talked to Lang and came up to the Bibb mine.

"The slaves!" How could anyone do that to human beings? He got up and remembered what Hyde had showed him inside. He hadn't even looked at the money. Just how much was it worth to a man to be shot and stomped and nearly killed?

A hundred-thousand dollars? Maybe not that much. He checked the weapon at his side. His own Colt Double Action. It felt good having it there. Automatically, he replaced the fired rounds from the piece and holstered it.

In the office, he looked at the cash box. They were twenty and fifty dollar bills. He had no idea how much cash was there. The sack of gold double eagles was real. Maybe two hundred of them. An ounce each that would be about 13, 14 pounds. He hefted the sack. More like 20 pounds. Three hundred and twenty double eagles. That would be more than $6,000.

"Yeah, we're getting there," Morgan said. He looked in the safe and saw the silver bars. There weren't ten of them, there were twenty. He rubbed his jaw. Gold was worth $20.67 an ounce, set by law. Silver, best he could remember, was about $1.30 an ounce. So a pound would be worth about $20. The silver bars were worth about $200 each.

Not worth carrying around. He took two of them for Dunc to use in his jewelry business. Morgan decided the money he had found would about settle his financial account with the shooters. He closed the safe door and twirled the dial, then carried the goods out the front door. He found his horse right where he left it.

Morgan put the two silver bars in one saddlebag and the stacks of greenbacks and the double eagles in the other one. Then he took the borrowed rifle and the shotgun and headed back down the trail toward town.

He expected all of the walkers would be in town or beyond by now, all ready to get as far away from Silverville as they could.

It took him about three hours to make the ride to town. He went slowly, trying to think through the whole thing.

Two loose ends. Bibb and Pickering. Pickering first, the bastard. Pickering shot him when he was down and helpless. Evening up time was due. Now he remembered it all. Pickering would not have a side-shooter to soften up his target this time the way he did with that shootout in the street.

Morgan rode right up to the back door at Dunc Davies' house and tied his horse. Before he could get the saddlebags off, Faith came running out the kitchen door.

"Thank God!" She threw her arms around him and kissed him.

"Inside, woman. You want to ruin your reputation?"

She grinned. "I don't care. You're back!"

He tugged the saddlebags off the horse and put them over his shoulder, then shooed Faith inside. Once there, with the door closed, he hugged her properly and kissed her.

"How is Dunc?"

"He's feeling better. Doc was by this morning, early. Said he looks good and that there isn't any infection, yet. We're hoping."

Faith tapped her toe on the floor. "Well, tell me. What happened out at the mine?"

"I found your friend's husband. He should be home by now. Bibb was running that place with slave labor. The only way you quit was to die. Let's go in and I'll tell both you and Dunc at the same time."

He went through it all. Right down to getting his memory back.

"So now I remember everything." He looked up at Faith who was standing above Dunc. She reddened a little. He went on. "I know why I came here, who I am. Everything. And I've about figured out how much I'm charging Bibb for having me gunned down."

Dunc grinned. "How much?"

Buck showed them the gold and the bills and the two silver bars. "This much, however much it is." He picked up the two silver bars. "These aren't worth hauling around. Only worth about $200 each. Thought you might like to have some silver to use in your jewelry business. Melt it down, make rings, things like that."

Dunc grinned. "I've done a few things. Silver comes in handy." He frowned for a minute. "Don't worry, I'll be sure to get rid of the mine imprint on that bar. Thanks."

"Oh, that also pays up my board and room for another two days. Speaking of board and room, I could use something to eat."

"You haven't had a thing to eat since breakfast

yesterday!" Faith said frowning. She ran toward the kitchen.

Morgan took out the stacks of greenbacks and found them already sorted into the various denominations. He counted the bunches and Dunc wrote down the amounts. When they were through they had a total of $3,485.00.

Morgan looked up at the watchmaker. "Dunc, if you had your druthers, what would it be? Looks like this town'll be lucky to have silver for another year or two. What then?"

"I always have liked Sacramento. Been there before. Give a good bit to have a shop downtown, do watch repair, sell some fine timepieces and a whole passel of clocks. Course, have some rings and stones and jewelry things."

"Sounds like a good future there," Morgan said and stood. "I better get washed up and oil my Colt and put the long guns away. That little shotgun is a dandy. You rest up now and we'll have you back to work in a week."

Morgan held out his hand. "Thanks for saving my skin back there. I'd have been dead for sure if you and Faith hadn't come and hauled me out of that muddy street."

Dunc snorted. "Don't mention it. Do the same for a stray dog if'n he was hurting." Dunc said it, then grinned and blinked to keep the wetness from seeping over the sides of his eyelids.

Morgan ate two meals, had three cups of coffee and sat in the sun out in the backyard for an hour. Then he went inside and touched Faith's shoulder and she turned around and hugged him.

"Now that you remember everything, you're probably riding away. I mean, you came here on a job. You do it and leave, right?"

"Right, usually. Sometimes I get lazy and stay awhile."

"You look real lazy to me," Faith said. She kissed him hotly. Then pulled back and whispered in his ear. "I want you in my bed so much that I can hardly stand not ripping your clothes off right now."

Morgan grinned and kissed her quickly. "You just keep your knees together for another day or so and we'll see what we can do about taking care of those wild, sexy desires of yours.

"I have two personal items of business first." He held up the stacks of greenbacks. "Oh, do you have a safe place where you can put this."

"Sure. How much is there?"

He told her.

"Probably more cash than the Silverville bank has right now. I'll put it away."

He kissed her forehead and took the long duster coat from the coat closet and put it on. Under it he slung the double-barreled shotgun and fastened the top two buttons. The big gun was entirely hidden. He waved at Faith and walked out the back door. The shotgun might come in handy. He had six extra shells still in his pockets. He rode straight to the Hard Rock Cafe and walked inside. The barkeep looked up and started to make a signal when Morgan stopped him.

"Pickering in the back room?" Morgan demanded, his tone had that deadly, no nonsense edge on it.

"Yeah. Alone."

Morgan pushed around the bar, checked behind him, and then went through the door quickly, his six-gun up covering whatever was ahead. It was a short hall with one door open to a storeroom. The other door was closed.

He unlatched the knob, then kicked the door inward.

Pickering sat at a table, pouring a shot of whiskey into a drinking glass.

"Don't even drop the bottle," Morgan said. "Pickering, you don't have five guns backing you up this time."

"Don't need them. I don't work for Mr. Bibb anymore."

"You're forgetting me, back shooter. I want a large piece of your skinny hide full of double-ought buck holes. You and me, right now. We're walking out the back door to the alley. Move it, now!"

"What good that do you?"

"I won't get your blood all over this fine room. Out!"

They walked down the hallway, with Morgan protecting his back all the time. At the alley door, Pickering stepped out, then slammed the door toward Buck and took off on a run. Morgan stopped the door with his boot and rammed it outward.

His first .45 shot hit the running Pickering in one of his long legs and he crashed into the dirt and rolled twice. He came up on one knee.

"Now, now!" Pickering screamed.

Two men in the alley fired revolvers at Morgan. Both were behind trash bins or burn barrels. He had no cover. He took two steps and dove for a large wooden box. One slug grazed his right shoulder before he got behind the cover.

He fired once more around the box, catching Pickering as he hopped toward the sturdy protection of the saloon's outhouse. The round nailed Pickering in his other leg and flopped him into the dirt.

Morgan pulled up the shotgun and when one of the back up men tried to run to another safe shield, Morgan fired. The 15 .32 caliber sized balls slashed through the air in a widening circle. By the time they got 30 feet to the running man, seven of them jolted into his flesh.

Two hit him in the side, two more in his neck and three in the side of his head. He spun to the left, hit the dirt and rolled three times, then dropped through the gates of hell.

The second gunman who must have been there to protect Pickering, crouched where he had moved to behind a large cardboard box. Morgan snorted at the protection. He pushed a new round into the ten gauge and then fired into the top of the box.

The slugs lifted it and blasted it over the crouching man's head. The second round from the scattergun pulverized the gunman before he recovered from the shock of being a wide open target. The .32 caliber balls drove him backward into the side of the furniture store and he died screaming.

Pickering held up his hand. "I got two shot up legs, I don't have a weapon. Get me to a doctor and I'll tell you all you want to know about Bibb. He's your next target, right?"

"Start talking," Morgan said, remaining behind his cover.

"Damn, you hold all the cards. Yeah, you're right. He used slave labor. Got most of the Chinks from Sacramento and San Francisco. Promised to pay them two dollars a day. All they got was cold rice and chicken soup until he worked them to death. The Mexicans he brought up from down south somewhere. Same deal. Two dollars a day. He never paid them a cent."

"He live in his office on Main?"

"Right. He's got two sawed off shotgun guards in the front of the place, one in back. Also a big black goon who can't talk but who can break a man in half with his hands. Does what he's told to do."

"What's this Bibb character like?"

"You've never seen him? He weighs about 400 pounds. Eats eight meals a day. Has a chef he brought from San Francisco. Likes little Chinese girls, I mean young ones, 12 or 13. I've never seen him walk. The big Nigra wheels him around in a chair that becomes his bed. That's about it."

"The cook live in?"

"Yeah, but you call him a cook and he'll scalp you."

"Anything else?"

"About it. The guards work 24 hours a day. They take turns at night."

"All right, Pickering, you earned it easy. Get up and walk."

"Walk? I'm shot in both legs."

"So they aren't broken, walk. Your choice, walk out of the alley or die where you sit."

Pickering whimpered with pain as he stood, then walked slowly down the alley. It was three blocks to the side of the mountain where the houses ended. They went another two blocks beyond the houses and Pickering stopped.

Morgan walked up within six feet of the man and glared at him.

"How many men you shot in the back when they're helpless, Pickering?"

He didn't answer. "Go ahead, get it over with. You didn't make me walk out here for my health."

"You haven't suffered enough. Your men shot Dunc Davies. The old man never even met you."

Morgan shot him in the right shoulder, high up where the .45 slug rammed into the joint and turned Pickering into a blubbering hulk.

"Finish me!" Pickering screamed.

Morgan didn't say a word. He watched the man. "At least I know that you'll never mash up another man and then shoot him in the back."

"Get it over with!"

Morgan lifted the reloaded shotgun and pulled both triggers at once. The thirty .32 caliber balls from the two rounds tore off Tim Pickering's head and sent it rolling down the slope for 20 feet.

Morgan turned around and walked back to town.

His next stop was Janish Lang. It was nearly three o'clock when Morgan knocked on the front door of the house where the mine owner lived. A woman said her husband was still at the mine. Morgan was welcome to go out and talk to him there. She gave him directions.

Fifteen minutes later Buck stepped up to the building that had a sign which read, "Big Strike Mine Number One." He pushed open the door and went inside.

Two men worked at desks and one of them looked up.

"I'd like to see Mr. Lang," Morgan said.

The clerk went to a closed in office, knocked and went in. A moment later he was back and nodded.

Morgan went into the room and shook hands with Lang. It was a stark, undecorated office.

"Is it true, the stories I've been hearing around town about the Silver Queen?"

"What stories, Mr. Lang?"

"About the slave labor mostly. I've heard there were over 50 men working up there in leg irons."

"That must be true then, Mr. Lang. I'm afraid the

mine is out of operation right now. Seems there were several explosions up there. The guards and the foreman and the mine general manager must have been caught in the blast."

Lang sat down and scowled. "I didn't mean for you to kill anyone up there, Morgan. I just wanted a report."

"I'm giving you a report. Everything else up there that happened was on my own. They were killing one man a day, working them to death. I saw them shoot down a man trying to get through the eight foot high barbed wire fence. The guards and bosses up there weren't men, they were animals. That was my good deed for the day."

"Pickering?"

"He won't bother you or any of your men anymore."

"I suppose you killed him, too."

"I just know he won't bother your men."

Lang rubbed his face. "Now I'm sorry I brought you in here. You're worse than they were. I'll have this on my conscience for a long time."

"While you think about it, think of Wid Garrison. Wid was one of the white slaves. He'd been up there for months. He said since they started the slave operation, they have killed over 60 workers. Murdered them. Worked them to death," Morgan said.

He looked at the miner. "You're a good man, Lang. But good men don't clean up nests of rattlesnakes like Bibb brought in here. It takes a specialist. I was the man you needed. I did the job. Now, I'm here to collect my wages."

"Yes, yes. I'll pay you. Then I hope you get out of town."

"That seems to be my business, Mr. Lang. By the

way, you need another good miner—I'd suggest you contact Wid Garrison."

Lang nodded. He counted out ten one hundred dollar bills from an envelope he had prepared and handed it to Morgan.

He rubbed his face again with his right hand. "Sorry I said all those things. You did what I asked you to do. I was just . . . I was at the end of my rope. I didn't know what to do."

"I got my memory back, Mr. Lang. At least I know for sure who I am now. I can live with that." He turned and walked out of the room.

Morgan rode his horse to the back door at the Davies house and tied her. He hurt as he eased out of the saddle to the ground. He hadn't hurt this much for two days. Most of the tension was gone, the nervous energy that kept the pain beaten down had evaporated with the life of Pickering.

Now all the pains surged back in his chest and back and leg. He got to the kitchen and met Faith. He held up his hand. She had to help him get out of the long duster.

Then he dropped in the chair. Faith brought a whiskey bottle and a glass and sat them on the table in front of him.

He nodded, tossed down a shot and coughed. He shook his head and drank the next one slower.

Faith sat close to him. "You don't really like the killing, do you?"

"Not always. But sometimes when I see vicious, terrible men causing others suffering and pain and death, then I don't mind at all evening up the score for the ones those men had killed. Pickering was just as bad as the others. He was twice removed from the actual scene."

"Is it over?"

"Almost. I have nothing to do until midnight."

She caught his hands and brought them to her breasts. He gently pulled them away and kissed her.

"No, I have to stay angry. I'll take a ride. I'll eat supper if you cook something, and I'll kiss you goodbye like I might never come back, which I might not. Then if I do, I'll be done with it, paid off and finished, and we'll make love all night and decide what to do tomorrow."

"Do you have to go out? Couldn't you just call it off now and stay here? Why take a risk of being killed again?"

"Don't argue with me. This is the way it has to be, that it must be. The odds are that some day, I simply won't come back. I never figured that I'd live forever. I don't know if I've made a mark, left the world any different than when I came into it.

"But this is the way it has to be. I can't let the biggest villain of all get off free to dirty up another town somewhere. I can't let him ride away unscathed."

"We can get the law on him," Faith said.

"Not likely. That would take a month. By then he'd be in Colorado or Alaska or Montana looking for another sucker game to play on people."

"Kiss me once more and I'll cook you supper."

He kissed her, not feeling good about it. But she seemed satisfied and went back to the roast she was cooking on top of the stove.

"I'll be back in an hour," he said. He went out the door and rode into the light timber south of town. There he took out his Colt and did some target practice. He put thirty rounds through his weapon, some off a fast draw, some firing six rounds as quickly as he could pull the trigger.

When he was satisfied, he went back to the house

and tied up his horse. Inside the meal was ready. They both took trays in and ate with Dunc. He appreciated it.

Dunc looked at Morgan. "You got another bone in your gullet?"

"One more, Dunc. One more damned big bone to fix, then I'll be able to breathe easy. I'll be back late tonight—if I can make it back."

"Oh, damn!" Dunc said, and stared at Morgan with sad eyes. He knew it was going to be a tough job.

Chapter Fourteen

Two hours later, Morgan was at his observation point. He had climbed the fire ladder in back of the two story hardware store and walked to the front where he had an ideal view of the one story building across the street with the Silver Queen Mine sign on it.

Lights glowed in the front office until just after nine o'clock. Then they went out. Morgan thought of burning out the fat man, but if he did and the fire got away, it would also burn down half the town.

The wooden buildings were built one against the other one, sometimes having a common wall. The torch plan was out. Smoke bomb so they could think the place was on fire? No, one of his guards would find such a device and throw it into the street or the alley.

He had to do it the hard way. The big bastard who ordered the slave labor was not going to get off free. He was the one who had put the gunmen on Lee Buckskin Morgan, and Morgan wasn't going to put up with that going unanswered.

By now Bibb must know what happened out at the mine. He couldn't ride out and take a look. Not without a carriage and two horses. Then he'd have to get into the carriage.

Bibb might have sent someone out to check it for him by now.

What other options did he have for getting to the fat man? There were no openings on the roof. Other business firms pushed up against each side protecting it. Defending the place would be simple. One shotgun guard in front and one in back.

So he had to eliminate one of the guards. How? A woman, a fire, a dog, a shotgun blast, a knife. Yes. It had to be a knife, quick and silent. Face to face with blood spurting into his face. The kind of killing that takes guts.

Dynamite!

He thought about it. He could put a two stick bomb on the front door and the back door, time the fuses to blow at almost the same time, then dash inside during the confusion. Maybe. He climbed down from the roof and walked past the front door of the mine office. He checked the minute and second hand of his watch.

Then he ran to the closest end of the block and down to the opening of the alley behind the mine office until he got to the back door. He checked his watch again. It had taken him 43 seconds to make the run. He could set the rear fuse a minute faster than the front one. Three minutes on the front, two on the rear.

Yes, he'd try it.

He went to the hardware store's back door. It was solid with a bar across the door from the feel of it. The windows on the first floor had bars on them.

The second story windows did not. He stared at them for a minute, then looked around the loading dock. He found what he wanted, a stack of 50 gallon water barrels. There were six of them. The window was 12 feet off the dock. He stacked up three of the barrels and the top of the third one extended up almost ten feet.

Morgan put another barrel next to the stack of three and stood on that one. Then he climbed to the top of the third one and reached the window. It was locked with a turn device. Morgan used the side of his fist and broke the foot square pane of glass without cutting himself.

He reached inside and unlocked the double hung window and slid it upward. He crawled through. He was in the second story storage room.

Below in the back room he found the underground vault where the dynamite was stored. The top had only a half-inch iron lid on it and no lock. He lifted it and found an opened box of dynamite. He took out four sticks, then thought a minute and took out two more. He found fuse and caps close by in another box. One piece of fuse he cut off at three feet, another at two feet. He then cut four more pieces four-inches long.

In his shirt pocket he put six of the thin copper blasting caps, the detonators. In the front of the store he took a sack and scratched out three handfuls of roofing nails, inch long with large round heads. He found some tape and put a roll in his pocket. Then he put everything back the way it had been and checked the back door. It had a bar on it.

He went back out the way he had come in and closed the window and locked it. Only the broken pane would show tomorrow. He took the barrels down and placed them as they had been and faded into the darkness down the alley. He sat there on the ground and taped the two-stick bombs together. He used a pencil stub to punch a hole in the powder and inserted the dynamite cap into the hole. Then he took the other two sticks of dynamite and cut them in half with his knife.

Around each of these half sticks he taped thirty of the roofing nails. When the powder exploded the nails would be blasted out in a deadly spray, cutting down anyone in the way.

He rigged four of them with the detonator imbedded in the stick ready to receive the fuse. The four-inch fuses should burn for fifteen seconds. That was time enough for a safety edge, yet not enough time for someone to find the bomb, grab it and throw it back at him—he hoped.

The last thing he did was push the proper length of fuse into each of the hollow ends of the dynamite caps. Then with his explosives all ready, he found a place to watch the alley window of the fat man's place and waited.

Someone blew out the lamp just after midnight. Morgan moved at once. He walked around to the front of the building and wedged the two-stick bomb in the fancy handle on the front door. He saw no one on the street.

A saloon a block down erupted with three men staggering out and shouting, but they moved in the other direction. Buck shielded a match and lit the three minute fuse. He ran then, moving quickly down to the end of the block and down to the alley and hurried up to the fat man's back door. There he pushed the second two-stick bomb against the base of the heavy door and lit the two minute fuse.

Morgan pulled back from the sputtering fuse and ran fifty feet down the alley and slid in behind a large wooden packing box. He didn't want to light a match to check the time. Slowly he counted down the rest of the two minutes.

He was at 57 on the second minute when he heard the blast at the front door that rocked the little town and probably blew out a window or two. He had just nodded his head when the blast just down the alley lit up the space for a moment, then the billowing roar of the two sticks came and a shock wave that slapped at the box and swept on past. He heard pieces of wood falling and stood and looked at the back door. He brought up the double barreled shotgun and raced for the spot where the rear door once stood.

Now it was a shattered mass of kindling, only small sections near the hinges remained. Some of the door had been blasted inside the room smashing into a wall. A form ran into the void holding a long weapon.

Morgan brought up the scattergun and triggered one round. He was close enough now. The double-ought buck smashed into the rear door guard, jamming him backward against the wall where he hung for a moment, then the big slugs jolted on through his body ending his earthly experiences forever.

Morgan darted through the smashed door and saw a light still burning down a long hallway. A form came out of a room on the left. He wore white pants and screamed in some foreign language. French? He ran toward Morgan. It was obvious he was scared to death and not a danger. Morgan let him charge past him and then he saw another figure down near the lamp. This one held a shotgun. Morgan dropped to the floor just before the weapon went off.

Even as he fell, Morgan triggered the second barrel of his own scattergun. He heard the other man's pellets slanting over his head, drilling the space where he had been with death dealing lead. His own round was fired from a low angle, coming upward. Two of the .32 caliber sized shot caught the shooter under the chin and ripped his head upward. Four more hit his chest, jolting through ribs and into his heart and chest, dumping him in the hallway, another dead piece of meat.

There were two more protectors to worry about, Morgan thought as he stayed where he was. He reloaded his shotgun and checked the handgun in its leather. It was still in place.

The hallway was deathly still.

A noise came from the front somewhere. Then all was still. He heard a team and rig somewhere in the front, through the blown off front door perhaps, out on the street.

Nothing moved.

Morgan got to his knees, then to his feet. Something was not right. There should be some movement.

He heard wheels rolling, squeaking. Pickering had said the fat man was wheeled around by the big black man.

He was leaving! Morgan surged down the hallway. His foot hit a wire across the hall and he slammed quickly to the floor as a shotgun blast boomed just over his head. Three or four of the spreading pattern buckshot bounced off his shirt and kept going. The weapon had been tied to a chair in a room to the left and aimed gut high.

Lucky. He had been damn lucky. He heard the team out front again and more squeaking of wheels. Morgan moved forward, watching the doorways now. There were three more between him and a larger opening near the front.

There still had to be the third shotgun guard somewhere and the big black. Where were they?

He checked the next room, empty. As he peered into the hall from the floor level, he spotted a face moving back from the doorway to the next room.

The door was open. Morgan pulled out one of the half sticks of dynamite from his pocket and lit the four-inch fuse. He held it as it burned halfway down, then flipped it into the room across the hall where he had seen the face.

Six seconds later the half stick went off, sending out thirty roofing nails like large pieces of shrapnel. The explosion seemed greater inside the building. Dust and smoke billowed from the room followed by a scream and then a frothy, bubbling sound, then silence.

Morgan jumped to the doorway and looked in through the dust and smoke. A man lay crumpled against the blown out window's frame, his body studded with the roofing nails, a dazed, surprised expression on his dead face.

Ahead, he heard reins slap on the backs of horses. Morgan ran through the rest of the offices, through a kitchen and a bedroom, then the outer office with its blasted in doorways. He caught sight of a carriage weaving down the street as it raced south out of town and toward the Sacramento road.

That had to be Mr. Bibb getting away. Furiously, Morgan raced back inside and checked each room he hadn't been through. There was no one else there. He ran outside and down a half block to a saloon. Three horses stood outside with reins around hitching posts and their heads down, sleeping.

He picked the one with the broadest chest and pulled the reins. Morgan vaulted into the saddle and jerked the just waking up horse around and aimed him down the street. Bibb and his carriage couldn't get far. Morgan had only the shotgun and his pistol. No long range work this time.

He charged forward, galloping the surprised beast for two blocks, then stopped dead still. He could hear a rig ahead of him still south on the stage road.

Morgan let the mare settle down to a mile eating canter and worked along the blackness of the night road. It was easy to follow with the help of light from a half moon. A carriage even with two horses couldn't go fast very long.

He relaxed in the saddle, counted the double-ought buck rounds he had left, six, and made sure his gun was in place. Now all he had to do was ride them down.

When he was sure the mare was well warmed up, he put her into a moderate gallop again. This time, as the trail led up a small rise, he could see the carriage ahead. The horses were walking up the hill. Morgan kicked the animal with his heels and it raced ahead.

He nearly got there before the rig reached the top but it went over the rise and just before it went down the other side a wink of light showed and a booming sound of a hand gun drifted back to him. He was still a hundred yards away, five times out of the range of the weapon.

Morgan pushed his mount faster up the hill and paused briefly at the top searching the rig below. Then he spotted it racing down the incline too fast. He watched as the carriage swung to the far side of the road, ran two wheels in the shallow ditch a moment, then came up and went to the other side where the front wheels hit something and the whole carraige tipped up on one side, then rolled over, breaking some of the traces and knocking down one of the horses dragging the rig.

The whole thing came to a sudden stop and the downed horse screamed with what must be a broken leg.

Morgan rode down slowly, the shotgun across his saddle, his finger on the trigger.

Someone moved below, and before Morgan got to him, the big man limped off into the night. A Negro. He was gone and out of it. He wasn't about to get killed for the fat man.

Morgan remembered the hand gun and when he was within twenty yards of the wreck, he got off, tied his horse and sat on the ground watching. Nothing moved for five minutes. Then the horse screamed again.

A pistol shot exploded shattering the stillness. The horse lifted its head, then rolled over and died.

"I hate to see an animal suffer," a voice said from the upside down carriage.

There was a silence again, then the fat man broke it. "You gonna sit there all night or come help me get out of this tangle?"

Morgan laughed. "Figure you aren't going anywhere. I can wait until daylight and make sure you don't have the six-gun anymore."

"You must be this Lee Buckskin Morgan I keep hearing about."

"The same."

"You ruined my mine," Bibb said.

"And set free your fifty slaves," Morgan replied.

"And killed my four managers, twelve guards."

"They knew the risks they were taking when they

signed on."

"This is getting us nowhere. Mr. Morgan, you're an intelligent man. Also good with dynamite and that shotgun. I propose a truce. Let's talk about a bargain that will make you a rich man."

"We've got all night to talk."

"Look at it this way. I made some money here, I gambled going after too much, too soon, and I lose. So I cash in my chips and move on to another situation. I have money in Sacramento. You get me safely to Sacramento, and I sign over the Silver Queen to you, lock, stock and silver bars. The whole thing is yours."

"Is that all? I hear the Queen is about worked out. That your ounce per ton figure is way down. You're dealing a stacked deck, Bibb."

"Not at all! The vein is getting wider all the time. We have two veins, with a potential of a million dollars. You go in with some capital and hire good men and it can be making money in a month. Then you sit back and get rich."

"How can I get you to Sacramento? I hear you don't sit a horse none too good."

A chuckle came from the wreckage. "True. I tend to weigh down one horse. All I need is another carriage and driver to get me to Sacramento. We're only about fifty miles from that town. You can go back to Silverville, hire a carriage and horses and meet me here in an hour. I'll work my way out of this tangle. I'm not helpless. Then we ride to the capitol."

"What's my guarantee?"

"I'll put it in writing. I always have pen and paper with me, a failing of mine. A travel kit. That's where I got the pistol. Derringer, in fact. I'll write out the bill of sale, giving you total rights to the mining claim, the mine, the below and above ground buildings and all equipment, and any silver still on site. It will be a legal and absolutely unbreakable bill of sale for the sum of one dollar."

"Sounds legal enough. How do I know you won't tear it up before I get back."

"Oh, I'm an honest man, Mr. Morgan. I honor my guarantees, stand behind my word."

"Rather have a little more assurance than that. You write out the bill of sale. And throw out the pistol where I can find it. Then when I have it, you fold up the bill of sale and push it out through the carriage there."

"All of this isn't necessary. . . ."

"It is if you want to get to Sacramento," Buck snapped. "When I see that the paper is written, I'll go back aways and light some matches and read it. Then will be time enough to go back for a carriage."

There was a long silence, then a big sigh. "All right, all right! I hate to bargain. I'll write out the bill of sale now. I, too, will have to burn some matches so I'll have light to write by. I trust you won't shoot me as I'm making you a rich man."

"Never do that, Mr. Bibb. No sir. I've never been rich. I been poor. I hear rich is better."

"Indeed it is, Mr. Morgan. Do you see my light? Even now I'm writing out a legal bill of sale."

Morgan waited. He could see the light now past part of the torn top. He had all night.

It was ten minutes or more and a lot of burned matches before the call came.

"There, I'm done. All legal, proper and in an envelope. I signed and dated it. You saw where my light was. You work up toward me there and I'll throw out the derringer. When you're satisfied that you have it, I'll put a rock in the envelope and pitch out the bill of sale.

"You have me at a serious disadvantage here. There is not a chance I'll hurt you. You're my one lifeline to get to Sacramento."

"Yeah, I think you're right," Morgan said. He kept low and crawled toward the spot he had seen the light. In the pale moonlight he saw an arm come out and throw something. It hit a rock and bounced toward Morgan.

A minute or two later he had the derringer. It had been fired both times and the spent rounds were in place.

"Fine, Bibb. Now throw out the bill of sale."

The arm came out again and threw a white item. It sailed and landed closer. Morgan waited, then found a stick and pushed and dragged the envelope toward him. He lay in a slight depression offering him cover. He still didn't trust the man, even though he had never seen him.

Morgan took the envelope and crawled away, got behind solid protection and opened the sealed flap. He read the letter. It was in a fine hand in ink, dated and signed. He was no lawyer but it looked legal to him. He folded it and put it in his pocket.

"I read it, Bibb. It looks legal. How is that other horse down there? I haven't heard anything from it."

"Poor creature died in the crash, broken neck I'm afraid."

"A shame. Too bad your black man wasn't a better driver."

"He was frightened of the animals. I told him to slow down. He's powerful with his hands, not with his head."

"A little more about you, Bibb. I'd guess that you've milked a few good mines before this way?

Almost like highgrading it?"

"Goodness, yes. I'm a specialist. I move in, buy up a good mine, take out the best ore as fast as I can and then sell it off while it's still somewhat profitable. The sucker who buys it thinks he's got a rich one."

"Why the slaves?"

"Profit, my good man. Profit. Why pay a miner a dollar a day when I can get one for free? That's an extra thouand dollars a month in profit."

"But you worked them to death. Didn't that defeat your purpose?"

"Depended on the time schedule. I had another two more months of good highgrading here. Then I'd be gone. All we had to do was keep the secret for two more months. That was Pickering's job. But thanks to you he failed miserably."

"I've got a surprise for you, Bibb."

"I like surprises. What is it?"

"You'll see in a minute."

Morgan had moved bck up to within 30 feet of the wreck. Now he took out one of the half stick of dynamite nail bombs and lit the fuse. He threw it as soon as it was burning. The device landed just short of the buggy wreckage and ten seconds later it exploded with an ear splitting roar since the dynamite was resting in the open.

"What the hell?" Bibb thundered when the noise had died down. "You're supposed to go get me a carriage so we can drive to Sacramento."

"Sorry, Bibb, never trust a gunman."

"You promised!"

"Not really. If I did, I lied. You can sue me," Morgan said. "I keep thinking about those fifty or sixty men who died in your mine."

"They weren't *men*. They were Chinese and Mexicans," Bibb said.

"Men in my way of thinking."

Morgan lit the second bomb and threw it. It dropped through a hole in the side curtain of the smashed carriage and exploded within four feet of the 400 pound man.

The roofing nails blasted into his bulk, but only one did any damage, that lanched into his neck but missed a vital artery or vein.

He bellowed in fear and anger "Stop this! I made you a rich man."

"In a highgraded worked out mine?"

Morgan threw the last bomb. It went on the other side and fell behind the seat partially deflecting the explosion. Two of the roofing nails blasted into Sylvester Bibb's face. One thundered through his left eye and into his brain. The second hit point first and drove an inch and a half into his forehead.

After the last blast, Morgan heard nothing from the wrecked carriage.

He waited an hour, dozing now and then. When he thought it was safe, he lit a torch of some heavy grass and weeds that had turned brown, and went up to check. He found Sylvester Bibb dead and growing cold on the rear seat of the wrecked carriage.

A leather carrying case four inches thick and a foot and a half square was clutched in his arms.

Buck tore the case free and carried it back to his horse. He was less than three miles from Silverville. Buck rode the distance slowly, letting the animal walk. In town, he tied the mount at a different saloon than where he had found him. Then Lee Buckskin Morgan walked back to the Davies' house, the shotgun in one hand, the leather case in the other.

He'd look and see what was in the case tomorrow. Yeah, tomorrow would be plenty of time.

Chapter Fifteen

It was almost four A.M. when Morgan came to the Davies house. There was still a light on in the kitchen. He tried the door and found it locked. He knocked.

A moment later the door opened and a revolver barrel poked out.

"Who is it?"

"Lee Morgan."

"Oh glory!" Faith rushed into his arms before he could get inside and close the door. "You're still alive. We heard about explosions and shootings and gunfights, all sorts of wild things going on tonight." She touched his face tenderly, then kissed him hard on the mouth.

"Oh, first, Pa turned bad, and two men took him over to the Doc's house on a door. Doc says he's got a touch of relapse, and he wanted to keep him there in his sick room for a day or two so he can watch him all careful. But he says not to worry. Pa will be fine."

She kissed Morgan again and pushed hard against his body with hers. "Now tell me what happened. I been waiting up for you. Went to sleep with my head on the table for a spell."

He told her as she heated up some coffee. She watched him wide-eyed, then stared at the bill of sale.

"It ain't legal, is it?"

"Far as I know. Looks right. I'll show it to a lawyer tomorrow if there's one in town."

"Good! Now you'll be staying here and I can have you every night! You got a silver mine to run!"

"Not likely. First we find out if the bill of sale will hold up, then we see if there's any silver ore still in the mine. Then will be time to decide what to do with it."

He looked at the case on the table. His cut arm had broken loose again, he knew. He could feel the wet blood inside his shirt.

Morgan took the case and tried to open it. There was a small lock and a place for a key. He shrugged and reached in his boot for the long knife and cut the leather flap in half. He spread the sides of the case and looked in. Stacks of greenbacks. The outside showed hundred dollar bills. He fished out some envelopes that looked like they held grant deeds to property.

There were half a dozen railroad stock bearer bonds that were unnamed and good as cash.

"Looks like Bibb was running out of town with all the money in his bank account." Morgan's eyes slid closed and he nodded.

"Time for bed for you," Faith said. "We'll count everything in the morning."

"My arm," he said. She took off his light jacket

and shirt and scowled.

"You hurt it again."

"I'm still alive, that's what counts most."

She put the salve on it, then wrapped it up with some more of the strips of sheets she had torn.

Faith took him to her bed and helped him undress, then he dropped on the sheets and never moved.

"Tomorrow you're not going to get off so easy," she said.

She kissed his lips gently, then undressed and snuggled down naked beside him pushing back until she touched him. Then she slept as well.

Faith was up at seven with a fire going and ready to make breakfasst whenever Buck woke up. At last she went in and sat beside him awhile, then she peeled the light covers back and kissed his lips gently. He mumbled. She kissed him again, then slipped into the bed beside him.

Her hand found his crotch and caressed him and stroked him. Quickly he was hard. Faith took his hand and put it on her breasts. Automatically he began to fondle them. He smiled in his sleep. She moved his other hand down to her own crotch and he grinned and opened one eye.

"Am I being seduced?" he asked softly.

Faith jumped. "How long have you been awake?"

"Since the first time you kissed me. I've been enjoying it."

She hit him with a pillow, then slid back beside him. "Why don't you continue?"

He did, setting her on fire, burning her into a white hot coal and then a white ash that drifted away on a light breeze. She opened her eyes and knew that she didn't ever want to move again. She would simply stay here on her back with him inside her and resting gently on top of her with her arms clasped firmly around his back.

"Hey," he said softly.

She opened her eyes and the spell was broken, but this one was almost as good.

"Yes, beautiful man. Yes, best lover in the world. Yes, I'm here and loving a man I love and not afraid to say it."

"We have work to do. First breakfast, and then the lawyer, and then see the Garrisons. I have a job for him."

"What kind of a job?" she asked.

"Not sure yet, depends on what the lawyer says."

"Dunc says I have to to go the shop today and stay open from ten to five so people who left watches to be repaired can get the ones that are ready. We better hurry."

She made a quick breakfast, then they dressed and Morgan realized that he had worn the same clothes ever since he came to town. He had arrived with no duffel. Today he'd buy some new clothes.

First thing would be the clothes, he decided. He settled for a new shirt and a brown leather vest and a hat, low crowned and brown. No red diamonds on the head band, but he'd watch for one of those.

The only lawyer in town was named Oliver Bowden. He looked at the bill of sale for a long time and turned it over.

"From what I can see it looks legitimate enough. All the required items are there, the intent, the compensation, the signature, the date, the location and complete description of what is being sold. Yes, if I'm representing you, Mr. Morgan, I'll work hard to make anyone prove that this is *not* a legitimate bill of sale."

"Fine, you're my new lawyer." He gave the man a twenty dollar bill for the consultation and another hundred dollar bill for a month's retainer. Oliver Bowden almost collapsed from surprise.

"Dear me, this does seem to be an excellent situation," Bowden said. "Just call on me when you rename the mine and set up your operation."

Buck called at the bank and discovered that Mr. Bibb had closed out both of his accounts the previous day just after noon.

His next stop was to see Janish Lang in his mine office. He showed Lang the bill of sale, and Lang looked up surprised.

"I don't understand."

"He's been highgrading the mine. Tearing out the best veins he can find, working everyone to death, and then ready to dump the property while it still looks valuable but is a shell. We stopped him well before that time."

"How did you ever get him to sell the mine, and for nothing more than a dollar?"

"He wanted me to take him to Sacramento."

"Oh." Lang looked up, confused. "And did you?"

"No. Mr. Bibb suffered a fatal injury when his Negro attendant drove a carriage down the first hill out of town and lost control. The rig crashed, killing one horse and breaking the other's leg. It was destroyed. Mr. Bibb wanted me to come back to town, get another carriage and horses and drive him to Sacramento where he had funds, he said.

"After he wrote out the bill of sale his injuries proved to be fatal."

"And you had nothing to do with that?"

"I wasn't driving the rig, no sir."

Lang took a deep breath. "Things change so rapidly around this business."

"I want you to make an inspection with me of the Silver Queen, see if she's worth saving and working."

"Why me?"

"Because I can trust you, and because I want you to be a fifty-fifty partner in the operation. You know mines, I don't. You can run a mine, I can't. I would suggest we leave as soon as possible and take along Wid Garrison, who was one of the slaves working in the mine and should know it well.

"If this all works out, it would be my suggestion to hire Mr. Garrison as the general manager of the Silver Queen."

"I don't know. I'd be in competition with myself."

"Not at all. It would be a logical expansion for your operation."

"I hear most of the buildings were wrecked. Take a lot of money to put it right again."

"True. I'm ready to put up five thousand dollars in cash. With another five thousand from you, that should be enough capital to get the operation going and into production."

"Damn, you've thought of everything."

"I try, Mr. Lang, I try."

They took a buggy and stopped by at the Garrison house. Wid was sitting on the steps whittling. He recognized Lang and stood up and brushed off his pants. Then he saw Morgan and raced out to meet him.

"Wid, good to see you again," Morgan said.

Wid grabbed his hand and pumped it. "Never was

so glad to see a mortal being in my life as when you slipped into them barracks up there."

"Wid, we want you to come back up to the Silver Queen. Me and Mr. Lang here are the new owners of the mine. Want you to show us around, see if it's worth getting back into operation. What's your first evaluation?"

"Oh, hell yes. There's lots of good ore in there. They had us grabbing only the widest veins. From what I've seen, a normal work day up there should last for at least three years just on the veins we know about now. Plenty of ore in there, yes sir."

"Good, grab your hat and let's take a buggy ride," Morgan said.

When they came back well after dark, the deal was consummated. Lang's own company lawyer drew up the partnership papers and they signed them. The bill of sale and the new deed would be signed over at the county seat as soon as they both could get over there. The next day work crews would go in to begin tearing down the buildings and putting up new ones, salvaging what they could.

The hoist house never had been used. They should be back in operation within a week. Wid Garrison had accepted the job as construction foreman and when the mine went into operation, he would handle the job as mine foreman, and general manager.

Later that night at the Davies house, Morgan and Faith counted the money in the leather case. The stacks of bills totaled $8,600. Bonds worth another $5,000 were in the case.

"The man did not go around without some

funds," Morgan said. He looked at the stacks of bills. "I had a talk with Dunc. He'd like to move to Sacramento and open a store there. I want you to be sure he does it."

She shook her head. "He's happy here. Why move? Besides, it costs a lot."

"No worry there. You haven't been paid for saving my life. Dunc might not take it, but I know you will."

"Take what?"

"Remember that cash I asked you to put away somewhere?"

"Yes. It still scares me to have it in the house. It's $3,485.

"Right. That and another $1,515, makes it an even $5,000. That's what I'm paying you for saving my life. I know, I know . . . it's not very much, but I'm a cheap guy."

"You . . . you can't do this. Dunc would never take it. I mean, all we did was what anyone. . . ."

He kissed her. "You take the cash or I'll never kiss you again."

She laughed softly and kissed him. "I'll take it, but Dunc is going to have a cow fit, I mean, an absolute heifer of a stomping around."

"I'll tell him while he's still sick. Oh, we have another job, to count those gold coins. I need $5,000 worth to set up the Silver King mine."

They counted the double eagles. There were 324 of them, for a total of $6,480. They put $5,000 worth in the canvas bank bag and pushed the rest to one side.

Faith was awed by all the money.

"I've never seen so much money in all my life. Do I have to think that it's stolen?"

"Absolutely not! This money is in payment by Mr. Sylvester Bibb for compensation to me for his almost killing me. The price is low. I should have charged him more.

"Now, if you don't have any more questions, let's get all this filthy money put away somewhere. Then let's eat something and then see if that bed of yours is big enough for two before we go see Dunc. He should be ready to come home today."

"And then you'll be talking about leaving, won't you, Lee Buckskin Morgan?" A tear slid down her cheek.

"A time comes when I'm due to move on. But not for a week or so. Have to get the new mine started, and check out the work force, and get Dunc well enough to move to Sacramento. That's going to be interesting telling him about it.

"I can put that off a while. We'll figure out what to do with the money later. Most of it will go into the bank. And I'll send a bank draft to my bank in Denver. If I have any left I might buy you a pretty new dress."

"Right now I don't want to think about dresses," Faith said as she pulled him into her bedroom and let her dress drop to the floor. "I'd rather think about not having a dress on, or anything else for that matter."

Morgan chuckled. It was great to have his memory back. It was so fine to have a beautiful, eager young woman undressing in front of him. And it was pleasing to think about what would be coming when he moved on down the road. He'd been thinking about San Diego lately. No reason. Might be time he went down there again and checked out his former friends.

"Hey, you're miles away," Faith said. She had pulled off the rest of her clothes. "Seems like I'm always undressing you."

Lee Buckskin Morgan grinned and kissed her. "Yeah, I like it that way."

SADDLER

The hardest-riding, hardest-loving cowboy whoever blazed a trail or set a heart on fire

#3: HOT AS A PISTOL by Gene Curry. Hated by the townspeople, Saddler had to work all day to keep the town safe from a renegade Irish family, a corrupt politician, and a deadly Confederate guerilla—and all night to keep himself safe from two criminally beautiful women.

__3037-3 $2.95 US/$3.95 CAN

#4: WILD, WILD WOMEN by Gene Curry. After killing a sadistic wagon master, Jim Saddler took over the wagon train carrying 50 buxom beauties to San Francisco. But after several deaths, torrential rains, and broken axles, it looked bad for the women and the wagons. But Saddler swore he'd get his women to California come hell or high water.

__3099-3 $2.95 US/$3.95 CAN